THE COMPANY
OF CROWS

Prepared for the press by Elise Moser
Cover design: Debbie Geltner
Cover image: Karen Molson
Author photo: E. J. Skelly
Book design: WildElement.ca

Library and Archives Canada Cataloguing in Publication

Molson, Karen, author
        The company of crows / Karen Molson.
Issued in print and electronic formats.
ISBN 978-1-927535-94-3 (paperback).--ISBN 978-1-927535-95-0 (epub).
-- ISBN 978-1-927535-96-7 (mobi).--ISBN 978-1-927535-97-4 (pdf)
        I. Title.
PS8626.O475C64 2016   C813'.6   C2015-908480-6
                                                C2015-908481-4

Printed and bound in Canada.

The publisher gratefully acknowledges the support of the Canada Council
for the Arts.

Linda Leith Publishing Inc.
P.O. Box 322, Victoria Station,
Westmount Quebec H3Z 2V8 Canada
www.lindaleith.com

THE COMPANY OF CROWS

A NOVEL

For Kim,
   great friend, great company,
   thanks for all!   xoxo

KAREN MOLSON

Karen Molson

April 17, 2016

The language of birds is very ancient, and, like other ancient modes of speech, very elliptical; little is said, but much is meant and understood.

— Gilbert White

For Lis

PROLOGUE

Thin grey lines fan out across the earthscape like a gigantic, tattered spiderweb. The routes—some asphalt, some gravel—dissect realms of trees and loop around the huddled flat-roofed buildings; farther east, they separate swampy thickets from clusters of houses. Each subsection of the web relays a different complexion of light. The colours can change by the millisecond; in late summer, wind can sweep green from a field of ripe wheat and whirl it into gold. But it's not yet the time for wheat.

One field below is dotted with square bales of green and yellow, the first hay harvest of the season. A rock wall separates the harvested field from the next section of land, which has a natural spring on it. Heavy rains once made the lowlands swell large enough to inspire a pair of mallard ducks to nest there. This whole expanse, left fallow this year, is already thick with horsetail and milkweed.

The crow beats his wings steadily. Down here are the channels where worms, beetles, and larvae writhe in muddy clumps. There, the drainage ditches cleave their way into culverts that gurgle under roadways. Far to the west, a haphazard assembly of white and beige trailers squats along pathways near the shore. A lake dances in the distance, alive with light.

He turns his head from the lake to the land. Along the road below him the vehicles stride, singly and collectively, like water insects. They clump together, separate, clump again.

Even the faintest scented summons to fresh meat eludes the crow. Fortunately, his weak sense of smell is balanced with superior eyesight. He adjusts his shoulders to bring his wings into a sharp tilt, descends toward a swath of warm asphalt. Under the dazzling sunlight, the tar gleams and flashes.

The carcass is flattened along the painted white line, blood slowly oozing from under its brindled fur. As he approaches the crumbly roadside he realizes he knows this fox. It's the same flame-coloured vixen whose breathy, desperate barks he's heard sometimes at twilight near the tree where he and his mate built last year's nest.

The asphalt is hot under his claws. He hops closer to the animal, but a car looms; he retreats to the safety of the gravel shoulder as it swoops by. Urged on by hunger, he tries again. When another vehicle is about to whizz past, he leaps lightly up once more, legs dangling; the gust of air blows past without dishevelling his feathers.

The crow is the first scavenger here. Though he can see well in two directions, the woods enclosing this part of the road might conceal competition for this meal. His senses are alert—he's conscious of a pack of coyotes congregating near the garbage dump. It's only a matter of time before the turkey vultures assemble.

The muscle tissue on the vixen's thigh is exposed. The crow works fast, vigorously stabbing at the carcass. He braces his claws against the spine for balance as he tears out small strips of muscle. He gulps down what he can, carries two larger morsels to conceal in an elm tree leaning by the fence line. He returns again and again in the breaks between streams of cars.

Soon it will be time to summon the others—his mate, their offspring and allies—to join him here. They can take turns gorging while he watches for competition. They will tug the lightened body further away from the side of the road, each will cache more of the meat, and if there's still some of it left in the days to come, they will squabble over the prize harvest of fresh maggots and glistening white grubs.

He begins to bend up and down, hoping to catch the eyes of kin scanning the vicinity. Four times he squawks the syllable-and-a-half of his own name, sending identical scrawls of turbulence into the air. Then he launches himself toward a clearing in the trees. His wings batter the air to find an updraft of wind. He climbs into the sky.

ONE

Clutching her pencil, her feet braced against the floorboards, Veronica Reid squints through the window at the moving landscape. Her father drives in long rhythmic spurts that make her back jounce against the seat. She's careful to point the tip of her pencil well away from herself. The day is already hot, and the sun beats incessantly through the windshield, melting the dimpled plastic that covers the front seats and making it stick to the backs of her thighs.

She drops her gaze back to the page. Words, glorious words, crowding into her head.

Upon my honour I would forsake my kingdom, if I had one, to be anything other than a prisoner in the passenger seat of this old car, anywhere other than lurching along this forlorn highway, heading to some piteous trailer park in the middle of nowhere.

The pleasure of turning everyday events of her life

into melodramatic incidents on the page makes enduring the events almost worthwhile.

I should sooner—

Her hand is jerked away when the car bucks against a pothole. She lifts her pencil, expertly flips it upside down, erases the jiggly line, and starts again.

I should sooner perish than be subjected to this fresh injustice. Surely I'll go mad with despair.

She gnaws on a thumbnail for a while. Emma Bovary goes mad with despair. Anna Karenina. Scarlett O'Hara. But the thing with heroines is that none of them are stricken with acne, have to wear braces or endure thick eyeglasses—or, God forbid, all three at once. The heroines are always beautiful, always headstrong, ever intrepid. Veronica feels like she becomes them when she's reading about them. Even more so since her braces finally came off two months ago.

She runs her tongue over her front teeth. It's not that she wants to be a heroine, but she'd love to be someone other than herself. Someone lucky, smart, or even pretty would be good. Or just a bit less of a misfit.

"It's a competitive world," her mother Marnie likes to say. "You just have to learn that people feel better about themselves when they can put somebody else down. Even chickens do it. It's called a pecking order."

It's a hard truth to accept, that meanness gets you ahead in life. No matter how she looks at it, that doesn't seem fair. In any case, if the world must be made of those who torment and those who are tormented, she'd choose to be one of the latter. Every time. If she could choose, that is, which she can't.

Each mile in the car brings her that much farther away from the aggressors. It's the only positive thing about her family's summer plan. No more boys' insults to dog her, no more great shows of girlie-whispering behind cupped hands in the locker room. The whinnying eruptions of scornful laughter she'd thought would disappear when she no longer had to wear braces.

For the last three months she's walked to school instead of taking the bus. Being trapped inside the bus was intolerable. Classrooms and hallways had come to feel like incinerators. To pass through them she'd have to hold her books tightly against her chest, head down but legs striding purposefully, moving like a sailboat with a deep, full keel firmly slicing through a sea of flames, hoping not to run aground.

Veronica closes her notebook, trapping the pencil, her close surroundings swimming back into focus. She steals a glance at her father, who is absorbed in driving. Colin's jaw is clamped, his eyes clouded in thought.

Here in the station wagon he's perfect company, seemingly content to stay silent while he negotiates the road. This grants Veronica the freedom to express her private lamentations in her notebook and, considering this, she feels a twinge of gratitude. His worn tweed jacket, folded on the seat between them, smells faintly of tobacco and something tarry and woodsy, like oakum. His presence in her peripheral vision—in his ball cap, blue-and-red plaid shirt, suspenders, and baggy trousers—is enough to anchor her in time and space. She is safe here.

Veronica slides her fingers along the door panel and finds the power-window switch. The snap still makes her jump, the sudden ripping sound as the glass jerks itself down. It's such a fatuous invention. She prefers the rolling-down sureness of the old way, the quiet connection between the circling knob and the sliding windowpane, one's control of the process.

They're passing the outskirts of Bancroft. The air smells different here than it does at home. She picks up her new glasses and looks through them, sees a long empty bicycle path running alongside a shallow, braided brook shaded with overhanging trees.

For a few minutes, the passing roadside dissolves into a blur of grey and green, bicycles gliding past a prominent sign advertising a cheese factory ahead. The brook narrows to a little wooden bridge, more overhanging trees, then the trees disappear, and behind the brook there are tilled fields, acres and acres of open space, and a smell like sour manure and smoke.

She pulls her glasses off again, presses the button—*nnnnnnnn*—and watches the window reseal itself. She squints toward the brook, but it's too far away to distinguish; in her mind there appears a blurred vision of Ophelia floating on her back, vacant-eyed, serene, and tragically beautiful, hair fanned out amid strewn daisies and violets.

Veronica keeps her writing concealed, her notebook in her backpack, her glasses shoved deep in her pocket. There's never anything to see out there anyway that's better than what she finds in books, or in her own mind. She closes her eyes.

The trailer park was her mother's idea. At home in Oshawa some weeks ago Marnie placed an open brochure on the kitchen table and flattened the seam with her thumb. They were in the kitchen, the boys abandoning the television for once, pressing forward to see the pictures.

"It's going to be a lovely place to spend the summer, and it's beautiful. Look. It's several hours' drive from here, on Lake Laggan. It's secluded—look at all the willow trees, here, and the beach. Mobile homes are spread out along this part, campers on the other side—"

"Can I bring my water pistol?"

"Can I bring my firecrackers?"

Instead of correcting their English, Marnie said yes to both of them. "And we'll even let your father bring his telescope when he comes on the weekends."

Veronica peered suspiciously at the brochure. "Mobile homes? I'm not going there."

"Don't be silly. The place is so popular that they have waiting lists, they told me. I was shown the last available—"

"Surely you jest!"

"—and there was somebody else considering it right there—"

"Tell me you didn't—"

"—and I rented it."

Veronica groaned.

"Why couldn't you have rented a proper cottage somewhere? We could even have gone camping like last summer!"

Last summer they'd camped in Algonquin Park, set up tents in what she thought of as real wilderness, an isolated paradise near a spring-fed lake small enough to swim across. A soccer ball and fishing rods for Dilly and Gumm, and a mesh bag for her, bulging with books she had chosen herself. Campfires for cooking, card games in the big tent by battery-powered lanterns, shadow-puppets that jerked along the inside tent walls. Best of all, woods, offering numerous places where she could make herself comfortable with one or two books, sitting with her back against a spruce trunk, cross-legged amongst the moss, bunchberries, and ferns, a bottle of 6-12 insect repellent in her pocket.

Her mother pointed out that being in a trailer would be drier, more comfortable, more convenient. The lake was close by, there was a safe beach for children to play on. She could make *real* meals on a *real* stove. No more squatting in outhouses; the trailer had a *real* bathroom. And instead of two weeks, this holiday would last two months—and what could be better than that?

Veronica opens her eyes again now, slowly sets her glasses back on, and turns back to the passenger window. Smears of dark on light become wires strung between telephone poles, upright posts strutting into the infinite distance. Blurs of colour become billboards spray-painted with graffiti, letters overlapping, plumped-up and colourful: *Make Love, Not War*, and *We are each of us a multitude*. A lone brick building where the words *Bridal Outlet* are peeling off the sign; a quickly glimpsed row of white gowns lined up in a window. Then an open field scattered with litter and shrubs. She has the uncomfortable sensation of becoming smaller and smaller in relation to the visual clarity that surrounds her.

Colin slows the car to approach lights at a crossroads, and Veronica notices a flock of small black birds perched along five parallel lines of electrical and telephone wire. The birds look like dozens of staccato notes crowded on a musical bar. Iridescence speckles their feathers in the sunlight.

Dazzled, she gropes for the window switch again and presses. The window starts down. The birds abruptly take to the air in a single collective movement, like a school of guppies in a fish tank. The car pulls forward and the aerial acrobats disappear behind them.

"What kind of birds were they?" she asks.

"Those?" Colin grunts. "Oh, those were just starlings. They're everywhere."

Veronica pulls her glasses off and lets them drop on the seat beside her. She opens the backpack at her feet. The fingers on her left hand close around the spine of Thackeray's *Vanity Fair,* while her right hand pushes her straight blond hair out of her eyes. She hates her hair.

Twenty minutes later, Veronica and Colin are eating Kentucky Fried Chicken and fries at a rest stop, paper bags spread across their laps. Veronica drops a greasy morsel on the floor and adjusts herself so she can reach and toss it out the window.

Colin turns on the radio and tunes in to a baseball game. The game must be nearly over, because the announcer is talking faster and his voice is getting higher and higher to be heard above the roar of the crowd.

Outside, a boy leading a black terrier on a leash tugs the animal away from Veronica's discarded piece of chicken fat. She watches as the terrier keeps turning back to look at the food, watches until the dog and the boy are out of sight.

It's hard to tell if the baseball game is over or not; the announcer is saying something about a riot and about the players using baseball bats to defend themselves from the fans.

Can this even be true? Colin, shaking his head, switches the radio off.

Just then the boy and the terrier re-appear, joining a family of four others gathered at a picnic table.

Colin lifts his drink and sips through the straw.

"I always had a dog. When I was a boy, that is. Your granny sure loved dogs."

"Emma—Madame Bovary had one. Named Djali."

"Jelly?"

Veronica spells it for him.

"He was a gift from a gamekeeper," she adds. "Madame Bovary told him all her problems."

"The gamekeeper?"

Veronica stifles a giggle. "Not the gamekeeper, no, the dog."

Her father scratches the back of his neck. "Maybe this fall we could adopt a puppy."

She stops eating and wipes her mouth. This is so unlike him. Does he mean it?

"Honestly? I mean, will you swear an oath?"

"I can't swear an *oath*, no. It all depends on your mother."

Veronica lets out her breath. "Alas."

"I mean, she would probably love a dog, too. But we'll have to see how things go this summer …." Colin's voice trails off.

"How things go?"

"It's what your mother wanted, this summer holiday. And—keep your eye on her, will you?"

"What do you mean?"

"Never mind. Forget I said that. It's not fair."

Veronica wonders if it's possible to will oneself to forget something. That would be the opposite of memorizing. But the brain likes to play tricks, like when a particular song you hate gets stuck in your head.

They clear up the mess from their meal and shove everything into a paper bag.

With the car back on the road, they resume their silence, carrying it casually between them. She looks out at the industrial landscape of the town's outskirts, the car dealerships and window factories blurred now by speed, the shapes of buildings sliding by, giving way to openness, ploughed fields, ditches lined by heaps of rocks until the highway widens and gusts blow into the station wagon and she has to press the window up again.

She's read that blind people compensate for their lack of sight by deliberately sharpening their other senses. With her eyes closed, listening to the familiar sound of the engine and the hum of tires on the pavement, she hears something else behind these sounds: an intermittent buzzing. It begins in the distance but seems to get louder, closer. Already her hearing is becoming more acute, just after a few minutes of concentration.

Will it someday become so sharp that she'll be able to discern the type of tree by the sound of the wind in its leaves? Be able to identify a person by the sound of their breathing? If so, surely she won't have to wear her glasses any more. She peels her thighs off the plastic seat one at a time, and they lift with the same ripping sound that the windows make when they're opening. The buzzing, which had receded, begins again, bumping against the inside of her skull. The sound merges with her other thoughts until she begins to feel drowsy and lets her head rest on the back of the seat.

There's a lurch in the movement of the car, and Veronica's eyes snap open. She strikes out to find the door handle. Her father's arms are thrashing and clawing at the air around his head, both hands are off the steering wheel, and the station wagon is veering at a crazy angle toward the far side of the road.

They come to a sudden halt, and a hot cloud of kicked-up dust begins to settle on the car and its surroundings. Veronica is breathing hard as she gropes for her glasses. Colin's rigid hands grip the steering wheel.

"Are you okay? Jesus. I'm sorry, I'm sorry."

They're on the gravel shoulder.

"I'm so sorry," he says again.

He unclamps a trembling hand to cup his ear, patting at a swelling welt where a bee has stung him.

Veronica's heart is still galloping.

"Did we almost die?"

"I'm so sorry," her father repeats. Veronica fears he's going to start sobbing, but he doesn't. She feels an urge to comfort him but doesn't know how, except to murmur, "It's okay."

For a time—it feels like forever—that's all he can say. "I'm sorry."

Colin clears his throat, and shifts to sit taller in his seat. His hands are trembling. He checks and double-checks the side- and rear-view mirrors, then looks at her.

"You're alright then?"

She nods.

He starts the engine, casts one last look over his shoulder at the empty road behind them. Veronica nervously scans the back seat for bees, but none appear. She's heard that after a bee stings, it dies.

"If you don't move, a bee won't bother you—"

"It's no use," her father mutters. "It's no use telling me that."

Veronica pictures the aftermath of a single-car crash. Red lights spiral. Police and investigators solemnly regard a station wagon that has flipped and smashed, the driver and his thirteen-year-old daughter have died, and no one can ascertain why. "There were no witnesses," the chief investigator says, "and visibility was excellent. So it's a mystery. We must contact the next of kin—"

Colin clears his throat again. "I can't help it. I—I stepped on a bee once—I was very young—" He breaks off, rubs his fingers across his chin stubble.

His moustache and chin stubble are new, having grown over a span of only a week. The hair on the top of his head has recently started receding, even though he's only forty-four. Veronica imagines her father with a beard like that of Dickens, and a watch-chain hung across his waistcoat which he touches lightly as he greets people along the cobbled street. In his left hand, he swings a thin walking stick.

Veronica says, "I understand."

She understands it wasn't inattention that caused the near-accident. She thinks about him driving these same roads from the city to the trailer park and back every weekend, and she's worried about him. He's always tired from staying up so late. Even when he's at his most alert, his mind always seems elsewhere, most likely contemplating some far-off galaxy, pondering the wonder of earth and stars, moons and planets.

Colin's preoccupations distress her mother, who's on her own most weekday evenings. Marnie's taken to mixing herself a cocktail before supper and a refill after dessert. When Colin comes home, she's usually in bed already. If he spies the open liquor cabinet door, he slams it shut, just hard enough for his displeasure to be felt, hard enough to wake anyone already sleeping. Veronica has often heard them arguing behind their bedroom wall. A few nights before the day he drove her mother and brothers to the park, Marnie had ranted at him. "You're never even here for *dinner* any more. You're either at work or at one of your astrology meetings! Then you're always too tired to— Okay, okay, astronomy. You know what I *meant*."

Veronica's mother knows the difference. Astrology is a pseudo-science, her father says. But when Marnie's ranting, she's apt to mix up words.

On their last night at home, Marnie had said, "At least at a trailer park I'll get to have a social life. And don't worry, it'll be dark enough for stargazing when you're there, because I know that's all you care about."

Colin's not an astronomer but an accountant. For the last four years, ever since Neil Armstrong and Buzz Aldrin walked on the moon, he's been infatuated with everything to do with astronomy. After work, he devotes himself to this most ancient science with the earnestness of a man who is making up for much lost time.

It was an interest that Marnie had welcomed at first, but she'd begun to complain as it took up more and more space in his life. He'd not only joined the local astronomy club, he'd started to attend their every event. Begun volunteering for them.

"He went and spent all our savings," her mother insists, "on a telescope."

It's the very same telescope, packed snugly in its custom-made trunk, which takes up half the space in the back of the station wagon now.

Whenever Veronica hears her father talk about his passion, she thinks he almost becomes someone else.

"It's infinite," he said to Marnie one time. "It's mesmerizing. I mean, the perfection of celestial geometry, in all its vastness and precision. Scientists are getting new data ... we're still charting new galaxies. Did I mention that sailors and explorers once used only the stars for navigation? And there's still so much that we don't know. Like black holes, for instance, the biggest mystery of all. Yet this is a time of striking breakthroughs in understanding. Think about it, all the perpetually travelling, moving, three-dimensional—infinitesimal—parts."

The first time she'd heard the word "infinitesimal," Veronica had gone to her room to say it to herself over and over again.

There's something on the side of the road ahead, a

mound that seems to be moving. The station wagon slows down, and the mound is a dead animal, and the movement is that of a bird, standing on top of it. A big black crow lifts up and flaps unhurriedly away, a dark strip of flesh in its beak.

As they pass it, Veronica looks down at the dead fox, the muscles on its haunches gleaming and bloody. The sight makes tears spring to her eyes. She sees the fox's lustrous red fur, its white throat, its swollen teats. There are fox pups somewhere that will starve to death, and she can't do anything about it.

TWO

It's almost four in the afternoon when Colin says they've just passed Longford Rapids.

Veronica puts her glasses on to help him look for landmarks (an old drive-in theatre, a primary school, a BP station) and street names. She notices a library on the main street and points it out. Finally, they see the enormous painted sign—*Laughing Willows Trailer Park*—with an illustration of two willow trees depicted as laughing people, their branches held like arms wrapped around their trunk-bellies. An arrow going up and to the right. One mile ahead.

They turn onto a gravel road with woods on one side and an electric power installation on the other, metal structures surrounded by a high chain-link fence, each section of which has a red sign depicting a white bolt of lightning and the words *Danger! Do Not Enter!*

On the other side of the road is an expanse of woods whose understory is thick with ferns and brambles.

She hadn't known there were woods here. If she could just get away from everybody and hang out in there, this holiday might not be so bad after all.

The road narrows and turns to the left, opening up into a parking lot with a flagpole at one end. They pull into an empty space. From the flagpole, a lane branches out in three directions down several long, low rows of trailers and motorhomes.

Straight ahead, a grassy park is shaded by willow trees and dotted with picnic tables. In the middle distance, two boys toss a Frisbee between them. Behind the boys, Veronica can see a slope that leads to a sandy beach rimmed by a quivering edge of lake. Lake Laggan.

Colin steps out of the station wagon, clasps his hands behind his head, stretches his arms and shoulders. Still in the front seat, Veronica removes her glasses and looks again at her surroundings. She sees forms in muted colours: brown, black, green, grey. Above, an alabaster sky. She puts her glasses back on, grasps her backpack, and climbs out.

Her father is slipping on his jacket, even though it seems too hot for tweed. His expression seems to be saying there's no need to hurry, now that they're here. He leans his back against the car, strikes a match, and lights a Cameo menthol. Then he glances at Veronica, eyebrows raised. She shrugs.

There's an eruption of laughter in the distance, and the sound of a referee's whistle. The wind sends a cloud of cigarette smoke over Veronica that makes her eyes water. She looks at her father, who's now changing his grip on the cigarette, fingers to thumb and finger, tapping off the ash in his practised, brisk manner. He seems far away, as though he's forgotten she's there. He brings the cigarette back to his lips and takes a long slow drag, holding in the smoke with his chest puffed out before he slowly exhales again. Eventually he tosses the butt to the ground and grinds it into the gravel with his heel. He tugs the right side of his collar—the side with the welt on it—up to his ear. Their eyes meet briefly, he shakes his head, and she nods. Neither of them will say anything about the bee incident.

As they walk toward the lane a pack of boys vigorously churns by on their bicycles, popping wheelies, gripping exaggerated handlebars, bouncing on their banana seats.

"That'll be *easy*," one of them is yelling to another over his shoulder. "Dare me!"

Veronica flinches before she realizes that their energy can't be directed at her; these boys are strangers.

Guffaws of laughter dissolve like contrails in their wake.

It'll be just a matter of time before these boys come to hassle her; she can feel it. Veronica keeps her head down as she follows her father.

Colin comes to a stop in front of a blue-and-white Corsair trailer propped up at each end on concrete blocks. It's smaller than she thought it might be. Steps of peeling paint are flanked by latticework that emerges from a scattering of gravel. The steps are nailed to a cluttered wooden verandah that spans the length of the trailer, shaded with a plastic awning. The grass on the small front lawn has been cut so short it's barely there. Folding chairs encircle a blackened crater enclosing the remnants of a cook fire. More dismaying to Veronica is the proximity of the next trailer, and the one after that.

Marnie comes out the front door to greet them, barefoot and breezy. Her pageboy haircut, freshly washed and curled, bounces on the tops of her shoulders. She's wearing tight-fitting slacks and a flower-patterned blouse. Her ebullient fussing feels insincere.

Colin takes Veronica's suitcase, carries it up the steps, and sets it on the verandah.

"Come," her mother says brightly. "Have a look! Put your things away, see where you'll be sleeping!"

The entire trailer could probably fit into half the living room of their house in the city. Where she's to sleep is a foam-covered bench that doubles as a sofa during the day in the open area of the trailer. Gumm is sprawled on it now with a comic. Marnie is pointing: the drawers under the bench are to be Veronica's. Gumm lowers his comic book, and cocks his head at his sister as she starts to protest:

"If you think I'll be sleeping here, you're sadly mistaken."

Gumm's lips silently repeat, *You're sadly mistaken.*

Veronica holds her ground. "No. No way. It's not private enough. What about my things? The boys—"

"For God's sake. It was really calm before you got here. Look, I cleaned out this entire cubbyhole for you.

22

Why would your brothers go after your stuff? It's more room than they get in their bunks. You should be grateful you have this oversized bed to sleep on."

All the while, Gumm has been continuously making faces, mimicking glasses with his fingers making O-shapes over his eyes, and chortling. Marnie's voice natters on. Veronica's hope is collapsing. When Marnie's attention flickers toward the kitchen, her brother pretends to rub a gob of snot on the cushion. Veronica reaches out to smack him and he squeals, twisting out of reach.

Marnie swings around, reignited.

"Now what? You just got here, and already—leave him alone. Some summer this is going to be. Where's your father gone now? Go outside, both of you, while I get supper on. Outside!"

Veronica heads back to the car where she locks herself in and flings herself down in the back seat.

"Nice of you to join us," Marnie says drily, an hour later. She's smoothing wrinkles from the plastic cloth covering the picnic table. "And nice to see you're wearing your glasses."

Veronica rakes them off her face with one hand and folds them into her pocket. "I detest them."

"Don't be so naive. You can't hate something that's necessary—you just have to get used to them."

Veronica thinks if she can squeeze them hard enough, they'll break.

Her mother's voice unexpectedly softens. "I know

you miss your friends. So do I, but I can make an effort. So can you."

"Friends are of small importance to me."

"I've already made friends with lots of people here. Grace, for instance."

"You call her your friend, and you've been acquainted for how long? In fact, I believe you said you only met her once, that time you first saw the place."

Marnie, her impatience reignited, glares at her. "I've told you, you *can* make friends, and there's lots to do. Will you stop looking like that. And stop talking like an old book. Just try, Veronica. Now help me set the places."

The tension between Veronica and her mother isn't new. For the last six months, Marnie's mood has been swinging from resignation to annoyance at the slightest provocation. As Veronica sets down the forks and knives, she realizes that anticipating this trailer-park holiday had, on the whole, made her mother more cheerful than she'd been in a long time.

Dilly and Gumm hustle to the picnic table, all knees and elbows and shaggy hair. Veronica knows that if she glances up, they'll kick her, so she keeps her eyes to herself. Her mother has made an effort: lamb chops and a medley of colourful vegetables, even a bouquet of wildflowers on the table.

"Next weekend when you're back, Colin, I'll make pie," Marnie says. She tips her head in Veronica's direction. "Now *there's* something I couldn't do if we were camping."

In the evening Veronica lies stiffly on the upholstered foam bench, staring at the ceiling. A steady light from outside squeezes its way through the gaps in the window blinds. There's enough light to write.

Along with my childhood, I have left behind my former belief in imaginary things like unicorns and mermaids. These beliefs have been extinguished for good. I can see what it's going to take now to resolve my dilemma is a miracle.

Miracles have been documented by many, not just one crazy person, so they must be true. Like that nun in the newspaper, Sister Agnes in Japan, who had visions and heard voices coming from a statue of the Virgin Mary. Even though the statue was made of wood, it started to bleed and sweat.

In Sunday school I remember the Bible story of Jonah being swallowed by the whale, and of course the miracle of Jesus walking on the water. Anything is possible if you just believe enough.

I love the enchantment that lives in each verse in the Bible, the cadence and authority of that old-fashioned English.

Forsooth, I do hereby proclaim, a certainty born from desperation is no less true. I will stoke my new faith with secret vows. Already my belief is underscored by the very rightness of miracles themselves. For I am someone who holds fairness and justice in high esteem, and miracles are imperative for either to exist for me.

When my eyesight is restored to 20/20 I will be so devoted I will seriously consider becoming a nun, and moving to a convent where I'll have limitless time and solitude to read—not just the Bible but all the best novels too.

After Veronica has stored her notebook away, she closes her eyes and tries to pray. She imagines the joy of having perfectly restored eyesight. She imagines awakening and opening her eyes one morning, able to see everything clearly. She will spring up, pull her clothes on, grab the cursed glasses, and set them down in the road in the path of an oncoming truck—or, better still, the school bus. Await the splintering sound. Released at last.

THREE

The mumbling voices assemble before Grace awakens. They float and bump and tumble into each other, simultaneously muttered conversations scuffing the inside surface of her skull. Another random ambush. Another siege.

A sharper voice flashes like a pair of scissors. The utterances twitch and bristle in their readiness to spring forward. Will she be able to dispel them this time? There's the sound of the scrape of swords as they're unsheathed.

Grace had trusted that by middle age she'd have outgrown these attacks. Instead, they're becoming more frequent.

Dr. Kerwin had said to breathe. If she can keep breathing the eclipse will pass, and she'll be able to lift her head from its hollow on the pillow.

Grace opens her eyes, darting a glance upwards to see if there's a note on the bedside table, one she'd written the night before. Get up. Get dressed. Make coffee. The notes release her from having to engage in the effort of thinking, of untangling the strands of possible actions. She'd prefer to blindly follow orders, especially if they're her own orders.

But there are no notes this morning. She empties her lungs with an audible whistling sound. The breathing exercise is working. The voices are starting to withdraw.

If she *had* written a note, a list, what would it say? Lift the blinds. Heat water for coffee. Switch the radio on. She heaves her body through the thick resistance of air to sit up.

The first morning rituals are comforting and familiar. They will get her started, they'll give her the impetus to wash up, to scrub away any evidence of the wild or unkempt, to look civilized. Dress in clothes that won't draw attention.

Her feet graze the linoleum floor. A reason and a reward: the taste of coffee and the familiar sound of the radio programs. Sound that will repel the phantom voices for good, at least for now, send them scattering. Distract the demons with news from the outside world. Good news or bad news, the reassuring sounds of the steady passage of time.

Outside, close to the bedroom window, there's a large black crow. She watches as the bird struts, glossy and imperious, along the edge of the lane. It makes for a candy wrapper and starts to peck and rip at it, tossing the shredded bits aside. Then something unseen startles the bird, and it gives out a loud, harsh cry that sounds like "Hrah!" and flies off.

In bare feet Grace walks the tightrope down the hall. She uses the toilet, examines her face in the mirror. (When did her hair become so grey?) Back in the hallway again she hears Ruby's soft snores coming from behind the curtain, the little alcove-room her elderly mother claimed from the start as hers.

Grace was glad to let her have something she wanted. For these days, their roles have been reversed. First her mother took care of her, now it's become Grace's time to take care of Ruby.

She pulls open the kitchen window shade, and a flare of sunlight pierces the chrome of the trailer next door. She reaches for the radio knob. One of the things that initially appealed to her about this particular trailer was its built-in radio and eight-track. Grace doesn't own any eight-track tapes, but one day she might. She keeps the radio low, so as not to wake her mother. She recognizes "Bridge Over Troubled Water."

A narrow space, the alley between two trailers, offers her a fleeting glimpse of the lake, the ripples on the water's surface.

The bag of garbage lands on the pile with an abrupt, implosive sound, a chance meeting of discarded glass and jagged tin.

"Grace? Is that you?"

Grace jumps, her hand fluttering to her throat. She wasn't expecting to have to engage with anyone. But the younger woman looks faintly familiar, the way her brown hair falls just to her shoulders, her clothes too tight in places.

"Do you remember me?"

Grace remembers. This person had been forthright then, too.

"Er—earlier this spring—were you here, looking around …?"

"I'm Marnie! And we did end up renting that blue-and-white trailer after all."

As Marnie points and swivels, her voice does an earnest tap dance next to Grace's ears. "My husband brought the boys and me up last Saturday, right after their last day of school. They're really excited to be here. Colin, my husband that is, brought my eldest later, her school had an extra week, she got here a few days ago. I was so hoping we'd bump into each other again. How have you been?"

Grace reaches up to shade her eyes from Marnie's scrutiny. "Not bad. Nice to see you again."

"Well. Summer's truly here now, don't you think? Another lovely day—" Marnie stretches both her arms out, still smiling. "Do you have plans?"

Grace hesitates, then tries a line of wry humour.

"Is it too early for a vodka martini?"

But Marnie doesn't laugh. Instead she looks both ways, and then says in a serious and low voice, "You're a woman after my own heart, Grace."

Grace is confused. Signals between humans are so hard to comprehend.

Marnie sighs. "Sometimes it's the only thing that feels good."

Grace swallows. "What is?"

"Like you said. Vodka and a splash of vermouth, with a speared olive." Marnie frowns. "Are you alright?"

"I'm fine."

There's an invisible dome of awkward silence; Grace shuffles her feet to step outside it. Now she needs to find an excuse to offer Marnie for her brainlessness.

"No, not fine. I mean, it's my mother. I have to get back. She is, you know, a handful sometimes."

"Ah, must be hard for you. Especially here." Marnie gives her a too-searching look, grimaces sympathetically.

Grace's defences go momentarily slack, temporarily weakened by Marnie's empathy and attentiveness, which remind her of Dr. Kerwin's approach. A waterfall of words slides out of her mouth.

"She insists on only wearing blue now. Blue slacks, blue shirts, blue underwear—she refuses to wear anything else. She's started to get aggressive—I give her a blouse or something that's not blue and she throws it at me!"

Marnie looks taken aback. "How extraordinary," she says. "What did you say her name was, again?"

Grace realizes she's said too much. She's released a huge, helium-filled balloon, and she can't snatch it back, nor know where the balloon will end up. She should have said something light and innocuous, though she can't think what. In her head a voice says, *Now look what you've done.*

"Ruby," says Grace, licking her lips. "Her name is Ruby."

"But why—" Marnie fumbles for words. "Ruby's so lucky to have you, but do you have any help with her? Can you maybe—hire someone?"

Just then a young man totters up to them with his arms full, balancing a box of garbage. There seems to be something wrong with one of his legs, or he's injured his foot perhaps. He lifts the cardboard box over his head to pitch it into the dumpster. There's a tattoo on the man's bare lower arm, a snarling bulldog wearing an army helmet, clenching a knife between its teeth. Under it, the word VIETNAM, only it's misspelled. Grace blinks. Sure enough, it says VIETNAN.

"Hi there, neighbour," he says to Marnie, grinning. Then, as if he's just noticed Grace, he says, "Who's your friend?"

Marnie looks flushed now, and there's such a strange energy coming off her that Grace doesn't know where to look. When Marnie says, "Grace, this is Milton," Milton extends a clenched fist toward her as a greeting. Grace lifts an uncertain fist to bump her knuckles against his, and smiles weakly. Great. Another one who knows her name. Grace reaches down to hold her flapping skirt against her knees.

"I really must go now."

"Listen," Marnie says hastily, turning back to Grace, "if you need a break or something, why don't you join us for supper on Friday? I promised the children a pie—"

"—I have a lot to do. I mean yes, thank you. Thank you."

Grace realizes as she's making her way back to her Airstream that she's just accepted a dinner invitation. She hadn't meant to. How to get out of it? Feign illness maybe. She tries the breathing exercise again but her thoughts keep churning with every breath. As we grow, we're taught table manners, how to button a shirt, calculate sums, sing the alphabet. Scientists decode minutiae, astronomers account for the universe. Yet no one explains how to negotiate the perils of human interaction.

She's just accepted a dinner invitation. Dr. Kerwin would be proud.

FOUR

Crow Hrah perches at the highest vantage point over-looking the trailer park. This single oak towers above the spruce and cedar trees that are all so familiar to him. By alighting here often, he reasserts his dominance over his family, though he would never stop the others from keeping him company on the lower branches. For now, he's here on his own. From this choice spot he's able, with one bright eye, to monitor any interesting activity between the sweep of the hill and the beach. With the other eye, he maintains his surveillance over the trailer park inhabitants.

Close to the water, the yearlings are playing games, testing their skills: some spring up and land again, their claws opening and closing on the shifting sand. Two of them become temporarily anchored in it up to their bent ankles, tugging at sticks. Gusts of new wind comb their neck and belly feathers.

The wind had been born that morning, soon after the sun came up. Hrah and his mate had paused from preening each other to watch it curl itself up from the belly of the lake, nudge along a section of the log boom, and circle against itself as it rose over the shallows. They'd watched as it became a breeze, lifting moisture from the lake and stirring the wildflowers. Then the wind had veered up and out, in its flight claiming the first, high-pitched morning voices from the park.

These fragments of sound are now dispersing, mingling with airborne pollen. Hoarse corvid voices that he recognizes are proclaiming themselves to be in the woods. Hrah answers the calls with his own declaration, the same one-and-a-half syllables drawn out for emphasis, and lifts off his perch to glide windward over the trailer park. He can see boy-humans down below on their bicycles as they begin to ride across the compound property, gathering momentum as they cut across the dirt lanes that divide this part of the space into quarters. He is aware of their earthbound trajectory, knows what they are doing: purposefully marking territory. He has survived enough seasons here to know it's a ritualistic practice engaged in by different boys every year, presenting slight variations of the pattern of these five bent heads, ten pumping legs.

He wheels back and lands on a high cedar branch behind the parking lot.

An engine starts up, and a car eases out of its space. On the asphalt there's something glistening that might be edible. He sees that the dumpster is filled with some new bulky packages, the kind encased in thin, rippling membranes that will be easy to tear open.

Over the span of the next hours, flies will be drawn to the dumpster's offerings of rotting diapers and discarded tin cans. They will be followed by the wasps who will drowsily inspect the sweetest congealments and the stickiest leavings. Greasy bones, fatty morsels of meat, rotting fruit, chip bags, and bread crusts await the crows.

He bobs in anticipation, and the branch sways under his claws.

FIVE

This trailer park, alas, seems the most unlikely place for a miracle to happen. It's so insignificant here. On the occasion of my restoration of perfect vision I shouldn't want to be standing in front of some sorry sight like a patch of weeds, a skateboard ramp, or wet clothes hanging on a fence. Would it not be so much more fitting to have something visually transcendent, brilliant, and utterly memorable? A sight that is worthy of this magnanimous, extravagant gesture on the part of the Almighty? But what beauty might I possibly come upon in this unnatural place?

Dear Diary, that's what I was thinking late last night. But since then I've reconsidered. After all, Jesus was born in a pretty unremarkable setting. And His birth was flagged by a star.

As a consequence I have a new habit now, that of looking at the sky. One never knows when a miracle might happen. There has to be a way, there will be a way. If I can just believe enough.

The advantage of the sky is that I can turn to it from anywhere outside, night or day. It's a vast, nay, infinite space in which some unprecedented vision might materialize, something splendidly illuminative.

Perchance a golden angel, or a resplendent rainbow.
Something only I will see.

Veronica puts her pencil down, closes the notebook, and slips it into her backpack.

When the vision arrives in the sky she imagines she'll stifle a gasp and fix her gaze upon it in rapture. She'll keep the gift a secret for a precious, perilous while.

How long after that, she wonders, until someone notices she can see just fine even though she's not wearing the detested spectacles?

In the evening, Veronica's flashlight makes a bobbing disk of light on the gravel, illuminating her path just enough to prevent her from bumping into anything, to keep her feet from straying onto somebody's property. She pauses sometimes to steal long glances at the sky. Past the length of her arm she can't see anything clearly in any direction, but in the dark neither can anyone else.

The evening's humidity clings to her skin. A moth blunders into her hair; she calmly shakes it out. A kicked stone bounces away with a satisfying thump and skitter. The shapes of objects ahead of her, farther away—a bench, a garbage can—are comfortingly fuzzy. From her left, about a hundred yards away, comes the sound of a piano; the notes trickle into her ears. A weak beam of yellow light glances from an open window in a low, sprawling building that's larger than several trailers put together.

She blinks, and the window-image becomes a bouquet of blooming jellyfish.

"Don't dawdle," Marnie calls out through the dark. "You wouldn't want us to lose you."

Veronica straightens her shoulders and glances skyward again. "Why can't Dilly slow down?"

"Come along. We have to show you the way to the canteen, at least."

Boredom and heat, in equal measure, have drawn them outside. Her mother and brothers have gotten considerably ahead of her. Veronica takes out her glasses, slips them on, and trots forward to catch up with her family.

There's a tall, thin woman poking at the remains of a campfire in her front yard. Sparks spring up from the glowing coals and vanish. Marnie warbles a cheerful "Good evening, Mrs Carmichael," and the woman looks up and murmurs hello. Thin ribbons of smoke vanish behind her.

Puddles of colour daub the dark grass lawn in geometric inclinations. The windows of Mrs Carmichael's trailer are made of stained glass.

They're there. The canteen stands on a well-trafficked curve where two of the main lanes cross. It's a small trailer just like many of the others, except this one has an awning that spans the length of a sliding window, and a menu— *Tuck Shop Sensations*—chalked on a propped-up sandwich board. Dilly is already sitting on the only stool. His flashlight is jammed into the hammer-loop on his overalls; one foot is kicking against the trailer wall.

"That'll be a dollar," says the girl at the counter, "plus the magic word. And I *don't* mean abracadabra. Or Open Sesame."

Dilly kicks the wall with increased vigour. The girl shrugs. She's deftly wrapping a sheet of brown paper around a stack of nickels in front of her. Veronica notices how her thumbs fold down the ends of the rolled paper at the top of the wrapped column, creasing the overlap into perfect, flat thirds.

"Why aren't there more stools?" Marnie asks.

"Stolen," says the girl, looking up. "So if you see them—"

"Is there a reward?" Gumm is eyeing the roll of nickels.

"Yeah," the girl retorts, "you'll get to sit down."

Veronica studies the teenager's face: she's probably a few years older than Veronica. A glorious tempest of red hair strains to escape from a paisley scarf. The girl's dazzling green eyes flicker from Dilly to Gumm, her eyebrows slightly arched. She's holding both boys at bay with the tilt of her head alone. Dilly squirms.

"Okay, okay," says Dilly. "Please." He stops kicking the wall.

The girl nods, turns, and lifts a cone from the top of a tall stack. She holds it away from her, tilts it under a metal spigot, and pulls a lever. The machine growls softly as chocolate ice cream slowly flows down into the cone. She adjusts the lever, swings the cone up, then down, and again, so that the pointed tip of the ice cream forms two perfect, looping swirls. Veronica watches, shyly admiring.

Dilly unexpectedly says, "Thank you," when the girl hands him the sculpture.

"You're welcome. Next?"

Gumm's looking the other way, so their mother gestures at Veronica. "What'll it be? A milkshake? A Mae West? A Popsicle? Cracker Jacks? How does it feel to be able to read the menu now? Go on, order anything you want."

"Anything you want," repeats the ice-cream sculptress, smiling right at her. Veronica's face grows hot and she quickly turns her gaze to the menu.

Marnie smoothes out five dollars on the counter, and the sculptress says "Thank you. I'll give you your change in a moment," and she tucks the bill into a shallow apron tied at her waist. Veronica, clamped between shyness and indecision, wills herself to say something, anything, as the girl waits. In the gulf of Veronica's silence, Dilly starts kicking the wall again. Gumm moans loudly, and flicks his fingers impatiently at his sister's arm. Hurry up.

"Hey," says the girl to Gumm, "do you have a train to catch or something?" She turns back to Veronica. "I'd go for the new flavour if I were you." She picks up another cone and reaches back to the machine. "Malted milk," she says, over her shoulder. "It's so new it's not even on the board yet. As a special bonus, chocolate-dipped. Trust me."

Veronica watches as the girl turns the glistening cone upside down and partially submerges it into a vat of melted chocolate. Keeping her eyes on the confection,

Veronica starts to say, "I am beholden—" when it suddenly occurs to her how odd that might sound, and instead she says, "Thank you."

Gumm is rolling his eyes. Dilly twirls the stool, thrusts what's left of his cone at Veronica, and scowls. "Why didn't *she* have to say please?"

The chocolate cracks softly open under her teeth and a cold, velvety sensation migrates across her tongue.

The girl sends a look of encouragement and approval to Veronica and then turns to Gumm. "For you, I recommend licorice."

"I hate licorice," he says.

"That's the whole point," she replies, and starts filling up another cone, oblivious to his protests. When she finally hands him a malted milk ice cream as well, he says "Oh," and "Ha ha, very funny!"

Veronica pretends to stroll casually, to be occupied with her ice cream, and starts to sidle farther away from the canteen, into some shadows. She hears the tuck-shop girl saying to Marnie, "You can have an account if you like. You just have to register at the office. Apply with the park superintendent." The girl stretches her long neck and looks down the lane—could she be looking for Veronica?—before she counts out the change.

On the way back, Veronica walks slowly, dawdling behind her mother and brothers, aiming her flashlight at the gravel, forgetting to look up at the sky. The ice-cream sculptress had said, "Open Sesame." Might she too have read *The Arabian Nights*? She might be staying here in the

42

park. Veronica finishes her ice cream and thinks, maybe she could get a job in the tuck shop as well, get to know that girl. She could learn things such as how to make those ice cream loops and how to be so self-assured. Surely Marnie will approve of her seeking something interesting to do; nay, she'll even be glad her daughter's showing some initiative, making some pocket money.

Veronica is about halfway home when she's distracted by an unfamiliar voice. Down one of the side lanes, where the campers go to fill their water containers, there's an older man clad in dark sweat pants and a white tunic standing under the lamplight, calling out to anyone who will listen.

"As His children we have an obligation to thank the Lord for all our blessings!"

Three people move past Veronica and disappear, their still-empty water jugs bumping together as they hasten back from whence they came.

"Go then, and sin no more!" he shouts after them, then sets his gaze on Veronica. She doesn't move.

When he comes closer, she lifts her flashlight and illuminates his body; one of his hands is swept across his round belly, and the other is folded behind his back as he takes a low bow.

"Swain, swain."

He straightens up again, and Veronica startles. She doesn't want to aim her light into his face, that would be rude. Could he really be saying "swain"?

"*Sssswain*, at your service, gentle damsel," he says.

There is a beat of uncomfortable silence. They are alone. "I beg your pardon?"

"No need to be alarmed. I have come to ask you if you have seen the light."

"You need light?"

Veronica has glimpsed his eyes, as small and dark as raisins. She can smell his breath: alcohol, like her mother's breath smells sometimes. She still grips the flashlight, but her legs won't move. He presses himself forward, swaying sideways in the darkness. A small chuckle erupts.

"To that light I do not refer, but indeed, to the light of eternal salvation. I beseech you, cast away your transgressions and ye shall be saved—"

This time, as he sways forward, his head almost grazes hers. But before Veronica can step back he reaches for her free hand and presses a small object into it.

"For you, young maiden," he whispers.

She points her light down at a medallion, an image of Jesus, His hands spread open, the creases of His long robe cast in two-dimensional relief. She turns it over. On the back, an engraving: *YE MUST BE BORN AGAIN.*

Her heart starts to beat faster. Does this have something to do with her miracle?

"Bless you, in the name of the Lord," says the swain gravely.

Veronica thinks quickly. Is this an angel in disguise? Does he have wings? Yet something about him reminds her of Fagin in *Oliver Twist*. Appearances can deceive. Saint Fagin?

Apprehensive, she meets his eyes, regards his face briefly in the light. Is something expected of her now? She turns her gaze higher, to the sky; no, she's not ready for this yet.

But she *can* speak his language.

"I—I am much obliged indeed, sir, for this." She holds out her left fist, indicating the medallion. "I shall see you again. Anon."

Veronica ducks her head and hurries home, feeling uplifted. Surely he's a saint disguised as a misfit, just like Jesus. He asked her if she had seen the light yet. What else could be be talking about, but her eyesight?

The Reid family's rented trailer—or mobile home, as Veronica's mother calls it—takes up the first outside-corner lot of the holiday community. The allotment's border faces a field of shallow, undulating hills, where a number of mature willows are green and golden as holy robes. The lake in the distance seems to be softly inhaling and exhaling, its scalloped surface beaming and twinkling all the way to the horizon and up to the changing sky. Veronica shades her eyes with one hand as she looks. She fingers the Jesus medallion in her pocket.

People are coming. Two girls talking, laughing. Keeping her eye on them, Veronica takes a few steps back under the awning. One, wearing cut-offs and a halter top, passes a cigarette to the other, who's in bright flared pants and a headband. This one has the look of the girl at school who jammed the lock in the toilet stall one time and made

Veronica crawl out. She lowers herself swiftly, her back sliding down the trailer's outside wall; she secretly watches the two girls as they cut through the inside of the Reids' corner lot. Who are they to trespass like this, or to cast skeptical little glances at their trailer? They look as though they'd like to tug the pleated curtains open with their eyes and peer inside the private, untidy spaces her family inhabits.

The curved side of the patch of grass here is constantly encroached upon, the edge worn bare by all the traffic. Scuffing shoes, flapping sandals, rolling bicycles, stroller wheels.

The neighbours and their trailers crowd too closely from the outside, but there's the same cramped feeling inside, where she's one too many people for the amount of oxygen in the space. Why can't privacy be measured like oxygen? In such an environment, she must conceal what's good and true, like her hopes and beliefs. She must protect them from becoming smothered, from withering in the light of others' too-close, scornful glares.

Veronica rises again and descends the verandah steps. She turns into the yard and almost right away her gaze falls, as though for the first time, on the storage shed. It's a plain utility structure behind their trailer, at the end of the strip of irregular paving stones bordering on their back yard. She comes closer. The door is unlocked. Inside, two sets of shelves support a collection of rubber boots, a life jacket, a picnic blanket, barbecue briquets, a leaning shovel, and a rake. The shed has a plywood floor and one window for light.

She barges back into the trailer and finds her mother tucking something swiftly under a seat-cushion as she enters. Marnie is smiling at her.

"I was wondering where you were. How're you making out? Starting to feel at home yet?"

"I appeal to you—entreat you—to allow me to transform the shed into my space. I mean to say, even to sleep there."

Marnie's smile vanishes. "No."

"Please."

"No."

"But why not? It's terribly important to me. You wouldn't have to take the shelves out. There's adequate room next to them, I could use the piece of foam that I sleep on now—"

"No."

"Why ever not?"

"It's unnatural. What's wrong with ... because it's unsafe. It's not meant to be slept in. And besides, where else would I put the folding chairs?"

"Fine then. I'll sleep in the hammock. On the verandah."

Veronica sees the battle between decorum and convenience playing out on her mother's face. Could she really be considering saying yes to the porch as a possibility?

"Think about it," Veronica says swiftly. "There's a roof to protect me from the elements, and that mosquito net we have, you know, the one that's suspended from a hoop. Lights are on close by, to discourage loiterers I'm sure. Yet—and here's the best part—nobody will be able to perceive that I'm there, for the hammock is concealed by shadow. If there's any disturbance, well, your bedroom window's next to where my head will be. I could call to you. On cold nights I'll take extra covers, or come back inside."

Veronica thinks of one more thing.

"I'm going to be fourteen," she says. "You can't really stop me."

Marnie has exhaled, but now she's just staring at the wall behind the stove. She mutters something that sounds like, "I just can't do this any more."

Veronica waits.

Her mother relents. "You're bound to have your own way," she says. Her lips form themselves into a knot. "Aren't you."

SIX

Several days have passed since Veronica's encounter with Saint Fagin. Each morning she's awakened under her netting in the hammock with new hope, pulling the layers of gauze apart and gazing up to the sky to discover her vision. Each time she's been disappointed anew, but she keeps steadfast in her faith.

Mornings and afternoons, at different times, she's hoisted her backpack and gone looking for the swain, feigning nonchalance, wandering close to the place she first saw him, her heart hammering. What was it, exactly, he had said? Something about seeing the light? Should she look for a church close by? Should she seek out Mrs Carmichael, with the stained-glass windows in her trailer, and therefore probably a believer in miracles? Should she start reading the Bible? (But where would she get one of those, without drawing attention? Maybe Mrs Carmichael has one.)

As she walks, she's intensely aware of the secret

medallion, savouring the pleasant sensation of its weight in her pocket, its solid teardrop-shaped heft, gently bumping against her thigh.

A pair of crows lifts from one of the willow trees in the park. Veronica watches the first lead the second as they fly over the compound, then angle off in the direction of the main road.

She's seized by the idea of making a bird feeder to attract them and be able to watch them more closely.

An empty milk carton will do nicely, and there just happens to be one in the kitchen. Veronica asks Gumm if she can borrow his pocketknife, but he snatches it from his back pocket, flips it open, and says, "I'm using it." From his other pocket he seizes a piece of wood and starts whittling.

Veronica opens the kitchen drawer. The bread knife will work. With one knee on the bench of the dinette, she saws intently along one side of the carton, turns it over, then, with the knife tip, works in a puncture near the centre of the pleated top.

"Look at the two of you, playing with knives," says Marnie, coming down the hall. She fastens her watch and reaches up to finger her bauble earrings. Her eyes are outlined in blue eyeliner, and her lipstick looks recently applied.

"Anyway, I just wanted you to know I'm going out for a while. I won't be long."

"Where are you going?" Veronica asks.

Marnie looks away. "Just out to see a friend, that's all."

She points to the shavings that have fallen on Gumm's thighs and are beginning to scatter on the floor.

"I hope you're going to clean up your mess after you're done."

Gumm looks down and shrugs.

Veronica says, "Mine's finished now."

Gumm matter-of-factly folds his blade back into its handle, thumbs it back into his pocket, and rises from the chair. He demonstrates the slingshot he's just made. "I need an elastic band," he says.

"As long as nobody loses an eye," replies Marnie. She looks at herself in the little mirror above the stove one more time and is gone.

Veronica fills the carton with peanuts, then drags a chair across the lane and climbs on it to hang her bird feeder on a branch of a mountain ash.

Some distance away from the feeder, but still close enough to keep it in view, Veronica settles on the grass, her shoulder next to the fence, the lake behind her. At the sight of the rows of toothed leaves, the droopy flower heads, the woolly clusters of petals letting go and drifting to the ground below—all that detail—she thinks for a split second that her miracle has come. But then she reaches up and feels that her glasses are there. Not yet.

Troublesome as they are, at least my glasses will enable me to see the crows when they come. There must be other kinds of birds, surely, like starlings or sparrows. Or robins.

So far the only birds I've seen here are the crows. I am drawn to watching them raid the dumpster, seeing how deftly they hone in on what they want, how efficiently they claw holes in the bags with their feet, make off with their prizes. I hear them assembling noisily in small groups over the woods, I see them scatter again. Sometimes they make no sound at all, whether they're sweeping silently over the lake or strutting on the ground in the park.

I wouldn't mind being caught by surprise by my miracle while watching crows.

She wonders where the crows are now. What if their flight paths take them too high to be able to see peanuts? They would have to have exceptional vision, or especially sensitive smell. They might not even like peanuts. Veronica wrinkles her nose and waits. She's determined to keep very still; she's even brought a book to read, just in case nothing happens for a long time. The bird feeder, now hanging a little lopsidedly below the branch, begins slowly to revolve.

Is that a crow she can hear in the distance?

I wonder, could they be saying actual things to one another when they caw, in some kind of avian secret code? Can they tell each other's voices apart? And where do they sleep at night? In nests? I'll ask my father to take me to a library and I'll look for books on birds. And a Bible, so I can read about miracles. Can a person even check out a Bible from a library? If so, I could tuck the Holy Book between the bird books so no one but the librarian will see it.

A guitar tune flickers into her consciousness. It seems to be coming from the trailer where Marnie said the hippies are. There, the front door is flung open, and a shirtless teenage boy comes out with a ball, which he proceeds to kick upwards, over and over, with the tops of his bare feet. Veronica regards him skeptically.

A car enters the compound. It's a Mustang fishtailing along the lane as it passes the skateboard park. It's coming fast. Alarmed, she tries to scramble farther from the road, but she's clumsy about it and slips in the grass. Behind her, she hears the engine revving, as the car's back tires spit the gravel sideways. She recoils as the smallest stones sting her legs.

She rubs her legs, trying to figure out if the gravel attack was deliberate or accidental. The Mustang pulls away, then brakes at the curve and disappears around the back lane. A horn sounds. And out of the dust into which the car vanished, a phalanx of cycling boys appears, bustling along, gathering momentum. A wolf whistle pierces the air; their knees start to pump faster. Something that looks to Veronica like a lasso spirals above them. She panics and ducks. But it's not a lasso, she can see it now, it's a kite. One of the boys—it's Gumm—leans out from the others as they whiz past.

"Hey, Ronnie! Four-eyes! You look like an owl!"

Boisterous reinforcements, hearty whoops of approval, as the boys speed off.

So the torment's started here too, after all. Because of Gumm, who wants to impress his new friends.

Veronica takes stock of herself. Her legs are peppered with red marks from the gravel. She clutches her book.

They're coming back. If they say anything this time, she'll sacrifice the book, throw it into their spokes. She imagines the first disabled bike stalling the second one, then the third, until the riders have all crashed, twisted their axles, skinned their knees. That'll teach them. By the time they pick themselves up, she'll be long gone.

A breathy jeer: "Hey, grease-face, Ver-ronnie, your epidermis is showing!"

She launches her book, which lands with a dull thump in the dirt, guffaws of laughter rippling behind the vanished boys. She goes to retrieve it, humiliated. What's an epidermis? It doesn't sound like a word a kid would make up. She yanks her glasses off and, with her head down, stalks into the park, headed for the beach, where the cyclists likely won't follow. The grass is crinkly and dry under her bare feet. Over a sun-bleached hillock, past some empty picnic tables, into a pool of shade.

And all at once on the ground in front of her, there's a pair of long, bare legs, crossed at the ankles, toes wiggling.

She stumbles back a few steps. "I beg your pardon—I wasn't looking where—"

"—where you were going, I know. I saw you."

The voice is familiar, a deep rich tone that's almost musical, like a cello.

Veronica gropes for her glasses and manages to put them on. It's the ice-cream sculptress, sitting with her

54

back propped against a willow trunk. She's grasping the top of a sketchbook in one hand, and a black stub of charcoal is poised in the other. Her gaze is clear and amused.

"I was—being too hasty, forgive me—on my way to the beach—I should have been looking up, but—"

"I know. Well—I can't be in the sun. Look at me, I'd burn to a crisp." She puts her sketchbook down and wriggles a creamy, freckled arm for emphasis. "I'm Charlotte." Pulling her knees up and hugging them to herself, she adds, "I'm staying just over there."

She points to the closest row of trailers, parallel to the water's edge, next to a border of pines. Veronica looks, then glances back at Charlotte. Maybe she doesn't have to go to the beach after all. What would happen if she just sat down, right here? She's not sure about the civilities. Sweat prickles on her neck and under her arms.

As if she's read Veronica's mind, Charlotte moves her sketchbook out of the way and pats the ground next to her.

"And *you* are …?"

"Um—Veronica Reid." Casting a look back to scan for the boys (surely they won't come after her here), she sits. "Thank you. Were—were you drawing something?"

"Sort of. Well, just practising with depth of field, really." Looking playfully sheepish, Charlotte hands the sketchbook to Veronica. Charcoaled lines render the scene before them: a straight horizon line, the lake's textured surface, a thin margin of sand, blowsy willow trees in the middle distance, and, thrust into the foreground, almost absurdly large, the top halves of two bare feet. It is delectable to be laughing with her.

Veronica learns that Charlotte is seventeen, on her summer break from a specialized arts-academic high school in Toronto, and works part-time at the canteen in the park. While she talks Veronica tries hard not to stare at her animated face, her blazing green eyes. The low notes of her voice are striking chords that make the shade thrum; her mouth keeps springing out into sideways smiles.

Veronica gathers her courage. "Are you acquainted—I mean, do you know what an epidermis is?"

Charlotte appears to consider the question seriously. "It so happens that I do. It's your outer skin, the layer on the outside."

Veronica's shoulders slump. She smiles ruefully.

"The boys told me my epidermis was showing."

Charlotte throws her head back and laughs. "What a bunch of doorknobs. I don't know how they can stand themselves."

"I've never read nor heard that word before, though surely I should have, by my age."

"How old are you, anyway?"

"Thirteen."

"I only know that particular term because of life-drawing class. Mostly we draw feet, necks, hands, places where the skin stretches over bones. I try to make the drawings realistic … veins and freckles, wrinkles, and even scars, marking the epidermis. It's good practice. Do you have scars?"

Veronica nods and holds out her wrist.

"Bike accident."

She hasn't told anyone that the fall was choreographed by the gang of girls at school, and she feels too self-conscious to mention it now.

"It happened over a year ago. I had five stitches."

Charlotte turns Veronica's palm over and looks at the wrist thoughtfully.

"That's a good one," she says.

Veronica wants to ask her if she has a scar as well, but instead finds herself distracted by the nearness of the top of Charlotte's head, the side part in her curly hair, one pale pink ear.

Charlotte traces the mark lightly with her fingertip. "Must have hurt."

Veronica nods. Goodness shines out of Charlotte like a beacon. She wonders if anyone else can see this.

"You're staying here with your whole family?"

"My father comes on the weekends."

"Well." Charlotte nods. "You're awfully mature for your age. I like you."

Charlotte pauses and Veronica considers what to say in response to this compliment. But then Charlotte releases Veronica's hand to examine a frayed hem on the bottom corner of her blouse.

"My parents died when I was eleven."

Veronica feels a lightning strike of panic as she searches her mind for something to say. "Jane Eyre was an orphan, and, and Anne of—" she stops. "Charles Dickens writes—" she stops again. Then the words come out in a kind of squeak. "I mean, that's so tragic. What happened?"

"Little Nell? Little Orphan Annie?" Charlotte smiles. "It's okay now. Back then, it was the worst thing that ever happened. It was a car accident. Drunk driver."

"Both of them?"

"Instantly."

"Do you have a benefactor?"

"A what?"

Veronica blushes. "Nothing."

"We had to stay with our aunt until Peter, my brother, was old enough to be our guardian. I'm here with him for the summer, and when I turn eighteen— It's okay, Veronica, don't feel sorry for me."

Veronica's throat feels tight. Charlotte continues to reassure her. "It was a long time ago."

Charlotte has one more year left in art school, then she'll go to college.

"I'm drawn to the lyrical abstraction movement," she explains. "And I like making sculptures—mostly papier mâché. After I graduate I want to move to New York City and find a cheap studio apartment. It's where all the modern artists are going. I want to hang out with them."

"That sounds enchanting, so—glamorous. But um, lyrical abstraction—I don't know what that is."

As they talk, Veronica forgets to be shy or self-conscious. Under Charlotte's gentle encouragement Veronica finds herself telling her that her favourite subject is English. She tells her about the bullies.

Charlotte looks puzzled. "Why do they pick on you?"

"Because I'm different, I guess. My mom says they'll grow out of it. That *I'll* grow out of it. I don't know." She presses her lips together. "Now that I have to wear these wretched glasses, I won't stand a chance."

"Never mind them," Charlotte declares. "You look fine to me. Their loss."

"They know exactly what words will pierce me to the quick."

"You'll have the last laugh one day," Charlotte assures her. "Give me back your hand. I can read your palm if you like."

While Charlotte looks at the lines on her palm, Veronica sits quietly, feeling a stirring sensation, a mingling of apprehension and pleasure. The dappled shade shifts and flickers. A beetle is working its way through the stubbled grass by her thigh.

"Are you right-handed?"

"M-mm."

"Let me see your other hand. No, I mean both. I need to see both."

Veronica turns and shifts closer, using one palm as a pivot on the damp ground.

"You have 'earth' hands," Charlotte pronounces, turning them over in her own.

"You mean they're dirty?"

Charlotte breaks into her robust laugh again. "No, it's to do with their shape. The shape of your hands says to me that you're a practical sort of person, down-to-earth, with a strong life force. That's vitality. You have a true connection to nature and the outdoors."

"Do I? Really? What does the shape of your hands say about *you*?"

Charlotte releases Veronica's hands and holds out her own palm and long fingers, and as she turns them over Veronica regards the constellations of brown freckles on the backs of them, the skin dry and soft. "I have classic 'water' hands. Creative and emotional. When I was little, I used to try to rub the freckles off, but I don't mind them now."

Veronica exclaims, "Heaven forbid! They're beautiful. Anne of Green Gables had red hair and freckles. The boys called her 'Carrots.'"

When Charlotte smiles, Veronica is encouraged. She adds, "My father says that when you look at the stars, you're looking at the past. Can you really look at my palm and see the future?"

"I'll try if you let me."

"If you please," Veronica blurts, her heart racing. She stretches out her hands.

SEVEN

Hrah turns his head from left to right as he flies, recognizing all the familiar landmarks. He has a purpose. He carries a pair of peanuts in his beak, aromatic morsels enclosed in one soft, dry shell.

At every wingbeat, he can hear and feel the nuts rolling back and forth in their little round pockets of air: a soft, percussive rumble, the sensation of which he feels against his hard palate. He is headed for a landing on a flat rock some distance along the lakeside, where he will strike open his prize. He will ingest the fragments of these nutmeats, head jiggled back to gobble them down.

His world is one of earth and air, granite and water, flora and fauna. Earth tells him stories of his ancestors through his dreams; the planet carries their memories through its orbit and cradles them in its revolutions. Earth holds the past, while pockets of still air enclose the present. Wind brings the future. Distant oceans breathe in and out, drawing in all the pulsing rivers, measuring the tide of time.

He reaches the flat rock, sets his prize down, looks around to make sure he's alone. Then he pins the peanut against a small cleft in the rock with one claw and lowers his beak to puncture and rip the shell. In seconds, the nut-meats are plucked out cleanly. He leaps up and launches into the air again.

He waits for the yearlings' and other family members' calls. Once they appear from wherever they've gone, he will lead them back to a new food source, near the edge of a sand pit, where a queue of bread crusts awaits. It will be his opportunity to teach them to carry the crusts to the river's edge and soak them briefly before gobbling them down.

He sees two humans moving away from the boat dock, one with straight, straw-coloured hair, and the other one with a mane of ruddy curls. They're wading waist-high through the wilder earth-growth, blossoms tangled in co-lourful profusion. The girls are bending to grasp the flow-ers, breaking them off, gathering bunches of stems in their arms. Woodsmoke curls up from the campground's edge.

EIGHT

Grace is playing solitaire, placing the cards one at a time in a smooth line on the kitchen table, when she hears the crack of gunfire. She jumps. Someone's been killed. She swiftly folds her body down from the bench to the trailer floor and draws her knees up tightly to her chest, her back crammed against the cupboard. She dares not pull the shade to look out her window; it's fully dark outside, and if anyone's out there with a rifle, she'd rather not be seen. Then comes the whistling noise of a bomb falling. Is it possible they're under siege? The cracking sound of an explosion. It will wake Ruby. She should double-check to make sure the door's locked. Is the metal cladding of the Airstream Land Yacht thick enough to stop a bullet?

After a minute the gunfire erupts again, and she hears Ruby groaning behind the wall. Her chest tightens. She crawls into the hallway, and with dread reaches up to draw the front edge of Ruby's curtain.

"Oh, Gracie. Where— Why, you're kneeling!"

Grace is partially relieved. "Oh—yes. But—did you hear—"

"Tell me, what are we celebrating?"

"Mother, don't panic. I'm not sure what's going on, but I think—"

"I can hear fireworks. Is it Canada Day or something?"

"Canada Day. Oh my God. Fireworks. Of course."

But Grace can't make her fingers stop shaking. An image burns like a brand in her mind: the silhouette of a gunman crouching close to their trailer, the side of his face pressed against a rifle, one eye looking down the long barrel. An Airstream window in his sights. A puff of smoke rising from the end of the muzzle.

Someone after them.

"Did you hear me, Gracie? I said I'd like to see them."

Grace is startled; she locks eyes with Ruby. "See who?"

"The fireworks."

Grace thinks for a minute. "Right. But we'd have to go out. It's—it's late, do you even know how late it is? And you're not dressed."

"It's dark. No one will notice if I'm dressed or not."

In the old days, Ruby cared very much about whether she were dressed or not. In the old days she was far more sophisticated, much less impulsive. Back then Ruby was still possessed of most of her faculties. But the last time she wanted to go somewhere late in the evening was last fall. It was a bingo night at the last trailer park they'd stayed in. Over the last ten months, Ruby's physical and mental condition had changed markedly. Has Grace's own condition worsened in that short time as well?

"Gracie?"

"Right. But Mother—surely you can't walk that far."

"How far?"

"I expect it's in the park. I mean, I don't know where else."

"We can go as far as the park, can't we?"

Grace doesn't want to let her mother down, not ever, certainly not now. "Perhaps we could take the wheelchair."

"It's settled then."

There's another rat-tat-tat noise in the distance, and Grace hesitates. She remembers she's left the wheelchair folded under an awning behind the trailer. When she thinks of going outside to get it—even in the face of the logical explanation for the noise—apprehension fastens itself to her rib cage.

Ruby rises unsteadily and reaches for her slippers. She turns her expectant gaze to Grace, who gets up and makes her way to the door. One thing at a time, Grace says to herself. Turn the handle, step outside, hand on the railing, foot on the step. She fights the urge to look up and down the lane. She tries to walk normally, stops herself from huddling too close to the trailer. She retrieves the chair and brings it to the front door. Then she's back inside. Victory.

Ruby leans heavily on Grace's arm as she finds her way down the steps in the dark, and Grace helps her into the chair before she turns back to lock the door. New popping noises erupt, and she looks up to see fan-shaped bursts of light flaring against the dark sky.

"It *is* happening over the park," she says. "Let's go then."

She likes that there are trees and hedges in this community. One of the trailer parks they'd stayed in consisted of rows of identical units set end-to-end across a big open plain, which she'd found demoralizing. Grace remembers that place for their social expectations also. The other tenants had kept at her to go to the nearby bowling alley, even though Grace wanted nothing to do with bowling, or with them. Then one day there'd been a fist fight between two of the women, one of whom called the Children's Aid Society to report the other. The informant came away with a broken nose, and Grace and Ruby moved out the next day.

In their very first trailer community, just over two years ago, there were specific, delineated neighbourhoods—some for the larger trailers and others for the smaller ones. In one of the poorer quarters, a van had been set on fire and had to be towed, still burning, into the parking lot. Not long after that, the trailer court had closed down for the season. Luckily Grace had been able to secure winter accommodation for them in the park landlady's insulated house.

They'd moved on after that, to another privately owned campground, where there was an elderly couple next door. The husband was quiet enough, but the wife had told Ruby to call her Anastasia, declaring that she was the escaped Grand Duchess of the Imperial Romanov family. Grace had thought Anastasia was a bad influence on Ruby, so they'd moved again. For the winter they'd settled into adjoining motel rooms where the mini-kitchen in Grace's room was adequate for preparing their breakfasts. They'd ordered pizza every Friday night. For all their other meals they went to a nearby diner or sea-food place.

Grace has never minded moving. Staying too long in any one place meant risking being found. But she thinks she's stayed in each of them now, all the trailer parks and motels that exist within reasonable driving distance of Ruby's medical clinic and her own Dr. Kerwin. There's nowhere else to go.

Now, looking down at her mother's thin shoulders, as she pushes the wheelchair along the lane in the dark, she despairs about their future. Even if a new trailer park or motel opened up, she'd still have to contend with get-ting Ruby on and off buses, helping her in and out of the little bathrooms on board, not to mention the taxis to get from bus station to destination. It would all be too hard, it would all draw too much attention. It was bad enough the last time, when they moved here to Laughing Wil-lows Trailer Park. But Ruby's practically an invalid now. Harder to be anonymous with an invalid.

Grace's sense of safety begins to erode when peo-ple start asking questions. And there's always someone, wherever she goes. Here, it's Marnie who makes her nervous. And now she's somehow agreed to pay a social call—to join the whole family for dinner, Friday night.

She's thinking of Marnie because she and Ruby are drawing near her trailer, the blue-and-white Corsair on the corner. There's a teenage girl leaning out from the porch railings. Must be Marnie's daughter. The girl is looking toward the park, up to the sky, her face illuminated by the strobe lights from the falling fireworks. She has a look of rapture on her face and doesn't appear to notice Grace and Ruby, doesn't seem to hear the gravel grind under the wheels of Ruby's chair.

Grace guides her mother across the lane and enters the park through the gap in the chain-link fence. There's a crowd ahead, the light in front rendering their bodies as silhouettes. Some are clapping and cheering, some shuffling and jostling for a better view.

"Why, it's a Catherine Wheel," Ruby says.

For a second Grace thinks her mother's referring to someone she's seen, someone here who she knows. There's a flicker of panic before she realizes Ruby's actually saying the name of the spinning mechanism in front of the crowd, the gigantic wheel spewing out sparks of gold and silver, expelling coloured flame.

"A Catherine Wheelchair," Ruby jokes, and Grace laughs.

People move aside to make room for them.

When the wheel stops swirling, the park drowns in darkness. Grace hears a voice say, "That's it, dudes, it's all

68

over now." Two boys start running back and forth, waving silver sparklers. A kid strolling through the crowd is selling them one at a time for a dollar; Grace finds a crumpled bill in her pocket and buys one for her mother. Ruby holds up the metal wand, and a man nearby leans forward, flicks his lighter. The sparkler spits into life. Grace watches it burn down, the descending crescendo of white light, the electric shocks of impossibly tiny explosions, the race of flame searing itself into the night.

NINE

My heart has become heavy with resignation.

What a let down, what a long, drawn-out, slow-motion trip of disappointment and disillusion. I had been so hopeful for my miracle last night. Fireworks would have been such a perfect backdrop. A firmament of coloured glass. Nothing else could top that, the drama of it, the perfect timing. What have I been doing wrong? Perhaps I'm cursed. Doomed to wear glasses for the rest of my life. How can I keep on believing?

After breakfast, Veronica stows her notebook in her backpack. When Marnie directs her to go to the trailer of the couple next door and ask to borrow some lard, she doesn't have the energy to protest.

The sun is already hot. The long, buzzing drone of a cicada starts up in the mountain ash. Veronica looks and listens hard, but she can't hear or see any birds this morning.

A string of frayed, sun-bleached cotton triangles sags along the neighbour trailer's chrome trim. A potted red geranium is propped in the window closest to the door. Veronica knocks.

A young woman opens the door in a clingy exercise outfit, exposing cleavage and toned midriff. When she sees Veronica she holds her hands in a prayer position and bows.

"Namaste. Hello, sweetie, what can I do for you?"

Veronica attempts to smile. "Good afternoon. I am here at the request of my mother." She gestures at their trailer. "She says we're sorry to disturb you but she wants to know if we may borrow some lard."

"You're Marnie's girl? I see. I'm Saffron. Lard, you said."

"Yes, please. She intends to make a pie."

Veronica's gaze flickers to the young woman's chest. The sight causes an unexpected spasm of pleasure between her legs, followed by jabs of shame, a swift alarm that it might happen again.

"I don't believe in lard, sweetie," Saffron says. "But a pie—that's pretty ambitious. You're welcome to borrow some of our Nut-Butter Bliss."

Veronica swallows her confusion. "I daresay—thank you, but I don't think that would be suitable for—I think pastry is quite particular—"

Saffron seems amused now for some reason, so Veronica looks away, takes her glasses, and wipes them with the edge of her T-shirt.

Then Saffron calls, "Milton? Milton!"

Putting her glasses on, Veronica sees a man poke his head around the outside end of the trailer. He emerges, sets down an armful of firewood, and lifts up his hand to shade his eyes. As he steps forward, Veronica notices his heavy limp. He has unruly dark hair falling to his shoulders. A tattoo on his forearm.

"Look who's here. This is Veronica, Marnie's girl."

"No, really?"

Milton comes over and looks her up and down. Veronica can see that, just below the hem of his shorts, a leather strap fastens an artificial leg to a stump where his knee should be.

"So you're Veronica." Milton extends a fist, bumps it playfully toward her. Then he points to the stack of wood. "Making room so I can back my boat in."

A swift image of Milton standing on an ocean vessel's pitching foredeck rushes into her mind. He stands with his weight on his good foot, his infirmity concealed under buckled shoes and woollen stockings that slide under dark breeches, and—as her gaze travels upwards—a fitted canvas doublet, a velvet tricorn hat with its trimmings of silk and taffeta. A scabbard swings from Milton's hip; his long, dark locks lift in the wind; the handle of his cutlass gleams in the sunlight. She imagines a parrot alighting on his shoulder and calling out, "Pieces of eight! Pieces of eight!"

The parrot's voice fades as Milton says, "We go for a spin now and again, eh, Saffron? We open up the throttle, throw caution to the wind. Hey now, young lady. We wouldn't mind taking you out, if you dig it."

"Think about it, sweetie," Saffron says.

The thought is terrifying. Veronica shakes her head

no, looks away.

"How come? You're not worried about this?" Milton leans down and touches his leg.

He gives a bitter laugh. "This little blessing is courtesy of the Viet Cong. Or should I say the US government. You don't want to know about that. Or maybe you do. Could be you're not old enough to hear my story. Don't look so worried, I still have one good leg. Sure I can't convince you to come out for a spin?"

"I—no—"

"Of course she will," says a voice from behind her. "Let's live dangerously! I'll come too, how about that?"

It's Marnie. Veronica hasn't even heard her come over. Veronica tries to catch her eye, but it's too late.

"Mother and daughter, far out," says Milton. "We'll make it a foursome. What are you doing this afternoon?"

After lunch, Veronica is pacing unhappily along the damp, hard-packed sand near the lake's edge. As her legs carry her back and forth, she hears the drone of a passing jet. She halts to tilt her head, and moves her glasses, alternating her gaze between the worlds of clarity and indeterminateness. The sky is littered with white clouds; the jet contrail slowly spreads into blurriness. She squeezes the Jesus medallion in her pocket.

Her gaze drops to a weathered signboard. The words are worn but still legible: *Swim at Your Own Risk*. She wonders if the warning refers to the lack of a lifeguard. Or more likely to the uncleanliness of the water.

Scowling, she tucks her hands into her armpits and resumes pacing.

Veronica and her mother are the only people on the beach this afternoon, though there are others in the park. Someone's carrying a shopping bag, there's a jogger in Adidas shorts, and a woman is pushing a toddler who's furiously kicking his legs in a stroller. A dark-haired couple comes into view; they're casually holding hands.

Veronica looks hard at all these people. None are Milton or Saffron.

"They're not coming. I told you it was a repellent idea. Let's just go home."

"Quit it, Veronica. Sometimes I just know what's better for you."

Marnie sounds flustered for some reason, though it's hard to really tell because of her sunglasses. She certainly doesn't look comfortable. Her lifejacket straps are buckled on too tightly, and she keeps adjusting her wide-brimmed straw hat to stop it from flopping down over her forehead. Beads of sweat speckle her arms; she smells of suntan lotion.

Veronica squats to pick up a stone and regards it in her hand. It's large, a rough egg shape, hard and dusty. She reaches her arm back and then swings it forward, aiming the rock at the far curve of the log boom. At the splash, a squadron of dragonflies lifts up, hovers in the trembling air, then vanishes.

Veronica feels the prod of her mother's elbow. She's pointing up the hill. Milton and Saffron have appeared at the top, Milton with his odd, uneven gait, orange lifejackets swinging from his hands. Saffron breaks into a happy trot.

Milton catches up with them and croons: "Are you the lovely ladies lookin' for a Lake Laggan boating adventure?"

Saffron's chewing a big wad of bubblegum. A yellow sweatshirt is tied at her otherwise still-bare midriff, and her hips sway as she comes closer. Her prematurely grey hair is coiled in a braid at the back of her neck. She takes one of the lifejackets from Milton and hands it to Veronica, smiling brightly. "Hi, sweetie. Want me to help you tie this on? Snug but not too tight, now—Marnie, you might want to loosen yours."

Veronica sees her mother turn coldly away from Saffron, as though insulted.

Together they make their way along the beach to the dock. Milton's boat turns out to be a tiny outboard-motored open skiff that's seen better days. Deep scrape marks graze the sharp, narrow hull. Fibreglass seats span the width of the vessel.

Milton holds his hand out to Veronica to help her climb aboard. The gesture feels old-fashioned, gentlemanly, and she accepts his hand. This time, much as she tries, she can't conjure up the pirate. Then her foot lands too far from the keel, and the boat rocks to one side, forcing her to grip Milton's hand more tightly. She lurches toward the bench nearest the bow, lets go of his hand, and sits down with a thump. Still on the dock, Milton helps Marnie aboard.

"Shift the towels, shove those tins over, that's it, swing your legs to the other side," Milton tells them. He braces two hands on a cleat as he swings himself aboard, and Saffron squats on the dockside, holding the mooring line. Milton leans over the motor and pull-starts the engine, then turns the throttle down to a slow purr. At a sign from him, Saffron tosses the painter and climbs in expertly after it.

The boat glides parallel to the shore, angling east from the park; the engine rumbles gently as Milton's hand on the tiller guides the prow over the shallows. He steers the boat around a fallen tree. An orange plastic jug bobs in a V-shaped space between the half-submerged branches.

The boat moves through a patch of eelgrass and arrow weed. A turtle slips out of sight with a plop. When Veronica leans out, she can see the bow cleave its way between the weeds, drawing a neat line in the membrane of the water. It looks like an iron pressing over thick silk. She tries to peer down, but a bloom of plankton obscures the bottom. Not plankton, surely, not in a lake. Pollen? They glide by a crop of swaying reeds, a dead fish floating amongst the fronds, its one unseeing eye facing straight up to the sky. A multicoloured brushstroke of gasoline twists and twines its way through the reeds, quiveringly iridescent where it rims a cluster of lily pads. Veronica remembers the starlings on the telephone wires.

Saffron leans over the starboard side of the boat and spits out her gum, which strikes the water with a soft splash. Her mother, turning and carefully adjusting her balance, leans close to Milton and says something

Veronica can't hear.

Stern, bow, starboard, port, the words orderly and definable on board ship, meaningless elsewhere. She closes her eyes, and the fibreglass skiff becomes a wooden schooner; the shallow, polluted lake becomes an ancient, unfathomable ocean. No purring motor but looming masts, snapping sails, and creaking timbers, a sturdy vessel battling real winds and swells. Keel. Bilge, grommet. *Treasure Island* words, *Robinson Crusoe* words. Yo ho ho and a bottle of rum. The lovely-sounding aft mast, mizzen. Boatswain, a word she'll never forget since she mispronounced it one day while reading a passage out loud at school. The teacher had interrupted the narration to correct her while the boys hooted out their derision. Bosun for boatswain. Not "boat-swain."

Saint Fagin had said "Swain, swain." She hears the words again in her mind, murmurs them to herself. It comes to her almost instantly and her eyes snap open.

"It's Wayne," she says aloud. "It's Wayne!"

Knocking noises, followed by clouds of exhaust fumes, erupt from the engine. Milton shrugs, adjusts the throttle, picks up speed, and gives them the thumbs-up sign.

Saffron turns to Veronica, her voice raised. "What was that you said, sweetie?"

"It's nothing, I just—I just recalled something!"

"*Recalled*?" Saffron shouts. "What?"

The revving outboard motor and the flying wind battle with the sound of their voices.

"I thought a gentleman was saying 'swain' for some reason! Like he was calling himself a swain! It's just that now I realize he was saying his name—Wayne!"

"Wayne, did you say?"

"Yes, why?"

Saffron's shouting something. But now Veronica can't hear, so she laughs politely, looks away.

And where has Charlotte been? Although Veronica has wandered through the park most afternoons, and twice checked the tuck shop, she hasn't seen her friend all week. Really, her friend? Would Charlotte deign to be her friend? She'd said she was mature for her age. Veronica remembers how she listened to her chatter and thinks of her relaxed, laughing manner. Charlotte had read her palm.

She had said, "I see you have a need for independence. You are inclined to be stubborn. Someone had a strong influence on you when you were young. Probably one of your parents."

Had her new friend been teasing?

Then she'd added, "Here's something more interesting: your destiny line has an intersection, just before it changes direction. As though something of consequence is going to happen to you—I can't tell if it's good or bad."

Charlotte had examined the line for a long time, turning Veronica's hand to the side and back again. What had she meant?

Tonight Colin will be back at the trailer with them, after five days working in the city. She's unsure if she should tell him about a vodka bottle she found wedged under the bench-cushion. And tonight too, there is to be other company for supper: her mother has invited her new friend Grace, from the Airstream trailer, to join them.

Veronica would love to track down Charlotte and invite her too. Does she dare?

The boat has picked up speed without warning, and now they're charging away from the shore, the bow jumping over waves, the keel bouncing and slapping. Then Milton abruptly changes direction, making Veronica's mother clutch the gunnel and shriek. "Please be careful! Oh my—Milton!"

Her hat sails off and cartwheels into the churning wake.

"No. Please!" Her mother is shouting now, her voice lost to all but Veronica over the sound of the wind and the outboard motor. "Stop! My hat! This is too fast! We've gone too far! Please, slow down!"

They skid across the bumpy surface of the lake, cool, wet pinpricks dotting Veronica's clothes, cheeks, and glasses. When a cold spray smacks at her bare arm and neck, a sense of exhilaration rushes over her. Anything seems possible. She tosses her head and lengthens her neck, her back bent forward, both hands now tightly gripping the front side of the boat. Droplets of water jerk and run together over her lenses, sending the lake, the trees, the houses, and the sky into smears of colour and light. If she lets go now, her whole taut body might lift up and fly. She won't let go.

Later, while Saffron attends expertly to tethering

the boat back in its berth, Milton reaches to help Marnie step out, and Veronica overhears her mother say to him, "Don't *you* have lots of hidden talents."

A few seconds later, the face Marnie presents to Saffron is a smiling one, but it seems as though she can barely look at her.

Veronica, puzzled, hastens to keep up with Marnie's long strides across the park. When they finally reach their trailer, her mother marches up to the porch and inside.

"Oh! Veronica! Wasn't that dreadful! You were right all along—it was a disaster." Marnie closes the door forcefully behind them.

Veronica says, "I don't understand. What changed your mind?"

"Oh, Saffron gets on my nerves, that's all. Something about her."

"You must admit though, it was awfully gallant of them to turn back and retrieve your hat."

"What kind of a *name* is *Saffron*, anyway?" Marnie mutters, reaching for an empty glass. She heads into her room, pulling the vinyl accordion door shut with an emphatic click.

TEN

Grace is chanting in a monotone. *"I breathe in abundance. With every exhalation I integrate trust. With every inhalation I deepen my awareness of the consciousness from which actions spring."*

Ruby swats feebly at her thigh. "Gracie, I can't hear a word you're saying. Take your sunglasses off."

Grace reaches up slowly to take them off. The mantras and the sunglasses go together: the words she chants calm her pulse, the dark glasses ease her mind's eye and alleviate the atmospheric transitions between darkness and light. She needs a sense of control over time and space, even though (both in her logical mind and in her heart of hearts) she knows time and space to be amorphous, terrifying, and ultimately incomprehensible. The sunglasses help, especially on those mornings when the sun rises so fast it catapults her dizzyingly into the day, or those late afternoons, like now, when this slant of the light pries and probes into everything, and she can't find anywhere to turn without further exposing herself to its intense explorations.

"I release resistance," she says, and places her folded sunglasses on a shelf. "Don't worry, Mother, I wasn't actually speaking to you—I was just saying my—my recitations."

"What recitations, Gracie? One for sorrow, two for joy? Three for a girl, four for a boy?" Ruby's tone is querulous and singsong at the same time.

"No. Those are nursery rhymes. You remember, mine are more like ... how to not lose my mind. Positive affirmations."

"Five for silver, six for gold, seven for a secret never to be told?" Ruby brings her forefinger up to her lips.

"That's right, Mother."

"Eight for a wish, nine for a kiss, ten for a bird that you won't want to miss?"

"Ten for a bird," Grace agrees. "One you won't want to miss."

Grace won't start a fight. As long as she can keep agreeing with everything Ruby says, today might close as calmly as it began. If she can eke out her patience, if she can hold fast to her plan, if she can keep on being the responsible adult here, then life can go on as she knows it.

It's so hard to reconcile this woman in front of her with the one who used to win all the games in her weekly bridge club, host fundraiser luncheons for the Garden Association, remember everyone's names and their favourite drinks. Now she's hunched in a wicker chair at the front end of the trailer, a skeleton in a blue dress, her knobby hands flopped in her lap.

"You'll be alright, Mother," Grace says gently.

"Eleven for health, twelve for wealth, thirteen beware, it's the devil himself."

Grace whispers, "*I breathe in abundance ....*"

Dr. Kerwin made Grace memorize the affirmations. They are his own creations, he tells her, a blend of Buddhism and modern cognitive psychology, something he refers to as syncretism. "Vipassana," he says, "insight into the true nature of reality meets a conscious, disciplined meditation."

He says Grace may not be able to embrace these concepts until she finds time to be on her own, to have interludes away from Ruby now and again. But Grace has only been able to bring herself to go on short walks—occasionally—and always at dawn, while her mother sleeps. She even waits until Ruby is napping before she takes out the garbage or carries a basket of laundry to the admin building's utility room, neither of which usually takes more than three minutes.

But now Grace says to Ruby, "I have to go out, remember? I won't be too long, I promise."

The woman from next door is coming to keep Ruby company. Stout, matronly Sylvia had assured Grace that it would be her pleasure. She'd fussed happily over Ruby ("Don't you look pretty in blue!") when they'd first met, and she'd told Grace that she used to work in a nursing home. But then, like Marnie, she'd started asking Grace prying questions, like where did they come from and how long were they staying, and Grace had done her best to lightheartedly deflect Sylvia's nosiness.

"You could say we're nomads. We stay in a place until we get restless."

Dr. Kerwin would say her encounters with Marnie and Sylvia are signs that she should try interacting with other people. In fact, maybe Sylvia would be a safer person than Marnie to practise on.

"Don't isolate yourself," he had said. "Remember, we can only really know the self by interacting with the other. Look for the opportunity to practise being with people. Think of a topic to talk about beforehand. Imagine you're writing it down in your head. Do whatever works."

He also advised her to become more tactile. "Grace, you're a woman clearly out of touch with herself. Touching another person—" and Dr. Kerwin put his hand on her shoulder and gazed meaningfully into her eyes, "will reconnect you with your own static energy."

"Static energy?"

For six months she's been going to see him once a week. She brings her mother with her, and Dr. Kerwin's perky receptionist, Faye, keeps Ruby occupied for a whole hour with simple games, cookies, and light conversation. Grace tries to focus on whatever Dr. Kerwin says, wants to believe him, wants to try hard to please him and get herself better, to recover from—what was it, what did he say she had? Mild psychosis with maladaptive coping disorder. Had he made this up? Grace is mistrustful of labels. But maybe this time, she'll act on this one morsel of advice she can remember, and it will be the turning point. How did he say to do this one thing, exactly? She thinks hard to summon his voice.

"When you meet people, reach out, take their hands, or give a little squeeze on the person's shoulder now and again. It will tell them about who you are, it will make other people more relaxed. This act of courage will be physically grounding for you."

Does Dr. Kerwin have *any* idea what kind of courage this is going to take?

Grace works her arms into her best cashmere cardigan. "I release resistance," she murmurs.

When Sylvia comes to the door, Grace takes her hands in both her own, which to her great relief seems to have the promised effect. Sylvia smiles.

"Thank you for coming," Grace ventures. "Make yourself comfortable. You'll need to make her some tea. You can keep my mother's legs warm with this blanket."

Sylvia lowers her voice meaningfully. "Remember, I've had extensive experience with the elderly."

"Ah, well, that's good then. And she likes to do these word-search puzzles."

"We'll be fine, won't we, Ruby?"

"My first name is Mrs," Ruby says.

The smile freezes on Sylvia's face. "Very well. Mrs," she repeats, and Ruby bows her head.

Grace clears her throat. "I really appreciate this."

The late afternoon light slips between the trees as Grace sets out for Marnie's trailer. Her footsteps punctuate her murmured phrases. She silently rehearses her greeting speech once more, and reminds herself what's on her list of things to talk about. There's someone coming her way, someone who will hopefully just pass by if she looks the other way.

"Grace."

A pale, earnest face of a man with dark eyes—real or hallucination?—bobs in front of her.

"Do I know you?"

"Name's Wayne."

"What? Why, how do you know my—"

"Grace," says Wayne gently, reverentially. "Grace is the unearned gift of God. The Lord Jesus is thy salvation."

No, no, no. She's unprepared for this. This kind of conversation can't be what Dr. Kerwin had in mind. She ducks sideways and then past him, her feet slipping on the gravel. The world is so full of weirdos. Her affirmations come faster as her pace hastens. "*I breathe in abundance. I am vast, I contain ....*" She slows down, pauses to catch her breath, willing herself to regain her composure. "*I deepen my awareness of the consciousness from which—actions—spring.*"

Grace doesn't slow down until she's sure Wayne's not following her. She's surprised how much this short sprint has winded her. Sharp stabbing pains in her chest. Is she having a heart attack? She's almost there—she can see Marnie's lot. It's a cool night, but she's too warm for cashmere now, so she starts to pull it off, forcing it when it doesn't come, yanking the cardigan's sleeves inside out. Her arms finally free, she grapples with the sweater to try to fix it, then gives up. She wads it under her armpit and takes a deep breath.

Marnie, wearing a voluminous poncho, steps down from the porch to welcome her. Grace reaches out to grasp the shape of Marnie's upper arm, just as Marnie halts. Grace can't read the expression on Marnie's face: it looks like some kind of intense, wild-eyed politeness.

Grace manages a faint smile and takes another breath. The words begin to roll out from her memorized script, the sentences unspooling smoothly.

"I just want to say how much I appreciate your inviting me to come tonight. It is such a kind thought, and I'm looking forward to meeting your family. What are your children's names, again? I'll do my best to remember them."

At the end of her speech, Grace squeezes Marnie's arm, as much to reassure Marnie as herself that this touching business comes naturally. The soft flesh yields, and Grace feels all the colour drain from her face. She pulls her hand back. It wasn't Marnie's upper arm that Grace had been holding on to all this time.

She turns away in a tumult of mortification, the impact striking her like shovelfuls of wet cement. Where to look to find the appropriate response? What next to do? Her insides have seized, and her wailing silent self is coiled with recriminations.

Seconds tick. She can't look at Marnie. Pretends there's a mosquito on her ankle, reaches down to brush it away.

Then, thank God, a man who must be Marnie's husband is striding over to her, smiling, and there're a couple of kids hanging back behind him, and two teenage girls over by the picnic table.

Colin shakes Grace's hand, welcoming her. "How do you do? Pleasure to meet you." He asks her if she wants a drink, and she answers, "Vodka martini please, if you're offering." Finally, drinks in hand, they're ambling over to the lawn chairs, where they sit down facing one another.

Setting his beer bottle down and clamping it between his feet, Colin moves to pull his pack of cigarettes from his shirt pocket. He holds the pack out to her; she shakes her head.

"Good for you," he says. "It's a bad habit. I'm trying to crack it, but everyone in my office smokes, so it's a challenge."

"Where is your office?"

"I work for a stock brokerage in Oshawa. I read balance sheets, assist with internal audits, that sort of thing."

Colin lifts his eyebrows apologetically, then strikes a match and cups his hand to shelter the flame. Grace watches him inhale. She still can't think of a single thing to say. Ruby would have known how to respond. Her mother at one time would have been able to carry on an informed conversation about smoking, accounting, stock portfolios, even the world economy, for that matter. With her versatility and sense of humour, Ruby made a positive impression on everyone she met.

Grace takes a gulp of her vodka martini. One of the

teenage girls at the picnic table lets out a squeal and, as if she's just remembered that they're there, Marnie calls out.

"Veronica! Bring some of those chips over here. Come and meet our guest, Mrs—Miss? Urquhart. Introduce your friend."

Grace starts to rise from the chair. "Please, she should call me Grace."

"This is my daughter, Veronica, this is Grace. And Charlotte, you may already know—"

Grace exchanges warm smiles with both of them.

The blonde girl, Veronica, is wearing big glasses with thick lenses. She has the same look as her father, the same stooped shoulders and frown, sort of closed-in looking, like a mole, or a mouse. She's holding a pair of binoculars in her hand. Charlotte hands Grace the bowl of chips. Charlotte's taller than Veronica, a few years older and more assured somehow, sturdy and capable, clad in denim overalls. Green eyes and a mane of curly red hair.

Marnie gestures at the binoculars. "Her father gave her those so she can watch the birds."

Colin shakes his head. "No I didn't. Actually I'm hoping she'll develop an interest in stars. With a strong pair of binoculars like that she can look at the moon."

Grace asks, "Why would you want her to look at the moon?"

"Why? Because it's so fascinating, of course. I have a telescope, but I haven't yet been able to persuade Veronica to share my love of astronomy. But imagine, if children can look at the moon through a pair of binoculars that will open their minds and lead them to be interested in more about our universe. Did you know that there are globular clusters that are probably billions of years—"

Marnie interrupts. "The children aren't allowed to touch the telescope."

Grace looks back at Colin, who's stopped talking. He's looking somewhere else and taking another drag on his cigarette.

The girls go back to the picnic table, and Grace wonders what she should say next. While she hesitates, Marnie speaks again.

"Have you any children, Grace?"

"No, no … never married, no children."

"Aren't you lucky," Marnie says, and laughs. Then she clears her throat.

"Excuse me," Colin says to Grace, then he gets up and leaves them, joining the two boys who are sitting on the steps pulling off their running shoes.

Marnie points out her sons to Grace. "My youngest one, that's Dilly, and on the right, Gumm. They're getting along, for once. Actually, they've taken to trailer park life like ducks to water."

Colin steps into the trailer and the boys start emptying the contents of their pockets on the step: Gumm shows Dilly a wooden slingshot, pretends to demonstrate it while aiming at Veronica.

"Boys! Go wash your hands!" admonishes their mother, and they grumble, but rise to comply.

"Those two have made so many friends, I just can't

believe it," Marnie says.

Colin returns with a fresh vodka martini and hands it to Grace.

At the picnic table, talk turns to the weather, and Grace is able to speak calmly again, to offer safe responses chosen from her mind's well-thumbed index cards. "Beautiful day it's been. We're due for some rain soon." At one point she senses that Marnie is staring at her, but when Grace turns in her direction, she quickly looks away and appears to be engrossed in serving the boys a second helping of jellied salad that they're protesting they don't want.

Marnie disappears into the trailer. Colin clears the table and sets down a stack of clean Melmac plates. Then Marnie re-emerges with a pie that must still be hot, for she's holding it in a pair of oven mitts.

"If you only knew the trouble I went to, finding ingredients for—"

Later, Grace won't remember anything Marnie served. For just then Sylvia appears out of nowhere, calling out Grace's name. Sylvia's breath is heaving.

"What a piece of work she is! Your mother said she doesn't need any help, thank you very much, and wants to be left alone. I did everything I could, sweet Jesus. Now I give up. Patience, I tell you! The language of her, the air turned blue! Fine, I said. I'll go. Now I've been assaulted! She threw her tea at me! I'm scalded, see?"

Grace, on her feet, throws a dismayed look at the gawking family at the picnic table. Her eyes linger on Marnie's round face and, in what feels like slow motion,

Grace moves one leg, backing away, and then another, before she says "I have to go, sorry," and bolts.

Grace finds Ruby on her knees in the front room, her backside swaying as she rubs a damp cloth over the rug. Grace steps forward to help Ruby to her feet.

"Let me do that. Wait."

"Go away."

"I've been away, but I'm back now. Come."

"Back now? I lost them again. Can't find them."

"What happened? What have you lost?"

"Back now. Gracie, will you find me my pills? That woman. I don't, don't care for that woman at all. I told her to go. What did she want?"

"Sylvia was just keeping you company while I was away. Didn't she make you some tea, Mother?"

"Tea? Hmmph! Tasted like a teabag walked through it on stilts!"

But Ruby allows Grace to guide her into a chair.

"There, that's better. You wait here, I'll find your pills and put another brew on."

While she's running water into the kettle, Grace remembers her first exchange with Marnie this evening. If only she'd thought of some joking comment, some self-deprecating remark to follow her terrible gaffe. Something clever, delivered with offhanded airiness, like, where I come from, that's how all women greet each other! They both would have laughed heartily, and the agony would be over by now.

Grace goes through motions that will get her through

the rest of the evening. She wipes the counter, tunes in to soothing classical music on the radio, murmurs reassurances to Ruby and affirmations to herself. Scrubs most of the tea stain from the wall. Tosses the carpet outside to await the next rain. Gets Ruby into her blue nightie and tucked in. Each minute becomes not the minute before.

Overnight, sleep—usually a welcome refuge for her—comes in fragments. Her body tosses and turns on her foam mattress. She dreams that a flock of pterodactyls detaches itself from a blackened sky, and that one by one they descend, crash-landing on the roof of her trailer.

ELEVEN

The crow beats his wings slowly, buoyed in the atmosphere, parallel to the earth. North-northeast his body deftly carves through the shapes of air, dispersing molecules and sending particles of light into little eddies that swirl thinly past the tips of his wings. As he reaches the edges of the trembling cedar tree and the upright pine, his gaze brushes across the next segments of landscape, the familiar crests and crevices, the seams where light meets shadow. Above the wavering waterline, where the lowest part of the land is endlessly nudged and caressed, is the crows' meeting place. He angles himself down, exactly as he saw his mate do a minute ago, quickly dropping to the water's edge. And there she is, regarding him from the higher ground.

Folding his wings snugly against his back, Hrah takes a few cautious steps over a heap of pebbles before he dips his beak down. He drinks in measured gulps, lifting his head to jerk the water into his gullet. Swivels his neck to regard the open space around him. Tosses back some more swallows before he spreads his claws widely in the sand and flexes them. Still feigning disinterest, he grazes his beak—one side, then the other—against a rough stone.

In the shade of the pine tree, his mate is straddling a snake carcass, pecking and roughly ripping at it. It's a small garter snake. Hrah hesitates: if he takes just one hop further now, she'll close her claws over the remains and spirit them away. Instead he scatters some water across his feathers and traces the tip of his beak along the contour of one wing. When he's finished preening, he pauses. Here, under the lapping shallows, there is often something to be found, something tasty or glittery, some interesting trinket.

His reflection is unsteady this morning, one bright eye with its pinprick of light winking down from the side of his cocked head. He sees the silhouette of his body undulate against the distant plane of sky. A small wind-gust disturbs the surface, and his shadow flickers over the water's multiple fragments. At the same time his ears pick up a distant sound of bleating, a chorus of two-pronged notes radiating from the southwest. The last of the Canada geese are leaving their breeding grounds.

His own nesting duties are over for the season. This year, like every year, very early in the spring, he and his mate constructed a new nest. Agreeing on a site, they anchored it with bulky, large twigs, filled the cavity with dead grass, and lined it with grapevine bark. This year, something new: she had shifted her body again and again, turning and turning, until the curve of the bowl perfectly matched the curve of her breast. The curve of the planet. Then, only then, did she lay her eggs.

This year they started with a clutch of five. Hrah's mate did most of the brooding. He would guard the nest once in a while, so she could go off to forage or bathe, but most days he simply brought her food—tree buds, seeds, salamanders, frogs, baby mice, bits of dead fish, or bread crusts from the dumpster—which she would seize eagerly from his beak.

During one of his watches, they'd lost two of their eggs to a horned she-owl. The event had prompted a mobbing; within seconds of his first cries, Hrah and his mate had been joined by a great many other crows, and for the next fifteen minutes they harassed and harangued the owl until she was driven away.

Later, the other three chicks hatched. Two would survive long enough to fledge. And now, many more seasons will pass before they seek mates of their own. He continues to keep his latest offspring close in the clan.

Hrah's mate rummages amongst some fallen leaves and selects a few to place over what's left of the snake carcass, concealing a stash to eat later. She lifts herself up, alights on the lower branch of a pine tree, and waits for Hrah.

But he, sensing movement, twists his head sideways. He sees a flank of boys advancing, without their bicycles this time, their legs scissoring across the last grassy slope to the beach. With urgency he flexes his knees and ankles and springs upwards. He beats at the air to reach the middle of the pine, where he will conceal himself. His mate unclamps her claws and propels herself after him, rising in a graceful arc to settle on a higher branch.

The boys split up at the sand's edge. The three smallest ones kick their shoes off on the beach and run crashing into the water, fully clothed. The other two, after conferring for a minute, collect pebbles and rocks from the sand, showing them to each other on outstretched hands.

The three boys in the water race from one side to the other in clumsy crawl strokes. Hrah watches them for a while, mesmerized by the water droplets wriggling and twinkling above their swinging limbs. To him, for a suspended moment, it seems as though the lake itself is alive—water wrestling with the boys' torsos, actively shoving and slapping against their shoulders and necks.

The vision will stay with him for the rest of his life as an omen: the sight of the lake rising and thrashing about—a whipped-up spirit—a sign of the most dreadful foreboding. For suddenly there's a swift whack in the green canopy above, and she is falling head first, wings splayed, her body grazing the tips of the pine needles on her way down.

"Got him!" a jubilant human voice rings out. The boy waves something made of wood over his head.

TWELVE

Looking up at the sky so much has made me see more of the crows. There will probably always be something about them that remains unknowable, I think, yet like my Dad's celestial wonders, there's so much more to learn.

Until I started sleeping outside, I had no inkling of what they get up to before most people are awake. At this early hour, three or four of them ride gusts of wind over the lake. They spiral down to the beach, pluck bits from the ground, strut around the park, all the while calling out to each other in spirited conversation. When there are two or more, one is always a lookout.

They're scavengers. They like to hide things by burying them, and sometimes, when another is watching, they pretend to conceal something then they dig it up again and hide it somewhere else. It is my privilege to know this, for I watch them when the sun comes up, before anyone else is awake.

I'll make a study of them and add these records to my observations. I wonder if I'll come to be able to tell them apart?

Veronica, who has been writing for a few minutes in her hammock, folds her notebook over her pencil when she hears her parents' low voices through the screen on their open window. The scrape of drawers opening and closing at this early hour means the weekend's over; her father's going back to work.

"I think you should just forget about it," Colin mutters. "Anyway, I don't know what makes you think she's a lesbian in the first—" The rest of his words are obscured by the sound of the zip on his suitcase.

"Oh come on, it's obvious, of course she is."

Veronica holds her breath, remembering the involuntary stab of pleasure between her legs at the sight of Saffron's pale cleavage the day of their boat trip. How in the world did her mother know about that? Veronica's fingers tighten on her pencil.

"She must be."

"Why must she be?"

"Well, for one thing, she's never been married."

Never been married? Veronica exhales: it can't be her they're talking about. Then who? *Grace.*

"Why must you argue with everything I say?"

"Tell me what you want me to do."

"I'm not asking you to do anything. I'm just saying."

"You were either giving her the wrong signals, or it had nothing to do with you. It's that simple. And if you're so preoccupied by it, then you should talk to her."

"But—"

"I have to go, or I'll be late. See you at the end of the week."

Keeping as still as she can in her hammock, Veronica pretends to be asleep as her father leaves the trailer.

He kept his promise on Saturday to take her to the library in Longford Rapids, where she'd been able to get a card and sign out a book called *Common Birds of Ontario,* and some Jane Austen novels.

One shelf away from Jane Austen had been a book called *The Plague* by Albert Camus. Its cover was most intriguing: a black-and-white drawing of a human form in a long black cloak, his or her face concealed under a mask of a bird's head. The figure was holding a thin stick in one hand and a doctor's bag in the other. Behind the plague doctor were several lines of medieval Latin script with distinctive loops and flourishes. Veronica had examined the cover for a while, then slipped the book back between the others on the shelf, thinking maybe next time. On a last-minute impulse she had pulled out *The Swiss Family Robinson* and *David Copperfield* for her brothers.

"Do you have a Bible, perchance?" she had asked the librarian, a woman who had a sharp, pinched face and dyed yellow hair.

A set of thin silver bracelets on the librarian's wrist had jangled together as she'd stamped the second book-card, tucked it back into its pocket and replied, "They're all checked out this week."

Veronica waits in her hammock until she hears her mother moving about in the kitchen, setting cereal bowls and spoons on the table. Listens for the bickering between the boys to die down, followed by her mother's insistence that they eat their whole breakfasts and wash their own dishes. Waits until the boys are gone. All the while rocking, thinking, reading the same paragraph over and over.

"Although the crow is familiar to everyone, very few have

much good to say for it. It is omnivorous and eats practically any-thing edible. It is destructive to crops, particularly corn. On the other hand, it destroys large numbers of insects. It is generally con-ceded that the harm it does outweighs the good."

The screen door bangs open, startling her. Her mother hurries by, thumps down the steps, and strides theatri-cally out to the lane, then stops, turns, and walks swiftly back inside the trailer.

A few seconds later, she's back standing on the porch.

"Are you just going to slouch there and read all day? Because I could use some help in the garden, you know."

Veronica stops swinging. Her mother's feet—in her scuffed, short-heeled shoes—are planted in front of her.

"Fine. I know how you feel about gardening. But you can do something else that's useful. Why don't you go over to Grace's? It's the Airstream trailer. See if ev-erything's alright with her mother. Offer to help. Ask if there's anything you can do."

Veronica closes the book and tucks it under her thigh, near the pocket with the Jesus medallion. She's still wear-ing the clothes she slept in: her favourite pair of tie-dyed shorts and the blue T-shirt that her mother says is too big on her.

"Well? Will you go there? Have you been listening to a word I've said?"

"Very well," Veronica says, "I'll go."

"You will?"

"Maybe I should change my clothes first."

"Maybe you should."

"It's the Airstream one, you said?"

"Yes." Marnie nods. "Silvery, longish, roundish. Thank you. Just ask if they're okay, if they need anything. See if you can help."

"If they need anything, such as what?"

"Like help, or something. For God's sake, Veronica. Just be neighbourly."

Veronica wonders if, as her mother suspects, Grace is a lesbian. For if so, and if the twinges Veronica felt on Friday mean that she is one too, then with Grace here she needn't feel so alone, so like a freak. Grace could be a potential friend, ally, confidante, even advisor.

What could Grace have done to get her mother so worked up?

Inside the trailer Veronica changes her underwear and puts on a clean shirt, then finds her sandals and slips them on. On the porch, she checks her backpack again to make sure her notebook is still there, hoists the strap to her shoulder.

A red squirrel spurts down the mountain ash, away from the feeder, its cheeks bulging with peanuts. Veronica watches as it leaps lightly for the fence and squeezes its body under it.

When she steps into the lane, the sun is warm on her shoulders. She hears a baby giggle behind a nearby trailer. Then a young woman's light laughter: "Good girl, good girl!" Another more distant voice is sharp and accusatory: "Does it matter? It's in the past!" Farther away, near the lake, a crow utters a series of urgent shrieks. She listens hard, but she doesn't hear it again.

Veronica feels nervous at the thought of calling on Grace and her mother. For years she's been afraid of elderly people, never sure how to act around them. When she was eight years old, in the foyer of the building where her grandfather lived, a group of shrivelled, feeble people sagged in their wheelchairs, gazing vacantly at their feet. One old man had a misshapen lip from which a long line of spittle dripped into a slimy puddle on his lap. He had reached his arm out and plucked at her cardigan and she had been terrified.

Apparently Mrs Urquhart is prone to hurling cups of hot tea. Veronica won't stay long. But she'd really like to know if what her mother believes about Grace is true. But how will she be able to tell?

Charlotte's been occupying more of her thoughts now, ever since she came to dinner on the night Grace was there. Beautiful Charlotte, bearing a bouquet of white windflowers for Veronica and a bottle of wicker-wrapped Chianti for Marnie, Charlotte telling Veronica funny stories of when she'd been a Girl Guide. Veronica daring to admit that she didn't want to come here at all but is now really glad she did.

She kicks at stones as she makes her way across the compound. The park seems quieter than usual this morning. Like her father, other people have jobs that they've gone to. According to Charlotte, there might be a job for Veronica at the tuck shop, if she doesn't mind taking the Friday night shift until nine and some Saturday afternoons. Her boss Jeremy had said the pay would be five dollars an hour. Veronica tries to imagine what she might be able to buy for Charlotte if she had a few weekends' worth of pay in her pocket.

Lawn ornaments adorn a succession of yards along the pathway leading her to Grace's trailer. A metallic windmill flashes as it turns lazily in the sun. There's a host of painted plaster gnomes with white curly beards and pointed hats: one holds a lantern, another an accordion. On the edge of a corner lot near the middle of the park, wind chimes hang from a wishing well's wooden filigree. Veronica runs the tips of her fingers along the chimes, and a tinkling murmur gently breaks the silence.

It has to be this one, the Airstream trailer, just as her mother described. Looking at it, Veronica thinks of the submarine Nautilus in *Twenty Thousand Leagues Under the Sea*. The arched, curved door and the shuttered windows look as though the whole vessel is sealed against moisture, air, and light. Rivets surround all the window frames. When she knocks on the door, she imagines Captain Nemo emerging in a diving suit. His eyes would twinkle, and he'd speak to her in a French accent, inviting her in, and then she'd have to sign a contract that promised she would never leave.

Just when she's about to give up and step away, the door finally yields to her knocking. The trailer exhales stale air.

The elderly lady standing there has tears on her cheeks, and Veronica immediately regrets having come.

"Oh, I do beg your pardon."

But Mrs Urquhart unexpectedly smiles, revealing a row of perfect white teeth. "I don't believe I know you. How *do* you do?"

Veronica gulps. "My mother asked me to pay my respects—but I could come another—Hello, is this an inconvenient time?"

Grace's startled face has appeared in the door opening. Her grey hair looks dishevelled, and pouches of dark skin sag under her eyes.

"I—uh, no, she's—we're fine. So, um, Veronica. What a surprise."

Grace explains that her mother is not crying. "She likes to bathe her eyes with used teabags."

Mrs Urquhart hands the teabags to Veronica. To her horror they are cold and wet, heavy with the residue of an old woman's ophthalmic secretions. Veronica wordlessly passes the teabags to Grace.

"Do come in, won't you?"

Veronica slides her damp palm on her shorts, opens her mouth to say no thank you, but stops. Mrs Urquhart, Ruby, is tonguing her dentures. Her eyes look dry now, but the cold tea-droplets are rolling into the creases that line her cheeks. The old woman's eyebrows are a pair of shakily-pencilled-in brown curves that don't match her coiffed white hair.

Inside the trailer, Veronica's eyes adjust to the gloom. Grace scuttles to the kitchen, where the small counters are stacked with discarded Swanson dinner boxes, potato-chip bags, and empty tins of spaghetti and meat sauce. With one arm she is trying to slide everything into a large garbage bag. Some of the contents spill onto the floor. Veronica looks away. Ruby is settling herself carefully, awkwardly, into a chair.

A macramé wall decoration in the shape of an owl hangs on the divider between the kitchen and the living room, and Veronica turns to examine it. It has a glittering bead for each eye, and tufts of frayed jute stick up for ears. A real tree branch with whittled ends is worked across the design at the bottom, forming the owl's perch. A second work of macramé, this one flowingly abstract in its design, is attached to the wall at the front—or is it the back?—end of the trailer. It looks unfinished. Veronica reaches to touch the strands of jute falling from the lowest row of knots and beads.

"Did you fashion these?" she asks Grace.

Grace looks up from tying the garbage bag and shoves it behind her. "I did. I do."

"They're lovely," says Veronica.

"I can teach you if you like."

"Would you?"

"I used to knit," chirps Ruby, "but my hands don't work any more."

She lifts them and shows Veronica her disfigured hands, knuckles swollen and stiff.

Veronica looks at the old woman's hands. "Do they hurt?"

"Yes, but—" Ruby lifts a vinyl purse next to her chair and peers inside it. "Oh. They're not here. Those pills really work, Gracie. We need to get more of them."

"Those pills are not for your arthritis, Mother. But they were supposed to last you a month. They couldn't be finished already."

"No. Sylvia took them. That woman stole them!"

Grace seems to flinch; she starts to say "Please—" to her mother. She pins Veronica with an anguished look.

Veronica touches one of Ruby's hands and murmurs, "That must feel dreadful."

"She stole my pills and she stole my pearls too."

"Pills, or pearls?" Veronica's not sure if she's heard correctly.

"They're not stolen, Mother. If you finished your pills, it's because you took too many. And you've misplaced the pearls, that's all. They were lost before Sylvia came over. I told you, they'll turn up."

"No. It's what I always say. *They'll do it if you let them.*" She seems so flustered, so adamant, that Veronica is taken by surprise. "*They'll do it if you let them,*" Ruby repeats.

"Who will? Do what?"

Grace clears her throat. "It—it's her way of saying 'take charge,' Veronica. Keep an eye on everyone and everything. It's just like 'buyer beware,' the same thing."

Ruby points a crooked finger in Veronica's direction. "You are squandering your youth here, my child. Mock my words."

"Mock your words?"

This is a lunatic asylum. It was a mistake to think she might find a kindred spirit in Grace. When Grace helps her mother to the bathroom, Veronica decides she'll make

107

up some reason to leave as soon as they come out again. She'll say something about having errands to run. No, her family's expecting her home to help with something.

A sparkle catches her eye. A light is glancing from something small and round that's jutting out from behind Ruby's cushion. She lifts the cushion and slowly draws out a knotted string of pearls. She cradles the pearls in her palm, admiring their lustrous symmetry. And when the women shuffle back down the hall, Veronica extends her cupped palm. Ruby's pencilled eyebrows leap up, and the creases at her temples briefly vanish.

"Oh! My pearls! Where did you find them?"

"Concealed between the cushions on your chair."

"You see?" Grace takes the pearls, drapes and carefully clasps them around her mother's neck. "There."

Ruby pats her throat and fingers the necklace with evident satisfaction. "That's better." She appears to think for a while. "Hidden? Maybe that woman *hid* them there."

"The clasp could have simply come undone, Mother."

"Nonsense, this clasp hasn't come undone in sixty years!"

"Never mind. You have them back now, thanks to Veronica."

"Mrs Urquhart," Veronica ventures, "if someone took your pearls and hid them, they would first have had to unfasten them from your neck, would they not?"

Ruby appears to think about this. "You're right—Sylvia might have done exactly that. While I was sleeping."

"That's not what I meant—"

"Mother," Grace says brightly, "why don't you tell Veronica the story about your pearl necklace?"

"The story?"

"Yes, where it came from and what your father said. You know."

"It was a present," Ruby murmurs, and stops.

"Go on, you remember."

"It was a present from my fiancé, at the time of our engagement."

Grace prompts her. "And then what?"

"You tell it. I don't remember."

"But it was always your story. I can't believe you don't remember. Alright, then. It was a big family," Grace explains to Veronica, "five sisters. The night my father brought the pearls to my mother, he went to visit her father, in his study, to get his blessing. He said, 'Sir, I would like your permission to marry your daughter Ruby.' And her father said, 'Which one's Ruby?'"

Veronica laughs. "Seriously? Was he trying to be amusing? Was he in earnest?"

Ruby nods. "He was quite serious, yes. He had five daughters."

"And what did your fiancé reply?"

Ruby's thick fingers flutter against her throat. "He said, 'Why, Ruby would be the one wearing these pearls, of course.'"

They laugh.

"My grandfather was a man of his time," says Grace.

Ruby nods. "I wear my pearls always. The skin oils

help the pearls keep their lustre. One day they will be Gracie's."

Grace takes Veronica to the unfinished work of macramé at the front of the trailer and shows her how to knot and work the jute strands. Square knots and then double half-hitches. Grace remarks on how quickly she is picking it up. Veronica finds she quite likes it, and asks if it might be possible to make a hanging bird feeder out of jute.

"Sure, you could make it with three strands of four strings of jute each, and attach a big hook at the top to hang it in a tree. Same as a plant-hanger, only you'd be putting seeds in the bowl where the plant would be."

An hour later, Veronica is stepping down the Airstream's two metal stairs. She turns back briefly to accept an invitation from Mrs Urquhart to come back soon. She blinks in the light as Grace closes the door behind her.

To her great astonishment, Charlotte is standing on the lawn. She's holding a dead crow in one hand.

"Good timing. Your mother said I might find you here."

Veronica's heart is leaping and falling at the same time.

"I remember you said you were interested in crows, and thought you might like to look at this one." Charlotte's face clouds over. "Some boys were tossing it in the air down near the beach. I made them give it to me."

THIRTEEN

Grace closes the door and stands with her back against it, her eyes adjusting to the unlit interior. She's relieved that the encounter with Veronica went well, and grateful that it's over.

"My father said, 'Which one is Ruby?' I remember that. Do you remember that, Gracie?"

"No, Mother, I wasn't born yet. I remember you telling me the story, that's all."

Ruby's cheek is pressed close to the window; she must be watching Veronica make her way back to her own trailer. But now Grace sees a new, gloomy expression fix itself on her mother's face.

"One for sorrow," Ruby says, her voice full of melancholy.

Grace sighs. She gropes for the radio and switches it on.

The noontime talk-show guest is talking about the growing trend of women's liberation. Protests and marches about abortion, equal pay, and birth control. Grace is about to switch it off, thinking the content is unsuitable for her mother, when the first voice is replaced by a more philosophical one:

"The revolutionary sentiment is clearly building momentum. Indeed, it can't be denied, although where it can go from here is questionable, in the face of the fact that women just aren't made for certain kinds of work!"

"The radical feminists, those women want to be just like men, but someone has to say it, they're not men!"

"There were so many different factions at the demonstration. And none of them agree on anything."

The voices float in and out of Grace's hearing as she walks around, opening the doors in the kitchen and the hall closet. She is rummaging amongst towels and face cloths, looking for her mother's missing pills, when one of the radio guests emits an unmistakable tone of scorn.

"Of course there would be squabbling. They're women. And that's why the antagonism started. Ironic, isn't it, that they end up in a brawl over whether violent action should be taken to promote peace. What a spectacle!"

"It's dead," Ruby says in a sad, resigned voice.

"I don't think they're saying it's actually dead, Mother. The movement still has a lot of life in it, as long as people like Gloria Steinem are around!"

"It's dead, it's dead," Ruby repeats.

Grace methodically opens and closes the kitchen's cupboard doors, still looking for the missing pills. She'll have to arrange a trip into town, soon, to buy some more.

FOURTEEN

Veronica follows Charlotte to the nearest picnic table, where Charlotte tenderly sets the bird down. Veronica's shock has given way to grief. Could this bird be the same crow she saw on her way here, eating the dead fox on the highway?

Veronica reaches out and prods the body tentatively. Its head flops to one side. The bird is larger and lighter than she expected, jet-black; its parts are still pliable.

"The boys were tossing it? How barbaric."

"Typical boys."

"They found it, or killed it?"

"I don't know."

"Oh, the poor thing."

Veronica caresses the lifeless crow's head with her fingertip. Then she gently turns the body over. A layer of down feathers is silky and light beneath the tougher chest feathers. The bird's talons are curled under, like a final gesture of surrender. The black skin on its legs looks leathery, but when she peers more carefully she sees overlapping scales. A sturdy beak that seems to be fused seamlessly into its skull. Beak to bone. A tiny fringe of bristly feathers covers its nostrils. She feels through her fingers how the shoulder joint swivels; she coaxes one wing open toward her. Holding it high above her head, she imagines a deep, suspended ocean of air.

"Phalanges," says Charlotte. "These bones here, past the shoulder, the ones like arm bones, finger bones."

Charlotte's freckles travel down from her forehead and gather on the bridge of her nose.

"Phalanges. I took anatomy class, remember."

"Anatomy of crows?"

"No, humans."

"Sounds like poetry," Veronica murmurs. "Phalanges. Do *we* have phalanges?" She's thinking about Charlotte's anatomy.

"Anatomy's full of good words," Charlotte says. "Like epidermis."

Veronica smiles sheepishly. "Do you have to draw naked people in art class?"

"Not yet. Maybe next year. I want to draw this crow, though. Do you mind if I take her home with me? I love all her different layers of feathering. I want to learn how to draw her surfaces."

"How do you know it's a girl?"

"Of course it's a girl, silly," says Charlotte. "I could tell when I first saw her, just by the look in her eye. Couldn't you?"

Veronica thinks Charlotte must be teasing her again, but she finds herself glancing down anyway. The bird's eyes are closed.

That evening, Dilly wants to go to the park with a soccer ball, but Marnie says no.

"It'll be dark soon, boys. How about we have a fire and toast marshmallows instead?"

"Okay, but I get to carve the toasting sticks." Dilly shoots a look at Gumm, who jumps up in protest.

"It's my knife!"

"I get to light the fire then."

"No!"

"Is that your third vodka?" says Veronica quietly to her mother, and looks at the glass still in Marnie's hand.

"What's it to you?"

"For one thing, we need a responsible adult to have a fire."

The boys' squabble has turned physical. A few light punches to Gumm's torso are followed by Gumm grabbing his brother's arm and starting to twist it.

"Let go or else!" Dilly yells. "Ow! Okay I'm telling! Ow! Mom! Gumm killed a bird! He did!"

Marnie blinks slowly. "He what?"

"He killed a big black crow. With his slingshot! It was him."

The next morning Veronica dreams that she is lying on her back on the bottom of a small fishing boat, drifting near an uninhabited shore of the lake. She laces her fingers behind her head and adjusts a puffy lifejacket under her neck. A dog is barking. The barks sound urgent, distressed. She struggles to sit up to see where the dog is, but the effort of trying to do so makes the boat rock alarmingly from side to side. Her hands scramble for purchase along the boat's slippery ribs.

The dog's barks begin to sound more like shrieks—no, more like bird cries. Then there is silence. Veronica listens hard, her eyes still shut as she slowly becomes aware that she's swinging in her hammock, hearing only the low, hollow rhythm of her mother's snores through the bedroom window.

It's there again: a hoarse, rattling cry. A crow.

The voice sounds so near that Veronica comes fully awake. She blinks hard, gropes for her glasses, swings her feet sideways, jerks at the mosquito net. The net catches on something in the dark and gives way with a ripping sound.

A bird abruptly disengages itself from a tree —oh, could it have been *her* tree, with the peanut feeder in it?— and then Veronica hears the lift and beat of feathers as it flings itself away. Alas, her sudden movement must have startled it.

Tiny flames of light faintly kindle the horizon with pinks and oranges.

Something's going on, something otherworldly. She creeps forward, soft thumps of bare feet on wood. The rhythm of her pulse. The sound of wings beating, chopping, a frenzied commotion as dark feathered bodies lift off into the surrounding air.

An indigo beach towel hangs on the porch railing; Veronica grasps it and wraps it over her shoulders. Her toe strikes a stack of comic books; the stack slides sideways and fans out across the floorboards. She slips her feet into unlaced running shoes and steps lightly down the porch onto the grass.

More crow cries pitch into the air and trail away in the direction of the lake. She moves as quickly as she can, hurrying for the trees, taking long strides. Finally, she conceals herself within the trees near the beach. She inches closer to the crows. There are more corvid voices—insistent, percussive sounds coming from different directions.

The underbelly of a thick mantle of clouds becomes visible, billowing purple and grey. Drifting remnants of these dark clouds, fugitives from a storm, reshape themselves into companies of flying crows, all seeming to be headed in the same direction. Strident diphthongs and short, rasping quacks ricochet across the lake. The cries of the flying crows are answered by those already gathered in a nearby pine tree. The clamour increases in breadth and volume.

Veronica tries to blend into the shadows as she gets closer to the noisy conclave. She moves stealthily, one slow, low step at a time, though her knees are starting to hurt. Surely any sound her footfalls might make at this point would be smothered by the crows' own cacophony. But her light-coloured hair might give her away. She stops, and ever so slowly shifts her towel-cloak up from her shoulders to the top of her head, gathering the fabric under her chin with one hand. She edges further forward, pauses, then another two steps. She lifts her head and freezes.

Crows fill the branches of the pine tree from bottom to top. She begins silently to count them, but six or seven shift their places and she loses count. The birds continue to reassemble themselves, unsettling, teetering for balance, resettling, until they evenly fill the tree. At once the raucous congregation falls silent.

Veronica can hardly breathe. There might be two hundred crows here. They are still, immobilized along the branches. There is a sharp, intentional quality to their stillness. Silhouettes of birds against a plum-coloured sky.

Long minutes go by; their silence is unbroken. The needles of the pine meld with the darkness of the crows. Their motionless shapes appear and disappear as Veronica blinks. She turns her head carefully to take them all in.

She doesn't know how long she's been squatting there. Fearful of moving and destroying the spell, she allows a mosquito to bite her ankle. A blackfly crawls into her ear and she grimaces, clamping her teeth tightly.

Drops of rain start to spit down, juddering the still air, striking branches, thudding softly into the grass. The intermittent rhythm gathers itself into a steady downpour. Veronica's glasses become rain-spattered, and her towel-cloak grows heavy. She thinks of Charlotte. Charlotte would have loved to have seen this. She'll have to tell her about it, all the details. She slowly lifts her hand to wipe her glasses, but not slowly enough.

The nearest crow abruptly scissors its wings. All at once the rest of the birds dislodge themselves. They grapple for space amongst each other, and Veronica feels wind buffeting her face as they collectively rise into the air, beating at the rain.

They disperse. The pine branches settle back into stillness, becoming greener by the morning light.

Later, Veronica stands inside the trailer, shoulders wrapped in the sodden towel, hair dripping, puddles forming on the floor.

Gumm blocks her way to the bathroom down the hall. "Lookit, Dill, look who's in big trouble," he says.

Veronica frowns with impatience. "What."

"Mom's got people out everywhere looking for you. Says you were kidnapped."

"She does not."

"Does too."

"Move. Out of the way."

Veronica inclines her head at Dilly, who has emerged from the boys' bedroom, looking wobbly and yellowish-green. "What's with him?"

"He's sick."

Dilly moans. Then he says, "Is it true you were kidnapped?"

"Kidnapped?"

"Uh-oh, I'm going to puke again."

Veronica pulls off her glasses and tries to dry them, ineffectually, on the edge of the towel. "Don't say 'lookit.' Don't say 'puke.' It smells gross in here. You're gross."

When she puts her glasses back on, her mother's shape fills the doorway.

"You! Where have you been? I've been frantic! We were frantic!"

"I went for a walk."

"Who goes for a walk in the rain? You could at least have left a note."

"It wasn't raining when—"

"I called and called. People came out of their trailers in their pyjamas to stare at me! How do you think that made me feel? Go, get some dry things on before you catch your death. For God's sake. I have to go call off the search now. What an embarrassment."

"Mom!" Dilly's plaintive voice wobbles out and hovers in the air between them.

"What search?" Veronica asks her mother.

"I've got the neighbours out looking for you everywhere!"

She takes this in. Then she lunges for Gumm, who is smirking.

"And what about you, *bird-killer*?"

"Shut up. Am not."

Their mother halts. "Gumm?"

"Dilly already told you last night," Veronica says coldly. "Only you probably don't remember."

Dilly wails. "Mom! I'm going to—!"

Marnie touches her temples and presses hard.

"Oooooh, Mom! Now!"

Thunderclaps shudder through the air in the trailer.

Her mother looks at Veronica quickly, then yanks at her umbrella and goes out the door. "All I know is, I have to call off the search now." She hesitates for a second under the porch roof, and steps into the pouring rain.

"Milton? Can you hear me?" Her voice trails off, and her shoes make squelching noises across the lawn as she shakes out and snaps up the black umbrella. "Milton?"

FIFTEEN

Grace enters the administration building with her sunglasses on and the hood of her raincoat pulled up. She quickly turns left down the hall, heading for the pay phone, making her way past a cluster of people standing outside the open laundry-room door. She hopes that no one speaks to her. They fall silent as she passes; maybe they were already silent before she came in. They also seem to be staring at her: she can sense their heads swivelling. "*Grace,*" she hears Dr. Kerwin's voice say, "*don't be paranoid.*"

She fingers the dime in her pocket, pulls out the paper with the taxi company's number on it and sees that someone's posted the same number on the wall above the phone. To bring the receiver to her ear, she has to push her hood down, and as she does so she thinks she hears one word singled out amongst the collective murmuring behind her.

Veronica.

Grace's dime falls down the throat of the pay phone,

and the sound makes her want to gag. She replaces the receiver and turns around.

"Missing since some time last night, man. She's about this high, blond hair down to here, yeah, have you seen her?"

It's Milton, who has followed her to the telephone and is standing behind her now, staring at her. She slowly pulls her sunglasses off.

"Have you seen her?"

Grace can only shake her head at him, uncomprehending.

Milton grows impatient, turns back to the others.

"We could all fan out from here, calling for her, in different directions."

Someone else says, "What's her name again?" "Veronica."

Grace folds her sunglasses. "What did you say?"

"The mother—Marnie—she says there were signs of a struggle."

"No."

Grace's hand comes up to cover her mouth. Images appear and flee in her mind. What might have happened? The pictures come faster and faster, flashing like a shuffled deck of cards: an escaped criminal grabbing Veronica by the arm, a knife glinting in the dark, a chloroform-soaked rag, a getaway car. Blood. The girl lying dead somewhere.

Grace should have known something terrible was going to happen. After all, the day had begun with a portent of doom. She'd been heading on her walk to the lake this

morning when she'd seen the congregation of dozens—
perhaps hundreds—of crows in what looked like a single
evergreen. The sight had made her think immediately of
Hitchcock's *The Birds*, a film she and Ruby saw in a theatre
about ten years ago. Birds gathering in silence, all muscular and aggressive, who were plainly waiting for the opportunity to peck her eyes out. Grace had hurried back to
the Airstream and checked that all the windows were still
sealed. She'd tried to shake off the image of Tippi Hedren
desperately trying to protect her face.

Dread seeps into her belly. She'd been poised to take
Ruby with her into town today in a taxi, to go to the phar-
macy to pick up her pills. What masqueraded as reality a
moment before—the tumbling thunder, the grey rain (giving her the assurance she could cross the compound and not
run into Marnie), her own force-fed stamina and courage
to leave the park, even the reassuring solidity of the telephone receiver—have either evaporated or turned out to be
illusions. Now a girl is missing, and everything's changed.

The crowd has become bigger, more having been
drawn to the universal vibration of disturbing news.

"What are we waiting for?" someone says. "We should
go look for her. Now."

"There were crows this morning," Grace says, and
immediately regrets it. Faces swivel to gape at her again.
Grace blushes. Their voices swarm around her.

"Did you see the girl?"

"Crows?"

"What are you talking about?"

"Has anyone called the police? Surely—"

"She can't be far. We just need to organize ourselves and fan—"

"Try to calm down. There's probably some other explanation."

"How old is she? Where's the mother?"

"Yeah. Kids go missing all the time. Nine times out of ten—"

A young woman in a skimpy top appears in the hallway, smiling, her bare upper chest and torso slicked with droplets of rain, her hair plastered to her head. They all turn to look at her as she lifts her arms for attention.

"False alarm, brothers and sisters, she's turned up, the girl is home!"

"Really?"

"That's right *on,* Saffron."

"Good news."

A man who'd been standing next to Grace steps forward, takes Saffron's wet hands and squeezes them. Two women spontaneously hug. Many seem disoriented by the unexpected turn of events, lost as to what to do next.

Backing away, Grace tries to clear her head, tries to return to where she was. But she can't conceive of going anywhere with Ruby now.

The rain has started to fall more steadily, smattering on rooftops, tapping softly on leaves, gleaming in the grass, being swallowed by the thirsty earth. Grace makes her way to the Airstream. She keeps her head down.

Inside the kitchen Grace shrugs off her wet coat.

Ruby is sitting at the Formica table, closely scrutinizing the back of a photograph. A photo album lies open beside her, next to a pair of scissors and a pile of cut-up pictures. They are black-and-white photos, scalloped edges gone slightly brown with age. In one image, a grinning young man leans on the rounded fender of a 1930s-era Rolls-Royce, a foot lifted to the running board, a hand jauntily touching the brim of his cap. A series of solemn children poses in pinafores and sailor suits. Four women sit along a bench, dressed in long white skirts, holding tennis rackets.

All the faces have been cut out. Ruby has a pen in her hand, and she's crossing out what's written on the back of a photo, writing something else under the scribbled-out words.

"Mother!" Grace reaches for the scissors.

"Hello, dear."

"What are you doing?" Grace picks up a photo of her childhood nursery school, one her mother has just written on, and turns it over. It says *"Our house, in Cannes la Bocca."*

"Just fixing some old pictures."

Grace picks up the open photo album, then gathers a handful of photo-pieces and sets them on top. The topmost piece says, in Ruby's spidery handwriting: *"Grandfather Nigel Whitehead 1895."* Grace turns it over. It's a photo of her own father, Roger Urquhart, who died just ten years ago. In other photos, some of the people's heads have been cut right off. She will have to try to match them up later, when Ruby's asleep.

"But I wasn't finished." Ruby is petulant.

"What have you done?"

"You're mixing them all up!"

"Mother—"

"But they're all wrong, and I wasn't finished fixing them!"

"I know, I know."

"Give them back! Give me that!" she sputters.

"I'm sorry. I can't."

Ruby's trying to stand up, trying to stay balanced, one hand gripping the back of the bench seat and the other the edge of the table. Ruby lifts her hand from the bench, swipes ineffectually at the air, and just then the table gives way. Grace sees Ruby's body pitch straight across and collapse over the empty space where the table had been; the photos slide down and scatter around her.

A sound escapes Grace, a strangled cry that punctuates her lurch forward, then her frightened hands are scattering lightly over her mother's body, brushing off the photographs. "Where does it hurt? Does it hurt somewhere?"

Ruby's voice is icy. "Help me up."

"Like this?" Grace hooks her arms awkwardly under her mother's armpits. "Should I pull up, like this?"

Grace heaves her mother up, staggers backwards briefly, and regains her balance.

Ruby, appearing painfully bent, palms her thigh, panting. "Help me over there, will you?"

Grace takes a deep breath and lets it out slowly, trying to calm her hammering heart. She supports her mother's weight and helps her step sideways.

"It's a miracle you didn't break something."

"Just leave me alone."

"Are you sure you're okay?"

"Don't touch me."

Ruby struggles into her chair. Grace passes her a word-search puzzle book and a pencil, switches the light on over her head. She picks up the photographs and fallen scissors and props the table back in place. Then she returns to the kitchen and fills the stainless steel kettle at the sink. As the kettle's contours begin to warm on the electric burner she picks up a dry cloth and starts polishing over its dullish smears, first one side then the other. The metal starts to gleam brighter. She lifts the cloth. A giant, bloodshot eye bulges out from under one wild eyebrow. The eye is looking back at her.

"Tea for two, and two for tea, me for you, and you for me," Ruby intones. Silence follows. Then she says, "My leg hurts. Did I fall down, Gracie? Mind you make the tea strong, won't you, dear?"

Grace fixates on the kettle, on the reflection of her horrifyingly distorted right eye, then slowly she turns her head to see the left. If this were a horror movie like *The Birds*, this would be the part where she'd start screaming. Her screams would rattle the glasses in the trailer's cupboards. The macramé owl would come to life and fly off the wall, its wings batting hopelessly at the closed windows. Her screams would mingle with the sound of the kettle's rising banshee whistle. She pulls her face away from her reflection and yanks the kettle off the stove.

Ruby slowly, emphatically, draws a circle over a word on the page, then looks up. "Tea will take the dampness out of our bones, Gracie."

Rain strikes the north windows as though flung there by unseen hands. Grace nods at her mother and reaches automatically for the switch in the wall, click, and the sounds of a talk radio show. People are discussing wines; a sommelier is offering advice.

"I would certainly recommend that one to go with cassoulet," says an authoritative voice. *"Mind you, make sure it's a 1971 and not a '72."*

"That's ridiculous," says Ruby. "That man sounds like he doesn't know the difference between a Zinfandel and a Valpolicella."

Grace lowers the volume until all they can hear is a low mumbling. She remembers Ruby's pills. Tomorrow, she might again attempt the trip into town. Today wasn't meant to be. She pours the hot water into the teapot, sets two cups down.

After a while the talk-radio show is over, and a song starts up. High, tinny voices curl and wiggle into the air.

"Sugar Baby, I'm in love with you.
Sugar Baby, tell me what to do."

Grace pours the tea and sets her mother's cup in front of her. Ruby scribbles something over her word-search puzzle and closes the magazine.

Grace sits down and, concentrating hard, uncurls her fingers from their tight grip on the teacup handle, forcefully readjusting them to a more comfortable, reasonable grip. She sips her tea and imagines herself walking back into Dr. Kerwin's office, imagines trying to describe what exactly's the matter with her.

"I'm so afraid," she starts. "There's something terribly wrong with me, and I need your help."

"Please," she imagines him saying back to her in a kindly tone, "take your time."

She searches for the right words. Then, finding that saying them out loud is impossible, she imagines asking him for a pen and paper. In her mind's eye she holds the pen over the paper, and her hand moves purposefully across it. But when she looks down at what she's written, she sees only lines of unintelligible markings: a trail of pictograms, hieroglyphs and runes, multi-syllabic dots and dashes. She tries to remember what she meant.

SIXTEEN

Veronica's reading in the living room of the trailer when there's a light tap on the door.

To her delight, it's Charlotte, who says, "I've come to kidnap you."

Veronica raises a finger in caution. "Shh!"

"Why are we whispering?"

"Mom and Dilly are sleeping. He's sick, she was up with him in the night. Gumm's grounded, and he's in the shower."

"Perfect timing then!"

"And how do you fancy that?"

"I just knew. Telepathy maybe. Or *Radar Love*, the new rock song already on its way to being a classic. Wanna hear it? Come on."

"I'd love to."

"And I want to show you my drawings."

"Oh yes—"

"Besides, we need to bury her. She's starting to smell

132

bad."

"Bury who?"

It's Marnie's voice, slurring from behind them. She's standing at the door. "Is it that crow business? I thought that was over and done with."

"Don't worry, we'll be back soon." Veronica moves closer to the steps.

Her mother, peering at Charlotte, says, "Who's this?"

"It's me, Mrs Reid. Me, Charlotte. Are you feeling alright?"

Veronica nudges her friend and slings her backpack over her shoulder. "Let's go."

They head to the park first. Then they take the back way to Charlotte's, between the park and the lake.

Charlotte's trailer is shorter than the Reids', though it feels bigger because of an airy, glassed-in porch room tacked on to the front. In the porch room, two wicker chairs sit next to a braided rug. Inside the trailer, the kitchen is on the left and the bathroom is at the front end. In Charlotte's bedroom there's a bed, a bureau, a night-table, and windows on two walls. A sofa in the centre folds out to become a bed. Charlotte shows her everything, opening cupboard doors, revealing storage spaces under the bench, the wardrobe built into the wall just outside her room.

Charlotte's sketchbook is open on the kitchen table. A bird is rendered in four different positions on the left page. She might be four crows, but she's one crow. She's seen from above; from below, in flight; here perched on a fence; there on her side, with her claws curled under. On the right page, spare, sweeping strokes show wing bones, with some detailed drawings of head and beak, claws. Veronica lets her breath out slowly.

"I had no notion! Oh, she's so lifelike."

After looking carefully at each rendering of the crow, Veronica turns the page slowly and looks at the drawings on previous pages. A barn wall, light streaming though the cracks between the boards. A yellow bird standing on the edge of an empty nest. A sleek dog sitting by a riverbank. Veronica remembers her dream. Soon she finds herself telling Charlotte how her hammock had begun to sway, how the crow calls had first awakened her. About following the crows to the lake and coming upon the birds' solemn gathering.

Charlotte is paying close attention to her words. "What do you think it means?"

"I don't know. It felt like ... something ceremonial. Like communion. As though they were all focused on one sacramental thing."

"Ho-ly," says Charlotte reverently. "I wish I'd been there."

When it stops raining, they turn to their real purpose. They wrap the bird up in a small towel, and place her in Veronica's backpack. Next they walk back to the Reids' trailer where Veronica procures her mother's garden shovel from the shed. Charlotte carries it over her shoulder as they reach the park and make their way to the crows' pine tree, the one nearest the beach.

Digging the hole is harder than they think it will be. The shovel hits too many roots and small boulders.

Finally, a little farther back, but still within the shadows of the pine trees, they find the earth more yielding. They take turns jumping on the shovel to deepen the hole.

Veronica unwraps the towel and lets the crow's body slide gently to the centre of the hollow. They both kneel and use the towel to push the soil over it.

Veronica swallows. "Should we say a prayer or something?" Her fingers rest on the medallion in her pocket.

"If you want."

"I think she should have a name. So she's not just any crow."

"Okay. What would you like to name her?"

"Mogle."

Charlotte smiles. "Mogle. That's good. I like Mogle."

"Do you know any prayers?"

"I'm a pagan. And pagans, you know, don't do prayers. They do meditations, and sun ceremonies. Dancing."

"It's just so sad."

"It doesn't have to be."

Veronica starts. "I remember something: 'Do not stand at my grave and weep. I am not there, I do not sleep.' I can't recall the rest. 'I am the wind ....'"

"I am the wind," repeats Charlotte.

"Feathers on the wind."

And so, through murmurs and hums, they improvise their own ceremony, inventing alternating phrases, repeating each other's words, inviting benevolent spirits that might be hovering nearby. Veronica is aware of new sensations in her body, of shrinking and expanding, falling and lifting.

The pine boughs nod and sway, loosening ripples of green.

After a while Veronica squats to place her palm on the ground over the buried crow. "We should come back and leave a mark here, a big rock or something."

"Sure. And we can bring flowers."

"Flowers? Or peanuts?" She stands up again.

Charlotte says she has to be off. "Hey, Veronica! Don't forget to miss me."

She says it like she means it. Then she's gone. Veronica grins, tucks her hands under her armpits, and looks at the ground. She tries to squeeze her elbows close to her sides, but they want to be up. She pushes them down hard but they keep jerking, springing involuntarily, wanting to open and lift her away.

On her way back to the trailer, Saint Fagin falls into step with her. Veronica slows down to look at him.

The swain—Wayne—seems to be dressed as a troubadour this time, his tunic bright green with swinging trumpet-sleeves, trimmed in red. She smiles.

Time traveller, shape-shifter. God's messenger who's singled her out.

He cocks his head, fixes her with an amused gaze and quietly says, "Do you know Tibullus? 'Fond hope keeps the spark alive, whispering ever that tomorrow things will mend.'"

Veronica blinks. "I beg your pardon? Ever tomorrow?" She starts to say, "Why, that's splendid—!" but he's gone.

SEVENTEEN

"Could you hurry, sir? We have a taxi waiting."

The pharmacist regards Grace over the top of his half-spectacles with an expression that might be registering skepticism or pity or both. He's been slowly turning pages in a folder on the counter while the meter ticks in the taxi. More importantly, Grace has an appointment with Dr. Kerwin in fifteen minutes. The last time she was late, Dr. Kerwin admonished her, said he couldn't make up for the lost time at the end of the hour, because he had another client coming in.

The pharmacist hasn't moved. "Lost, you said."

Grace sighs. "Yes. My mother loses a lot of things these days. But like I said, we're kind of pressed for time."

"I'm sure you are. But I am committed to my oath, and it is my responsibility to remind you to be very careful with this prescription. This is a very strong drug. You know, of course, it's a treatment for senile dementia, a particular kind of dementia. It's heavy stuff. In other words this drug could be quite dangerous if it fell into the wrong hands."

Why now? He's never given her a hard time before.

"I understand," she says, looking at her watch. He doesn't seem to get it. "But I really must go now."

"Perhaps you can let me know if they turn up."

What does he suspect her of? Selling them?

"I will."

"And wait. Before you go … someone was here asking about Mrs Urquhart."

Grace goes cold. "When?"

"About a week ago. I told him our records are confidential, of course. But I thought you should know." The pharmacist keeps looking at her, as though he expects her to say something. Finally, he picks up a large container, shakes some tablets out on the counter and starts to separate them, using a tongue depressor to slide them across the laminate. They rattle into a tray.

Grace's mouth is dry. So they haven't given up yet. She tries to swallow.

"What did he look like?"

"Medium build. Well dressed, suit and tie. Round, black-rimmed glasses. Says he might come back with a search warrant or a court order."

She is silent as he drops the pill container into a paper bag, folds the top.

The pharmacist regards her suspiciously. "We don't keep our clients' addresses in our records, but I would have to divulge the information that she is a client here, if I am compelled to do so by the law. You can pay for this at the front."

The click of the stapler at the top of the bag sinks sharply, like an ice pick, into her temple.

Grace is late for her appointment with Dr. Kerwin and agitated about the pharmacist's disclosure. She settles Ruby in the reception room with Faye, the doctor's bubbly assistant, who sports a beehive hairdo that's been out of fashion for years. Faye has already made a pot of tea in anticipation of their arrival. She welcomes Ruby warmly.

As Grace steps into Dr. Kerwin's inner sanctum, she tries to put her thoughts in order, tries to remember what she meant to tell her psychologist. Whatever it was has been displaced in her mind by a new fear. It might be safe to change pharmacies. It could be as simple as that. What's one more inconvenience, if it means protecting her mother?

Grace looks at her watch when she sits down.

"I'm sorry I'm late."

Dr. Kerwin swivels in his chair to face her. He has pleasant features, a small chin, and eyes that are used to smiling, or squinting into the sun.

"Grace. How have you been?"

She clears her throat, and the words cascade out in an agonized disorder.

"I was trying to do that thing you said, you know, touching people. I'd prepared myself, and everything. It all went wrong, I was trying so hard to follow it, what you said, but there was this poncho, then I squeezed this woman called Marnie, I mean I thought it was her arm—and then I could tell it was her—her chest."

Dr. Kerwin's response is matter of fact. "You have to go and explain it to her."

"Oh, but I couldn't do that."

"Now, now, Grace."

"But what if—"

"You *are* capable of doing that. Of talking to Marnie."

"But what on earth would I say?"

"Let's *practise*." He means role-playing. They stand up facing each other. Dr. Kerwin makes his voice about an octave higher. "*Oh hello, Grace, good to see you again!*"

"She wouldn't say that."

Dr. Kerwin lowers his voice to its normal pitch. "Oh hello, Grace, what brings you here today?"

Grace shakes her head. "No. She'll say, 'There you are, Grace, are you out of your mind?'"

Dr. Kerwin clears his throat. "Alright, try, ah, 'I've been thinking, Marnie. I'm afraid I might have accidentally touched your *chest* under the poncho.'"

"I can't say that!"

"I see what you mean."

They talk about it for an hour. In the end Dr. Kerwin's voice has become so gentle, so patient and low and soft that she can barely hear his words.

"Grace, remember you found the courage to reach out and touch her the first time. Could you not find the courage a second time, somewhere deep down, to explain your *mistake*?"

Thankfully there are no other patients in the waiting room when Grace emerges. But Ruby is frowning, brandishing a cookie at the receptionist.

"I can tell you, these are *not* Fortnum & Mason's Piccadilly cookies."

Faye looks dishevelled. Long strands of hair have come loose from her beehive "do," and her makeup is smudged. The plate of cookies is between them, but Faye doesn't offer one to Grace.

"There you go now, Mrs Urquhart," says Faye, as Grace puts her wallet back in her purse, "you don't have to put up with me any longer. Have a nice afternoon!"

On the ride home in the taxi, Grace and Ruby sit side by side in the back seat. Grace turns her face to the window, closes her eyes and moves her lips soundlessly. *I breathe in abundance. I am conceived by divine light. I am sustained by divine light.* She breathes in and out, slowly, deeply. Then she opens her eyes, looks down at her lap, and tries to make herself imagine facing Marnie. Her heartbeat instantly picks up, her breathing quickens, the blood starts pulsating in her temples. It's no use. She may as well give up on herself.

Grace pinches the top of her nose between her thumb and forefinger.

"What's the matter, Gracie?"

"I think I'm having one of my spells."

Grace's mother pats her on the knee, chuckling. "You'll be fine, Gracie. You're fine."

But by the time they get back to the trailer park Grace has concluded that Dr. Kerwin is right. She needs to get this over with or it's going to haunt her forever. And that's all there is to it.

She waits until her mother lies down for her afternoon rest.

When Grace steps up to Marnie's aluminum screen door, she sees Marnie inside, running her hands through her hair. She's shouting at someone.

"I've had enough! Why, why, why do you have to be so … You make me feel useless, all of you! It's already enough that your father's always missing in action. You were all his idea, I never wanted, you know, it was his idea—"

Grace steps backwards on the porch, and instantly crashes into a folding chair, which ends up on its side with her in it. She tries to get up again, but her limbs are somehow tangled in the collapsed chair.

"Grace?" Marnie's flustered face peering out the door screen. "Is that you?" To Grace's dismay, Marnie steps out hastily and presses her back against the shut door and starts talking.

"I didn't see you there."

Grace wriggles out of the chair and stands up. "I shouldn't have—"

"I was talking to my son. He's driving me crazy, pestering me to let him go out."

"I, ah, I'll come some other …"

"He killed a crow, of all things. With a slingshot."

"Who killed a, what did you say?"

A boy whines inside the trailer. "It was hunting

practice!"

Marnie turns and yells back, "It was unnecessary cruelty!"

The voice goes on. "*This* is unnecessary cruelty! What a warped sense of justice! You're stunting my growth! Let me out!"

Marnie's face is growing a darker shade of lavender.

"Come *on*! Mom! It was just a *bird*!"

Grace is torn with confusion and embarrassment. She stammers that she'll come back another time.

But Marnie seizes her by the wrist. "You don't have to go. You must understand, Dilly's sick. I've been up with him all night, and now this fight with Gumm. As if it's not enough to spend my whole time cleaning up vomit, cramming machines full of laundry—where I have to go again now—and people are saying it's my fault they're sick. All three of them. Dilly and two other boys who swam in the lake that day. If it's polluted it's not my fault. Boys will do—"

Gumm starts banging his head on the door, so hard that Marnie's body nudges forward from behind with each impact, and each bang is punctuated with single syllables: "Out! Just! Watch! Me!" Marnie lets go of Grace's wrist to place two hands against the door.

"I'm still your mother! I'll let you go out when I'm damn good and ready to let you go out!" She turns her face back to Grace, who feels too stunned to move.

Marnie says, "This summer is turning out to be so much harder than I thought it would be. You know?"

Into a sliver of silence comes a faint, weak voice calling out from inside the trailer. "Mom. Mom."

It's the younger one, with the other odd name. Dilly.

"Oh, no. Here we go again." Marnie swoops away from the door and turns to let herself in. But the second her body is out of the way, Gumm's hand is on the knob, and he wrenches the door open, shoves her sideways, and leaps off the edge of the porch onto the hard ground below. Sets off running.

Marnie throws her hands in the air. "I don't believe it. Why am I even here?" she says, looking hopelessly at Grace.

"I came to tell you something," Grace blurts. "I came to tell you that I'm sorry about the other day, I ..."

Marnie frowns, tilts her head.

"The other day, I was greeting you and I think I touched you somewhere by mistake. That's all. It was a mistake."

Grace holds out her hand and mimics the squeezing motion three times.

There's a brief silence, then a laugh erupts out of Marnie like a hiccup. "Is that so," she says. She crosses her arms across her chest and laughs some more.

Grace attempts to laugh with her, but it feels artificial, forced.

"Can I tell you something?" Marnie gives a short, bitter kind of sound. She listens for a few seconds for her son, through the door, but all is quiet. She lowers her voice.

"That was the first time I've been, you know, touched,

in a really long time."

Grace opens her mouth and closes it again. She's not sure if Marnie is laughing still, or if she's somehow started to cry. How can she tell the difference?

"Oh please, don't get me wrong," Marnie whimpers, "I mean, you know I'm married, and of course I like men, but Colin—what I'm trying to say is, that part of my life shouldn't have to be over, you know?"

Marnie's shoulders are slumped over, and she is clearly crying now, but in a muted, subdued way. Grace pats her pocket for a tissue while Marnie talks, her voice so low Grace can hardly hear it.

"I just feel so unattractive, so unwanted. I'm only thirty-eight. I asked Father Michael what to do—I was raised Catholic you know, Grace—and he said I had to accept my lot in life. My marriage vows didn't mention what to do when you're desperately unhappy, when your needs aren't being fulfilled, when your husband isn't even the same person you married."

Grace fixes her eyes on Marnie and tries her best to look sympathetic, to be encouraging.

"I hope you don't mind my being frank with you," Marnie says. Then, without waiting for an answer, she lowers her voice and leans closer to Grace.

"I came here so I could have a simple summer affair, to see, you know, if a man could still desire me. I thought it would be safe here, just a bit of harmless fun that could end when everybody goes home. You know, free love, and all of that. Believe me, I've been doing my darndest. I even tried to seduce Milton, but so far," Marnie blots her eyes and looks sadly at Grace, "it's hopeless. So the joke is, wouldn't you know it, the only thing I can manage is to be felt up, by accident, by a woman. No offence."

"I'm sorry," says Grace. "Really I am." She reaches up and pats Marnie, softly, carefully, on her upper arm.

"It's not your fault."

As Marnie sniffles and pulls herself together, to her surprise Grace sees Marnie's expression pass through several recognizable shades of sorrow, bitterness, and resignation. Grace keeps patting her, and after a while Marnie starts chuckling again, and her pageboy-curled hair begins to bob up and down.

Grace catches a glimpse of the absurdity of their situation. She suddenly sees the joke through an outsider's eyes, and Grace doesn't have to be Grace any more but just some ordinary middle-aged woman in a trailer park standing under an awning on a verandah strewn with collapsed folding chairs, sharing a laugh with one of her neighbours.

EIGHTEEN

The lake is restless and impenetrably blue. The curved line of the log boom jerks and bobs. Farther down, two figures in a canoe are paddling near the shallows; their voices undulate faintly over the flat slapping sounds of water against the bow.

Aloft, the crow is approaching from the west, shoulders set and wingtips trailing a cross-breeze. His gliding, outstretched silhouette creases and ripples beneath him. Sunlight scatters itself in prickling fragments upon the lake. The sky is the blended colour of robins' eggs. A white vapour trail is an eel's bleached backbone.

Since the day of the lakeside mourning ritual for his mate, Hrah's solitary inner life has been permeated by visions like this. The first one came to him while sleeping, his head tucked under his shoulder-feathers. He dreamed he saw a plump, grey vole wriggling through a tangle of thatch next to a stream, but when he stabbed at it with his beak, it startled him by rearing up and speaking to him in the voice of a crow. The voice was his mate's.

Here, she said. I am here.

Other visions come during the day, lifting out of his turbulent grief and manifesting his inarticulate, windswept fury. Once, shadows appeared on a wide expanse of grass and began to thrash until they became multi-dimensional and looked like sprawled horses kicking their legs. Another time, an arching plume of black smoke took the form of a benevolent avian spirit as it rose. Later, a mass of gnats became a miniature, crowded rookery. At dusk, tree silhouettes at one end of the woods assumed sepulchral proportions, and the entire forest seemed to emit an atonal moan.

The visions have been helping him symmetrize his life. By reminding him of the past and future, they tether him to the permanence of the present. The visions urge him to endlessly test the reliability of the forces of gravity, using acceleration, calculating magnitude. They guide him to plunge back up into the sky, to align himself with the sun, the angle of its warm rays slanting on his pinions. They summon him to yield to enduring magnetic and spiritual forces. Again and again his familiar shadow slides over the water, rippling over the earth, painting the leafy canopies.

Hrah spies a clump of black feathers under one of the willow trees, drops down to inspect the remains to see if they are hers. They are not. One afternoon near the railroad track, he is startled at hearing her voice again, but turns to see it is only one of the yearlings.

Throughout the first long light-revolutions that followed his loss, the non-breeding juveniles have stuck close by, as have the newest fledglings. They've been sharing food stashes and remaining nearby at night, taking turns on watch. Warding off evil with their collective presence, shuffling ceremonials amongst the foliage, sentries perched to face every direction.

The crow becomes wary and watchful as he approaches the trailer park. Here and there he sees people, some single and others in pairs and clusters, but not the loose alliance of boy-nomads.

He thrusts harder, wings surging, to gain height and perspective, lifts above the willow trees where all the leaves are trembling under the touches of the wind. From this height he can see the distant town and the grey scrawls of the roads that lead from it in the direction of the lake.

Then he sees the boys. They are riding their bikes along one of the roads, heading for the trailer park. He glides and descends for a closer look at their faces. He makes two sweeps overhead, looks and looks, but *that* boy is not one of them. He makes a wide arc in the empty sky and turns back, eventually gliding close to the ridge of trees where the yearlings await. They call across to him and he answers, their vocalizations joining in familiar utterances that scrape the air.

Then Hrah's voice changes: he emits an urgent shriek to alert the others. *Mob! Danger! Now!* There's that particular boy—*Drive him away! He's a killer!*—that human menace jogging along, stumbling on laces that flap from his running shoes.

NINETEEN

Ever tomorrow. What does it mean? It's hard to hold in her excitement. Hope is everywhere: it's in the little berries that are starting to form in the mountain ash, it's in the smell of cedar and woodsmoke, and the richness of the water's blue sheen. Hope even radiates from the Jesus medallion, the metal becoming so hot that Veronica imagines it could burn a hole through her pocket, branding her upper thigh with the words YE MUST BE BORN AGAIN. Indeed she feels reborn. Her glasses feel lighter on the bridge of her nose and, everywhere she looks, the sun seems to be illuminating new things: a bicycle, a sailboat on the lake, a child's wagon, a clump of cosmos.

Saffron has taken to doing yoga on a hill in the park in the early mornings. From the verandah, looking across the lane, Veronica can see her neighbour's movements silhouetted in the quickening light. The well-toned body moves languidly through a series of impossible-looking contortions. Saffron stays still without wobbling, each pose a culmination of self-control. In one of the poses, both arms and one leg outstretched, she looks weightless. A dark profile on the hill, she slowly descends to a crouch and then puts her hands flat on the ground. She props her body up to balance on just her hands, her knees tucked in to rest on her upper arms, her toes pointing back, her head slightly lifted.

Ever tomorrow, thinks Veronica. Anything is possible.

At ten o'clock, the canteen trailer seems to shimmer at Veronica's approach. Charlotte introduces her to the manager. Jeremy is tall and lanky, with an unruly crop of tow-coloured hair. When he smiles, Veronica can see his crowded front teeth. He rubs at a patch of stubble on his jaw.

"Veronica, is it? Yawright?"

She likes his British accent. Apparently he did a year of schooling in the UK, and when he came home he had the accent. Jeremy explains that he works at the tuck shop himself most of the time. Charlotte is part-time. Veronica is to apply for what Jeremy calls part-time relief. Only a few hours a week. He hands Veronica a piece of paper.

"If you'd like to fill out this form, I'll have a look at your qualifications. Charlotte says you're available Friday afternoons and evenings?"

Veronica nods.

"Have you worked a cash machine before?"

"No," she says apologetically, "I'm afraid not."

"It's okay," Charlotte says, "I can teach her."

Jeremy nods. "You're fourteen, Charlotte says?"

Veronica glances at Charlotte. She's not fourteen for

another three months.

"Yes," she replies.

"She's a hard worker," Charlotte says to Jeremy. "Mature and responsible. And she learns fast."

Veronica sits at one of the stools to fill in the application form. Full Name, Home Address, Education. Under Work Experience she writes, "Not yet." Under Hobbies she writes, "Reading, Birdwatching."

Jeremy takes her application, but he barely glances at it. "Jolly good then," he says. "Can you start tomorrow?"

Marnie's tossing bedsheets off the balcony onto the lawn when Veronica sees her. Her mother lets the last sheet drop, then she picks up a drink from the railing and takes a swig. Beads of condensation swim down the outside of the glass. She watches her mother wipe her wet palm on her forehead. Marnie notices Veronica.

"Where've you been? Just look at this place. You and Gumm, the pair of you, just as bad as each other. Dilly can't help it, he's sick. And you're old enough to know better."

"I thought coming here was your idea," Veronica says.

Marnie turns and picks up some soiled towels, which she drops on a tangle of folded chairs.

"What did you say?"

"That coming here was your idea."

"Yeah, so? What do you know about it? You're still too young to know anything. Oh, it doesn't matter. You, you won't listen to me anyway. Not about handling dead birds, not about sleeping on the porch. You leave without saying where you're going … God knows what else you're up to." Her mother walks away again, stalks inside and lets the door bang after her.

Veronica calls out, "I got a job." The door remains closed so she doesn't know if Marnie heard her. Veronica enters the trailer and waits for her mother to speak.

Marnie says, "Are you sure that's a good idea?" She has an empty glass on the counter and she's reaching for the vodka bottle.

"Are you sure *that's* a good idea?" asks Veronica.

Marnie opens the refrigerator door and pulls out a carton of orange juice, splashing it over the half-melted ice cubes in her glass, shoves the empty carton aside, and adds a generous dollop of vodka.

Veronica frowns. "Where's Gumm?"

Her mother takes a gulp of her drink. "Gone. Good and gone."

"What do you mean, gone?"

"Just gone."

Veronica turns, but something—some*one*—is blocking the light from the door.

"Who's gone?"

Colin has come up to the trailer unheard, his two hands grasping either side of the door frame now, his words entering softly, damply, through the screen.

"So this is what goes on when I'm not here."

Marnie's glass falls hard to the counter, orange juice splashes across the wall, ice cubes skid to the sink and tumble to the floor.

"What're you doing home?"

He opens the door and steps in, lifting his shoes over the ice cubes. "Marnie, it's eleven in the morning, for God's sake."

"You're never home. Why are you here?"

"What do you mean, why am I here? Why do you think? I want to spend some holiday time with my family. Where are the boys?"

"One's in there." Marnie points at the alcove where the narrow bunk beds are tucked against the wall. She takes a step forward, and her hands find the counter.

"But why, a day early?"

But Colin's heading straight for Dilly's bunk bed, and, bending over to the lower mattress, presses his palm to Dilly's forehead.

"Hi, Dad. You're back."

"That's a big ten-four, good buddy."

"Mash on your motor. Ten-thirty-three."

"Copy that. We'll see what we can do. Marnie. How long has he been like this?"

"I was just going to call a taxi and take him to the hospital, but now Gumm's gone, and I've got to go find him."

"I'll take him," Colin says. "I'll bring the bucket, a towel, his blanket. Fill that empty juice carton with water in case he's thirsty. We need to make sure he drinks enough. Obviously you've made sure *you've* drunk enough."

Marnie swallows. "I thought you said you couldn't take any more days off work."

Veronica asks, "Do you want me to go with you, Dad?"

Colin says "No, we'll be fine."

Marnie shoots Veronica a look of contempt.

"Did you phone him?"

"No!"

Colin says, "Leave her alone. I was just trying to surprise all of you."

Veronica waits on the porch while her father brings the station wagon around to the lane in front of the trailer. Marnie has placed a red plastic bucket and the last clean towel at the top of the porch steps. Then she emerges from the trailer with Dilly at her side, her arm over his shoulders, his unsteady body wrapped in a blanket.

"Thanks for taking him. Is there anything else you need?"

Colin shakes his head. Then he helps Dilly into the car and sets the bucket at the boy's side. He glances at Marnie before slipping behind the wheel.

"I don't know how long we'll be."

He hasn't yet turned the key in the ignition when Gumm bursts into sight from across the road, gasping, waving his arms over his head. Fresh blood is smeared down one cheek and covers his ear.

"What's the matter with you?"

"Birds are attacking me! Dad! Make them stop!"

"Oh, it can't be, Colin! Look! Veronica!" Marnie points upwards.

Veronica looks up too quickly, and her glasses slip a bit

sideways on her face. Four—no, five—no, seven! crows are circling above them. Their cries make little jagged rips in the air.

"Get in. Just get in. In the car."

Gumm does what he is told and shuts the door; the station wagon roars to life and starts away.

Veronica straightens her glasses. The crows have climbed higher in the sky. Still wheeling, the birds grow smaller as they lift above her blinking gaze, receding until the dark peppered specks are indistinguishable from the infinite blue.

Colin brings Gumm back to the trailer some hours later, drops him off on their front lawn, and drives off again. Gumm sports a gauze bandage running from his temple to his ear. When he enters the trailer, he goes to look at it in the mirror. He comes back out of the bathroom to show it to Marnie.

"The doctor said Dilly has to stay overnight. Dad's gone back so he can sleep in a chair next to him. They'll both be back tomorrow. Dad promised."

"The crows will be back tomorrow, too," says Veronica, "to finish you off."

Gumm sticks his tongue at her. "Liar. They will not."

"Don't be so sure about that."

That night in her hammock, Veronica reads her book by flashlight, wanting to stay awake until midnight, the end of "ever tomorrow." But she falls asleep before half-past ten. Friday morning when she wakes, her eyesight is just as bad as ever. She's crestfallen.

"Ever tomorrow" must have meant "same as ever, to-morrow." Ha, ha, the joke's on you, Ver-ronnie.

She can taste the disappointment. No more painstak-ingly constructed hopes, no more faith; she's obviously doomed to a life of misery, a life behind glasses that make her a laughing stock. At least that way she won't have to become a nun.

Early the next afternoon, when Colin and Dilly get back, Marnie makes a big fuss over her youngest child.

"Your colour's better, my love. What did the doctor say?"

"He said I'm a lucky boy."

Dilly's holding a new toy airplane, made of balsa wood, pretend-flying it over his head.

"They gave him fluids and antibiotics," Colin says. He's still standing at the door. He leans forward, sets a small bottle of pink liquid on the table. "Dilly needs to take a teaspoon every four hours. Keep it in the fridge."

Gumm comes into the hall and touches his head gin-gerly, fingering his bandage. "This still hurts," he says.

"Of course it does, my love," Marnie says. "But aren't you going to ask how your brother's doing?"

"Hey Dill," Gumm says. "I had to have a needle. Did you have to have a needle? For tet-nus. Makes your jaw lock up."

"Well," murmurs Veronica, "that would be an improvement."

"That's uncalled for, Veronica." Marnie turns back to Dilly. "How do you feel, my love? Would you like a piece of toast? Some apple juice?"

Dilly pretend-crashes his plane softly into the wall, then flops into a chair, drops the plane upside down in his lap. "I don't know."

Colin hasn't moved from the door. "They said he should take it easy for a couple of days. Lots of liquids, lots of rest." He frowns. "Marnie, look. We have to talk."

Gumm points to his bandage and says, "Two stitches, but I never got a plane."

"Speaking of stitches, that's it. I'm going," Veronica says. "I need to find a needle and thread. So while I'm gone, Gumm, you go too. Buzz off, why don't you. And you, Dilly, you're well enough to come sit outside for a few minutes. Go on, even you can give your parents some privacy."

She takes Dilly's free hand, leads him out, sits him at the picnic table, and tells him to stay there for a while. She sees Gumm stomp out of the trailer and protectively lift his arms over his head as he heads for the park. Veronica leaves Dilly and walks in the opposite direction, down the lane. Her father will confront her mother about the drinking, and then they can all just get back to normal.

Veronica's steps are bringing her to Grace's Airstream. She recognizes Ruby in the front yard, sitting in the shade, wearing a big straw hat and her string of pearls. Her feet, in blue slippers, stick out from under the hem of her blue dress.

"Hello, Mrs Urquhart."

Ruby looks up and her face changes, breaks into a wide smile. "Hello, hello!"

"Lovely afternoon."

Gnarled fingers are opening and closing stiffly, one trying to point at her. "You're, you're, that girl, that's right. We have a present for you."

"For me?" Veronica is mildly confused. "But that's very kind. Is your daughter home?"

Ruby nods and looks up at the trailer. "Gracie's inside." She raises her voice. "Gracie? Are you in there?"

Grace comes to the door at once.

"Veronica."

"I was wondering, may I have a favour? I tore some netting. Would you have a needle and thread I might borrow?"

"What's torn?"

"Just some mosquito screen. I've been sleeping outside, and since the rain there've been so many more mosquitoes, and they've been biting me at night without mercy."

"Mercy!" says Ruby. "You don't say. But why do you sleep outside?"

"It's a long story."

Grace says, "In my sewing kit, I'm sure I have ... Come on in."

Veronica follows her inside and sits down, but leaves the door ajar to let in some fresh air. She leans out of the doorway and waves to Grace's mother. Ruby waves back.

Grace emerges from what must be her bedroom, carrying a needle and a spool of white thread in one hand, a paper bag in the other. In the light from the doorway, she notices that Grace's fingernails are bitten down to the quick, and a fringe of pink skin rims her cuticles.

Grace shyly hands the bag to her. "We went to town the other day and I bought something for you."

Ruby calls through the open door in a tremulous voice. "Gracie? Are you there?"

"I'm here, what? Oh, but I thought you wanted to be outside. Mother, just five minutes ago you said ..."

Inside the bag are two balls of jute, a smaller skein of orange cotton, and an assortment of beads.

"Thank you, I'm so grateful! You didn't have to!"

"I thought you might like to make something of your own. I can show you how to make a belt, or a necklace, or a plant hanger, if you like."

"Or a bird-feeder hanger?"

"Or a bird-feeder hanger, right."

When Grace's mother is settled back on her living-room chair, she wants the folding table, on which a puzzle is laid out, set up next to her.

"You can help me."

So Veronica sits beside her at the table. The bottom edge of the puzzle has been completed, as well as most of the top, between which all the other pieces lie scattered.

The old woman fumbles with a piece, drops it, curses her clumsy fingers. Veronica picks it up and gives it to her. Ruby tries to place it in one spot, pulls it back, tilts her head exaggeratedly, then tries another spot.

"Voilà!" Her voice is triumphant.

Grace hovers nearby. "Veronica, I—does your mother know you're here? Has she said anything this week about, I mean, has she been okay?"

Veronica searches Grace's face. "No, why? I don't really converse with her."

"Because every time I see her, there's some kind of crisis."

Veronica picks up another puzzle piece and slips it between Mrs Urquhart's thumb and forefinger.

"Dilly is indisposed. Actually he's more than indisposed. She's been busy with him."

"Oh. You mean she's under stress because your brother's sick?"

"Yes, but only as a consequence of swimming in the lake. Dad even had to take him to the hospital. The boys—including him—spit and urinate in the swimming zone, so it's obviously contaminated."

"They what? How do you know that?"

"They brag about it. So now Dilly is ill. Ill Dilly, ill Dill, hear the rhyme? I call it poetic justice."

"Or *schadenfreude*," Ruby intones.

"Or both, it sounds like," says Grace.

Veronica looks from one to the other. "Suffice it to say that I'll not be doing any swimming." Then she adds, "I don't even want to put my feet in the water." She pauses, looks searchingly at Grace. "Boys are so disgusting, don't you think?"

Grace doesn't take the bait. "Well, I hope your brother's better soon."

Veronica tells Grace that she has a job. "It's just Friday afternoons and evenings for now, from four until nine. Today's my first day."

Grace's mother says, "That was a good stroke of business."

Grace says, "A job? But you're so young!"

"I could use the pocket money. And it's good experience. Try this piece next, Mrs Urquhart."

After a while Grace says, "Veronica, are you planning to go to the slide show in the common room? It's on stained glass. Tomorrow night."

"Mrs Carmichael's putting it on?"

"I think so, yes, I think that's her name. I'd like to take my mother there. Only, I was hoping maybe you could help me with her—if you're going, that is. She could sit on your other side. So I could watch the show too."

Grace digs a flyer out of a kitchen drawer, and Veronica reads it out loud. "'The World Through Prisms, Colour, and Light! Free Slide Show and Lecture on Stained Glass, Saturday Night.' Sure I'll go, I can help you if you like."

As she's stepping out of the Airstream later, Veronica hears Ruby's quavery voice again.

"Voilà!"

TWENTY

Veronica the part-time relief worker is relieving Charlotte, who's finishing her shift at the tuck shop. Charlotte lingers a while to show her where things go. She points out the items they're not allowed to sell to minors, demonstrates how to work the cash register and how to count the change back into people's hands. It all seems simple enough.

Charlotte waits with Veronica until the first ice-cream customer comes by, so she can show her how to run the machine and how to make two diminishing loops of ice cream on the tops of the cones.

"There are the regular customers," Charlotte tells her, "and a few who just like to chat. Jeremy might come by to see how you're doing. If you want to buy something for yourself, it's twenty per cent off."

It's a bonus she hasn't expected. Then a second bonus: Charlotte says she's going to come back before nine o'clock to show her how to lock up, help her turn the lights off, show her where to stash the cash. Veronica says she looks forward to it.

"Good luck, and have fun," Charlotte says. Then she's gone.

After about fifteen minutes, her first customer comes. It's Saffron.

"Fancy seeing you here, sweetie. Your mother doesn't mind you working alone?"

"No. I mean, I didn't ask her if she minded."

"Good for you. Make sure you be careful. Hey, didn't we have fun on our boat ride? Want to do it again some-time?"

"Sure, I guess. Thanks. So ... what can I do for you?"

Saffron rolls her eyes. "It's not me. It's Milton. He'd like a packet of rolling papers and two bags of Yum Yum potato chips."

Veronica finds she likes the authority she feels when she announces "That'll be two dollars and forty-nine cents, please," and afterwards counts the change back into people's hands. Most of all, she likes the fact that she can read her book between customers, pinning it to the coun-ter with her elbows.

As the sun goes down, it slants parallel to the lane and falls between the trees, lighting up the spread pages. Soon she'll turn the lights on behind her, but for now she's ab-sorbed in *Pride and Prejudice*. She's just begun the last chap-ter when a shadow falls over the page.

"Pray tell," says an amused voice, "who have we here?"

It's Wayne. She's still angry with him for misleading her. Ever tomorrow. Never ever, more like.

She lifts her chin. "Can I help you?"

"That depends upon you. Tuck Shop Sensations, eh?"

Veronica blushes. "This is my first day at work."

Wayne steps closer. "Then I'm honoured, m'lady, to share this momentous day with you." He makes a sweeping bow.

The chivalrous gesture makes Veronica giggle in spite of herself.

"Next thing you know," she says, "you'll be kissing my hand."

"At your service, young maiden," he replies, reaching his arm toward her, palm up. She looks away, embarrassed, but Wayne quickly snatches her by the wrist.

She tries to pull her hand back, but his grip is secure.

"Ow, you're hurting me!"

To her horror, he still doesn't let go. He's pressing his lips on the back of her seized hand—no, he's playfully biting it, making noises. Now, could he really be licking, nay, sucking, the skin on the back of her hand? In the midst of it all, he meets her eyes and winks. His wet tongue pressing back and forth—

"Don't!" she says.

She pulls her arm back as hard as she's able, tries to jerk it away from him, to no avail. She's scared now. Would screaming be an overreaction? She takes a breath, opens her mouth, and Wayne drops her hand. She pulls it back roughly to wipe it off, and looks down. The back of her hand is gleaming pink. When she looks back up at him, his eyes glitter in the light, as though he's in a trance.

"I'm just trying to declare myself," he says.

Veronica can't speak. Then, as though nothing unusual had just happened, Wayne asks her for some gum. She retrieves it automatically and places it on the counter with a shaking hand. He gives her two dollars and tells her to keep the change. Winks again and says, "Now I will take my leave." He bows and walks away.

Veronica washes her hand in the canteen sink, both sides, over and over again, scrubbing with a bristle brush that was meant for the floor. She keeps looking over her shoulder to see if Wayne might be still lurking, watching her, out there somewhere in the early evening gloom. She hunts in the cupboards under the sink for a bleach bottle. Her hand still feels unclean, but it hurts too much now to scrub any more. Her skin feels scalded, raw. It's the colour of a ripe plum.

She tugs her sweatshirt sleeves down to her knuckles, squeezes her fingers to hold them there. She opens *Pride and Prejudice* again, but she can't concentrate on the words.

Later, when Charlotte comes back and asks her how her shift went, Veronica tells her it was quiet.

"Did Jeremy come by?"

"No. Mostly I read my book."

Charlotte shows her how to balance the cash, count the new float, prepare the deposit, bring in the Tuck Shop Sensations sandwich board, which things need to be cleaned. Veronica tries to be attentive.

Afterwards Charlotte walks her home in the dark. Veronica tugs down her sleeves again, rubs her hands together, smiles meekly, and says goodnight.

Back at the trailer, everyone else is in bed except for Colin, who's set up his telescope next to a picnic table in the park. He's holding court before a small crowd; his voice carries faintly across to Veronica lying in her hammock.

She knows it's her fault. She's the one who said, Next thing you know you'll be kissing my hand. But surely, in the days of Mr. Darcy and Elizabeth Bennett, gentlemen expressing regards didn't latch their lips on and do things like that. Did they?

TWENTY-ONE

Last night, Grace had been afraid to go to sleep. This morning, she's afraid to wake up, for the voices have come to torment her again. The words twist and slur into overlapping phrases. She can't make out their meanings, and they're getting louder. She muffles a groan. Her own mind, once a place to escape to, is turning against her. The enormous effort to keep all the bad things locked out is barely manageable. The demons are readying themselves to swarm over her.

Grace shifts her head on her pillow and tells herself to calm down. She reminds herself for the nth time that a trailer park is the last place anyone would think to find her. They are safe here. It's the outside world that's dangerous. If they never had to leave, never needed to see a doctor or get a prescription or go out for groceries, they'd be fine.

Ever since the world started changing, it's become harder to hide. There are fewer safe places. International news on the radio is always about war: the Americans bombing Cambodia, the Nepali Congress hijacking that plane bound for Kathmandu. Here in Canada, Donald Marshall has been sitting in jail for two years already for a murder he didn't commit. Police aren't necessarily on your side, even when you've done nothing wrong. And you never know any more where there'll be news cameras, spies, or security personnel to answer to.

Grace had to fill out their names the last time she bought bus tickets. Luckily she thought quickly enough to give false names, and no one asked for any identification. But she doesn't know what might happen if there's a next time.

Then there's the pharmacist; he's had Ruby's real name all along. It's got to be time to change pharmacists. Perhaps it's also time to hire someone reliable—they'd have to be simultaneously loyal and discreet—to pick up and deliver prescriptions and groceries.

Or is it time to stop running?

At breakfast, Ruby startles Grace by saying, "This has been a very long holiday, hasn't it, Gracie? When can we go home?" And Grace feels a twist of remorse.

"We can't go home, Mother, remember?"

It's been months since Ruby has referred to home as being somewhere other than here. Grace had thought her mother had forgotten entirely about their old life. Grace shouldn't have to piece it all back together for her. For both their sakes she needs to say this out loud to Ruby, who is, after all, the reason she's doing this.

"Craig wanted to put you in that institution. Remember, Mother? He and Becky set you up. And you said you'd rather die than go there?"

Grace grimaces to think of them: her brother Craig, a lawyer, and Becky, a psychiatrist, thinking they could get away with it. They still might, for that matter.

Ruby's face darkens, and her blunt fingers start to fidget. "I remember. You say it's my money they're after. Not true, not true."

Grace sighs. "It *is* true, I'm afraid. Craig kept taking large sums out of your savings account every time they deposited a cheque for you. He made it look legal, but it's *not* right. What they did. That's why we're here. They live in your old house now, remember?"

Ruby had already signed the house over to them before Grace got wind of what her brother and sister-in-law were up to. Grace doesn't know what she'll do if her mother forgets all of this, if Ruby reverts to an earlier time when her son was the apple of her eye.

"I remember. But when can we go home, Gracie?"

Grace sighs.

It's getting harder on all fronts; she's afraid their time, space, and luck are all running out. Yet they've had three worthwhile years. And Ruby still has good days, certainly she does. Lots of them. Surely this life is worth fighting for, a little longer.

Grace pulls Ruby's prescription bottle from her dressing-gown pocket, anchors it in her left palm so she can clamp her other hand over it to open the new childproof lid, the latest security feature in her surroundings. Safety this and regulation that. Laws and rules, crimes and punishments. The lid finally pops off, and the pill container flies up and across the room, the green tablets scattering in an arc, like fireworks.

"Gracie!"

Grace leaps after the pills. Counts them. Cups her hand, tips them back into the bottle. Two are left in her palm. She hands one to her mother and pinches the other between her thumb and forefinger. She slips it under her own tongue.

Mid-morning Ruby says, "You know, Gracie, the worst thing about growing old is not feeling useful. I've stopped feeling useful."

Grace has just started on a new work of macramé; she lets the strands drop and turns to face her mother. "You're useful to *me*. I mean, to me, you're a useful person." She laughs lightly.

"Maybe it's lack of imagination," Ruby says.

"Yours? Surely not."

"I know. Have you any peas I could shell? That's what children and old women did when I was a girl. They shelled peas."

Grace shakes her head. "Afraid not."

"But Gracie, I can't play the piano any more, with these fingers. I can't knit for the hospital, can't embroider …"

Grace can't imagine how she'd cope if her own hands

became useless, unable to knot jute, unable to work a needle and thread.

Yesterday Veronica had come by looking for a needle
and thread. She's a strange girl, Grace reflects, those big
glasses making her look so awkward, and that odd manner of speaking making her sound slightly foreign.

"Even though I can't embroider," Ruby says again, "I
could probably still shell peas. Do you think I could?"

"We'll just have to buy you some peas, and find out."

"You make it sound like a make-work project."

Grace laughs again. "Are you happy, Mother?"

"What an absurd question. I just wish I could be useful, that's all."

Later, Grace decides she will make a fish chowder for
lunch. Because it's Ruby's favourite, she always keeps the
ingredients on hand. A bag of frozen shrimp, a can of
clams, a few potatoes, some butter, onions, garlic, lime
juice, parsley, a sprinkling of chives. Grace credits the pill
she took with her new mental clarity and motivation.

Is inspiration something that spreads? Could the space
it inhabits just keep on widening, in varied increments, ad
infinitum? Could she get used to this? These tantalizing
thoughts form a small vortex of possibilities in her head.

She hums to herself as she chops the garlic and peels
the shrimp. For now she is Queen of the Kitchen again.
It's just like riding a bicycle, how it comes back to her.
A lump of butter starts to slide across the warm frying
pan. The scent of sizzling garlic fills the trailer. She pulls
a bag of celery from the refrigerator. Tosses the shrimp

and clams in warm garlic butter, squeezes the lime juice, chops the other ingredients, sautés the onions, sprinkles in flour, adds coconut milk a splash at a time.

Ruby compliments her on the aroma, as Grace ladles the soup into the Limoges bowls with the hand-painted gold leaf rims and, when she tastes it, Ruby pronounces the chowder the best she's ever had.

After lunch, Ruby withdraws for her nap. Grace steps outside the trailer and sits for a while on the front step. She'll see if she can get Dr. Kerwin to prescribe for her some of the tablets Ruby takes. Would begging him for a particular kind of drug make her sound too desperate? How could she make her case? How could she explain why she stole a pill from her mother in the first place?

Grace knows that at some point her head will start to swarm again, and a thick muscular knot will form below her rib cage. The all-governing anxiety will prevail, discontent will begin to snatch at her with those swiftly-darting phantom fingers. The voices will come back, she'll be in someone's rifle sights, the pharmacists will tell her they have to release information, the police will come. Before too long, her life is bound to catch up with her.

TWENTY-TWO

"What did you do to your hand?"

"Caught it in the door."

"When? Let me see it." Marnie tries to grab her hand to look at it, but Veronica won't let her.

"It's nothing. It's just—it happened Friday night. At work."

"Did you see this, Colin? Look what she's done to her hand."

"Stop. I just banged it, that's all."

"I thought you said you caught it in a door."

"I did. I banged it in a door."

There's no way she can tell them the truth. The truth is too peculiar, too loathsome. Plus it was her own fault, she should have known better. She should certainly have known—although what Wayne did to her hand she's never heard of happening to anyone before, not in books, nor in real life. But then in books there are no trailer parks, no gangs of bullies; in books people don't say unintelligible things. Nobody goes to the bathroom. And girls certainly don't fall in love with other girls.

There are things to negotiate in real life that she has no idea about, because no one talks about them. She tries to think what she'll do if she sees Wayne again: look the other way, for a start. Say, "Don't touch me." Should she give him back his Jesus medallion? Report him to somebody? For doing what? One thing's certain: Wayne is no saint.

Her parents are arguing again.

"It's not funny, Marnie," Colin says. "If you're trying to say something, it's not funny."

"I told you, I didn't touch your cigarette."

"I put one cigarette right here. And it's gone."

"Well, *I* didn't touch it!" Marnie marches past them and down the steps, scans the ground below the railing. She bends over, holding one hand poised, as though the second she sees the cigarette she'll be ready to snatch it with a flourish and hand it up to Colin, her attitude demanding an apology. Instead she swivels her gaze over the bare ground and looks back up at Veronica.

"You must have taken it."

"I don't smoke."

"You're lying."

"Marnie," says Colin, "for God's sake. You're angry at me, not her. Angry because I found you drinking in the morning again—"

"Maybe the crow stoled it."

They all look up. Dilly's come to the doorway.

"Maybe the crow stoled the cigarette."

175

"Stole, not stoled."

"What crow?"

They all follow his pointing finger, across the lane to one of the willow trees. Then Dilly scans the rest of the park.

"Well, it's gone now," he says. "But it *was* here."

Before Colin takes her back to the library to return books and choose a few more, there's something Veronica has to do: get rid of what's in the back pocket of yesterday's shorts. She retrieves the shorts from their corner of the porch under her hammock, quickly shakes the half-dozen coins with the Jesus medallion into her empty running shoe, then shoves the shoe back. Now she won't have to touch any of it. For the money is contaminated. And the medallion—everything it's supposed to represent is false. Late at night she'll bury all these repugnant symbols so that they're gone. Good and gone.

Later, in the car with Colin, Veronica opens her window in case of trapped bees. Then she sits back and hugs her backpack on her lap. Inside are her binoculars, her notebook, and the novels she's bringing back to the library. As they pull on to the highway, she reaches inside and retrieves the binoculars. She trains them out her window and finds she can dial them into focus without her glasses on. She presses the eyepieces comfortably into the soft hollows below her eyebrows and scans the moving horizon for crows.

"Keep the strap on your neck if you're going to do that," Colin says, looking sideways at her.

"It is." She tugs on it to show him.

"Do you find them useful, then, your binoculars?" He asks this as though he's shy to know the answer.

"I've been watching the crows," she says.

"Is that right? What do you see?"

Her father's unusually inquisitive, but she doesn't mind. She puts the binoculars down. "Well, since you ask, the first remarkable thing I've noticed is that they watch *us* a lot of the time."

"Is that so?"

"It is so, yes. I'm making a study of them. Writing all my observations."

"Like what else?"

"They talk to each other. They say different things." Veronica glances at him to see if he believes her, and she's encouraged by his pensive expression. "They tell each other where food is. I think they even mourn their dead."

"Your mother told me there was a dead one."

"Did she say Gumm killed her?"

"She did, yes."

"The crows must be smart if they attacked Gumm. I think they knew who he was, they picked him on purpose. And because they're so smart, I'm more curious about them, so I'm trying to tempt them to come closer, so I can watch them better. That's why I made the bird feeder. Only the problem is the squirrels got all the peanuts, so now I need more. May we buy a big bag while we're in town? I'll pay you back when I get my first wages."

"I'll see what I can do. But you could just be

squirrel-feeding, you know."

Her father drops her off at the front door of the library and says, "I'll be back in twenty minutes."

"In the shell," says Veronica. "Peanuts in the shell. Thanks."

Veronica finds a book on stained glass for Ruby, and nearby an art-history book for Charlotte. Scanning the fiction section, she finds Albert Camus again and chooses two titles, *The Stranger* and *The Plague*. She considers whether she should borrow Stevenson's *Treasure Island* and Tolkein's *Lord of the Rings* for her brothers. She's not seen them reading either of her last choices for them. Here's a Dickens title she's not seen before, *Barnaby Rudge*. She adds it to her armful. Lastly, Veronica pulls a new book on bird identification from the reference corner and sets it on top of her pile. The librarian points to it, the silver bracelets on her arm sliding together.

"Technically I'm not supposed to let you take this one, as it's a reference book. But, hmm." Here the librarian pauses, holding Veronica's gaze, making her wait. "I think I'm going to make an exception in your case. You took such good care of your last books, and brought them back on time looking new, and I do like to encourage avid young readers … You can take them as long as you promise to bring this one in particular back next week. Can you promise me that?"

"Upon my honour," Veronica says, "I promise."

She helps Veronica fit all the books into her backpack. When she heaves it on to her shoulders, it feels to Veronica like the weight of joy; tangible, specific possibilities of vicarious journeys and knowledge and intriguing things, all measured here in her backpack by the pull of gravity; in this haul, the real substance of wonder and enchantment.

Veronica prepares to walk with her family to the admin building right after supper. They'll be early and will get good seats, her mother says. Dilly and Gumm complain that they don't want to go, but Colin tells them they have to. In the end the boys agree to go if they can bicycle over. They've just affixed playing cards to the spokes with clothespins, and relish the rapid slapping noises the cards make when the bike wheels turn.

Mrs Carmichael greets them effusively when Veronica and her parents enter the room. She introduces them to her son Jeremy, who's warming up the slide projector, fine-tuning the focus.

"Hi Jeremy," says Veronica.

"Yawright Veronica?" But when he turns he's looking past her, as though searching for someone else.

The young man turns back to the projector, and Veronica looks at the screen. The image of a medieval cathedral comes into focus, grows blurry again, comes back into focus. Other people start trickling into the room and claiming seats for themselves. Her mother's still talking with Mrs Carmichael.

After a while, Veronica moves up the aisle to the back of the room, pulling several chairs together so that they are touching. She shrugs off her backpack, sits down, and waits for Grace.

TWENTY-THREE

Entering the common room in the admin building, Grace doesn't take long to spot Veronica in the second-last row, beckoning to them. But to get to that row, Grace needs to make room for Ruby's wheelchair, which first has to roll up the aisle and past the slide projector. Grace must ask people to move out of the way. Chair legs jerk and scrape on the floor. She hates causing disturbances, even mild ones like this. Veronica hastens over.

"Sorry! I thought it would be best if we sat at the back—do you mind? Mrs Urquhart isn't hurt, is she?" Veronica touches Ruby's wheelchair.

"No," Grace says quickly. "The distance between here and the trailer was just too far for her to walk, even with her cane."

"Oh. Good. My friend Charlotte's coming, so I'm saving room for her, too."

"Of course," says Grace.

The room is airless and hot. Grace pulls off her

cardigan. Except for Ruby and Veronica, everyone here is sleeveless, and some are even fanning their bare necks and arms. Yet Veronica's shirtsleeves seem extra-long; she keeps yanking them down to the ends of her fingers.

"I brought a book, Mrs Urquhart," Veronica says, when they're settled in their places. "It's about stained glass. I got it from the library. Would you like to look at it?"

She hands the book to Ruby, whose misshapen fingers begin to pat at an empty pocket at her chest.

"You're a good girl. My spectacles have to be here somewhere."

"I have them, Mother." Grace reaches into her handbag. "Can you put them on yourself?"

"No. You do it."

Grace obliges, and then Veronica opens the book and lays it carefully across Ruby's lap. The last people enter the room and find seats. There's coughing and clearing of throats. Someone's closing the slats of a window blind. The air begins to smell strongly of patchouli.

"Who's wearing that awful perfume?" Grace's mother wails. "I think I'm going to retch!" Heads swivel.

Grace feels the colour drain from her face. Someone snickers.

"Don't hush me, Gracie! It's perfectly dreadful!"

Ruby shakes her head from side to side. Her hands are now firmly gripping the sides of the wheelchair. She looks like she's about to launch herself forward.

Veronica points at a picture of a cathedral window.

"Do you like this one, Mrs Urquhart? It's from Chartres, in France. One of the girls in my class at school comes from France."

Ruby corrects Veronica's pronunciation of Chartres. Grace, standing behind her mother now, fans her hands in the air above the wheelchair.

"What happened to you?" Ruby is pointing to the back of Veronica's hand.

"Nothing," Veronica says quickly. "I just banged it in a door."

"I have one of those too. Look," Mrs Urquhart says brightly, and hoists up her skirt. On her thigh is a massive purple bruise.

Grace starts forward. She begins to say, "Don't do that, Mother—" but just as the words come out of her mouth, a woman trying to get past them stares in horror at the bruise. It's Sylvia, the occupant of the trailer next door to the Airstream, Ruby's former minder. For one horrific and hastily aborted evening that Grace would rather forget.

"Well, well," says Sylvia.

Grace yanks her mother's skirt back over her knees.

"It's nothing," says Grace, remembering her mother lying on the floor amidst the cut-up photographs. "It's nothing. Just an accident."

Ruby looks at Sylvia with narrowed eyes.

"Put an egg in your shoe," Ruby says, "and beat it."

Sylvia starts to say something else, stops. Then she lifts her chin up and continues sidling past them to her chair, sits down in it, back rigid.

Veronica turns a page, points again. "Do you like this one, Mrs Urquhart?"

"And do you like *this* one, Miss Reid?" says a low, velvety voice. Charlotte. She is grinning, holding one of two orange rocket Popsicles in front of Veronica.

"You're here!"

"Wild horses," says Charlotte, "couldn't drag me away." She waves to Jeremy, who grins and waves back.

Veronica coughs. "You remember my friend Charlotte. This is Grace, you've met, and Mrs Urquhart."

"You can have my Popsicle, Mrs Urquhart," Charlotte says. "You look like you could use it."

Ruby's face lights up with pleasure as she attempts to peel the paper covering from the Popsicle. Charlotte helps her unstick the strips from her lumpy fingers.

By now a few people have re-seated themselves farther away. Grace moves into the seat on the other side of Ruby and the teenagers, lowers herself slowly. The effects of the drug seem to be wearing off. Trepidation is beginning to build.

"Careful with that, Mrs Urquhart," Charlotte says. "Don't get the juice on your glasses or you'll stain them. Get it? Stained glasses?"

Ruby chortles. She says, "Mine are rose-coloured glasses," and they both laugh again.

Grace tries to imagine what it must feel like to be able to share a joke with someone you don't even know. The patchouli outburst and the bruise incident seem to have been forgotten. Other than Sylvia, people are no longer staring at Ruby. How easy it seems for some, how they can just change direction from a joke or a gaffe and move on to the next thing, whatever life serves up to them. Sometimes life is a head waiter, handing her an envelope on a small silver tray. She takes the envelope. It's usually bad news.

Somebody really *is* handing her something. "Thank you," she says automatically.

Not bad news, but a flyer advertising more community events and fundraisers, to be held here in the common room. Easy flower arranging, choir practice, movie nights. Next week, a games jamboree followed by a decoupage class.

Grace tries to remember her affirmations, settling her gaze on one spot at the front of the room, but Marnie turns and looks right at her, smiles and lifts her hand. Grace waves back, then realizes that it's Veronica beside her whose attention Marnie wants, not hers at all.

Just then Grace sees Wayne sidle into the chair behind Veronica. He's so intent on watching Veronica with her Popsicle he doesn't seem to notice Grace near his side.

Veronica's absorbed in helping Ruby, trying to keep drips from falling into her lap. Then Ruby says something to Veronica, slaps her knee with a sticky hand, and the girl laughs. Sitting side by side like that, their heads bent together, the young girl and the old woman look like the closest of friends.

Wayne shifts his body in his seat and starts to take off his sweatshirt, which he lifts over his head and drapes on his lap. Grace tries to keep her gaze averted, though she remains uneasily aware of his movements. She hopes he won't speak to her. She wishes she'd brought her sunglasses.

Groups in the audience settle their attention on the front of the room as Mrs Carmichael strides across the space to a podium. Then another movement next to her catches Grace's attention, and she darts a glance in Wayne's direction. But her eyes soon fasten on what she sees: he's holding his hands under the sweatshirt on his lap, not still, but moving rhythmically. His expression is fixed on Veronica, or the back of her head, her left ear perhaps, or her neck.

For a second Grace is speechless.

Someone switches the lights off, and the room falls dark. A slide projector casts a square of light onto the far wall. A voice begins to drone at the front of the room.

"Thank you all for coming. My name is Florence Carmichael, and I am here to show and tell you everything I know about stained glass. To show and tell." There is a ripple of weak laughter.

Grace finds her voice. "Oh no you don't!"

She stands up, and in the dark somebody mutters "Excuse me?" and there's the sound of chairs scraping, and footsteps, and "Where?" and eventually somebody turns the lights back on. Florence Carmichael is walking across the front of the room, looking at the screen and back again, craning her neck, saying "What is it?"

Everyone in the room seems to be fixed on Grace, who's standing there in the next-to-last row, mute.

Even Marnie's expression is full of pity. Strangers blink up at her, waiting. Ruby, her face streaked with orange Popsicle juice, looks bewildered.

Veronica touches Grace's sleeve.

"Grace? What is it? What's the matter?"

"He was right there," she says, pointing to an empty chair.

"Who?"

"He—" But she can't say it. "Nothing."

Someone leans over and taps Grace on the shoulder, points to the chair. "There's not been anybody there, Ma'am. I've been here from the start and nobody sat where you say, not in the whole row—"

"Is everything alright up there?" It's Mrs Carmichael, her dry voice with an edge of annoyance. "Shall we just get on with it, then? Lights, please?"

Grace sits down.

TWENTY-FOUR

The stained-glass presentation is over, Grace and her mother have left already, and Charlotte has withdrawn to talk to Jeremy. Marnie nods to the boys who're clamouring to be off with their friends to build a bonfire on the beach. Marnie and Colin linger to speak with Mrs Carmichael.

Veronica seizes the opportunity to hurry back to the trailer, where she makes sure she's alone before she retrieves her stash of coins and the Jesus medallion. She grasps her mother's garden shovel and sets about digging and then burying the collection next to the far side of the shed. When she's finished, her relief is profound.

Colin is the last one back. Veronica sees him appear in the lamplight on the corner and step across the front lawn. He finds her there and looks pleased.

"There you are. Want to go for a walk? Look at the stars?"

Veronica looks at him. "Just me, you mean?"

"You and me."

"So you'll be bringing your telescope, then."

"Not tonight; it's too bulky for just the two of us to wheel over and set up. But bring your binoculars. I want to show you something."

Veronica reaches for her backpack and shrugs it on. Her father leads her toward the line of trees that marks the edge of the park. In the envelope of darkness that swallows the outskirts of the trailer compound, most things are obscured. She can't make out the lake on their right, though she knows it's there. The row of trailers where Charlotte lives is to their left. She keeps her eyes trained on the back of Charlotte's trailer as they pass. The lights are still on. She slows her steps and sees two people moving inside, just behind the main trailer window. Must be Charlotte and her brother. They disappear from sight, and Veronica hurries to catch up to her father.

Past the end of the row, facing the lake, is an expanse of open space where they can look at the night sky. Far below them, at the water's edge, she can just make out the inky rectangle of the boat dock.

Her father stands and regards the sky, his hand on the small of his back. He shifts and looks in one direction, then the other, clears his throat quietly. "We can start with Venus." He points.

"Is Venus the brightest star?"

"It's a planet. You can see it in your binoculars, but you don't need them to find it."

"Oh. I forgot it wasn't a star. Sorry."

Her father doesn't reply.

"And the Big Dipper?"

"Right there."

"I see it."

"Good. You'll always know where you are in the sky when you start with Venus."

They grow quiet. Then Veronica points.

"There! A shooting star."

"That's a meteor." Colin cranes his neck as though he's scanning for more. "There's no such thing as a shooting star. They're actually pieces of debris just burning themselves out in their last blaze of glory, if you will. At this time of year, the meteors ... Look over there. Do you see it? Follow the dots."

He points, then nudges the binoculars in her hands. She looks through them to where he's pointing.

"Want to know where that meteor most likely came from? Let me show you the constellation. It's a shape made of stars, like the outline of a ship's sail on a mast. That's Corvus, which means crow, or raven. Some of the stars there are Delta, Gamma, Epsilon, and Beta Corvi."

"Corvus," she repeats. "I can definitely remember that."

She'll try to remember as much as possible, to write in her notebook, and to tell Charlotte. How to find these stars in the sky again, and what their names are. Next time she goes to the library ....

"Some of the stars you're looking at are more than 150 light years away. They were born long before the earth was born," he adds.

"That's impossible to imagine."

At her father's suggestion, they sit on the bare grass, then lie down on their backs side by side, their faces solemn, the sky an upturned bowl.

Veronica rests the binoculars on her chest and blinks under her glasses. She counts two more meteors. A chorus of frogs and crickets, a fusion of speech and music, lifts around them. Veronica thinks about gravity binding their bodies to the turning earth.

There's something stronger than gravity that binds her to Charlotte.

She writes about it in her notebook later.

I am smitten. There, it is written.

TWENTY-FIVE

Monday morning, the air is motionless, with a grey, at-tenuated light that slices through cross-hatches of electrical tension. The Holstein cows on the other side of the ridge are lying down in a copse of trees. In the distance, the surface of the lake appears to glow.

Wheeling above the outskirts of town, scouting for roadkill, Hrah arcs to take a small detour over a cluster of houses with low, black asphalt roofs. He remembers the shape of one particular lot that sweeps back from the lake road and is fenced into sections. There's the patched greenhouse below him, the cone-shaped heaps of compost. Now he scans for the small rows of biodynamic sweet corn seedlings. Have they sprouted yet? He pivots his body to descend closer. Sure enough, there they are: the bright green fronds that distinguish themselves from fieldcorn through their shimmering ultraviolet striations, all but trumpeting their sweetness to him.

At once he calls out to his kin, last seen two fields

away. If they can hear him, they will leave whatever they are doing and join him in the corn patch. He jabs his beak into the ground and plucks out the first small plant, its clinging root spilling crumbs of clay and sand. His timing, as usual, is perfect: the pale yellow prize has softened and plumped itself up under the earth. This first, fresh kernel of the season is a luscious blend of sweet water, starch, and crunchiness. He hops along the shallow ridge, aims for the next sprout, gobbles it down.

The younger crows arrive, descend, spread out, and poke along the furrows. They take turns as lookouts on the fence post, watching for danger. With luck they'll all be able to gorge themselves well before they have to take shelter. Or before the angry farmer comes striding out to shoo them away.

Hrah cocks his head and tries to calculate how much time he has before the coming downpour will drive his family from their feast. Last year's non-breeding young, and of course this year's newer fledglings, will follow his lead. As the only elder now, it's his responsibility to know, listen, and feel; his duty to teach by example, to keep them safe from raptors, to watch for the farmer's approach, to keep his young charges alive.

Thunder rumbles, ponderously somersaults across the land mass, and shakes itself out upon the mantle of earth on which they forage.

The skin near his shoulder itches. Pausing between two rows of corn seedlings, Hrah uses his beak to flip over a wedge of dry cow dung and grabs a centipede, swallows it whole. Then he pokes at an anthill, grasps some ants and crushes them, smears the insects' acidic remains on his skin next to his shoulder. He reaches for more ants.

A river of wind picks up, first in little soundless wisps and eddies, and then expanding, rapidly becoming noisy, coiling, swirling. Dead leaves lift and scatter. A tattered piece of clear plastic skims lightly along the ground and then lifts up, becoming snagged on the barbed wire that's strung across the top of the fence. It twitches there like something alive.

A crow from another, migratory clan alights on the tallest fence post. Its aura marks it as male; his stretched-out neck and how his beak is tilted upward signal ambivalence: he is wary, though non-threatening. The birds regard one another but remain silent, spectrums of radiance reflecting from their contour plumage. These two have long had an uneasy alliance, but at this time of the year territories are less important. The alien clan's crow utters a single rattle call, then abruptly launches himself up and flies away.

Lightning slashes the sky, followed by a sharp eruption of thunder. Heavy droplets of rain begin to fall, scattering the electrical tension and striking dully at the earth. Hrah and his kin rapidly strike at and pull up the nearest clusters of corn seedlings, drop them and pick them up again to find their best grips, and lift off. They'll fly the mile and a half to reach the trailer-park woods, where they will shake the moisture from their feathers, hide their kernels and seedlings from each other, then wait out the storm in the shelter of the densest branches of the pine trees.

For a while, it seems as though the earth is drowning. There's a sense of timelessness that ebbs and flows as the crows are driven from the wind-battered trees. Nine of them have come to shelter inside the strategic culvert, perched side by side along a stuck branch. The ditch water chases itself in ripples and splashes, rushing beneath them; a muskrat bolts past and disappears out the other side. Butterflies and moths cling to the corrugated metal ceiling.

Wind scours the culvert's northwestern end, flinging rain onto the closest birds. The rain tastes like sulphur and salt. The storm spirals ever larger as it heaves its tenebrous bulk to the east. Together they wait, saying nothing, until finally the flow of water lessens. A salamander scuttles up the inside of the shelter, then, noticing the crows, freezes.

Hrah begins to quietly preen himself. Others sit perfectly still. None of the birds is interested in scoring a quick meal. The little reptile doesn't register in their minds at all. The crows who are closest to the edges turn their attention to conditions outside.

Hrah sifts his tail feathers, and a black plume falls, the third one this afternoon; it loops down, strikes the water, and is swiftly buoyed away. His feathers feel heavier than his skeleton, so plastered with moisture they are. His air sacs feel compressed. He gives his body an impatient shake. Another feather falls.

TWENTY-SIX

I scattered peanuts under the crows' mourning tree. I hope they find them before the storm comes. Before the squirrels find them. I wonder which are smarter, squirrels or crows? I learned about the constellation Corvus. I wonder why our distant ancestors called it that. I will look it up the next time we're at the library. It is daunting to think there is far more I will <u>never</u> know about the stars and the universe than the sum total of what I could possibly ever learn in my entire life. Still, I doubt there is a constellation named after a squirrel.

Observations about crows:

1. *They watch me.*
2. *I can't tell them apart, one from another, but they can definitely tell <u>us</u> apart. I wonder how they tell one an<u>other</u> apart.*
3. *They always see me before I see them.*
4. *They keep their distance. They act like they're accustomed to being chased.*
5. *They hide things from one another.*
6. *They mourn their dead.*

Veronica looks down at the back of her hand. It's not as red as it was yesterday, the skin now having faded to brown and moss-green. She'd secretly rubbed some bleach on it (ever since Dilly's illness, her mother has been using bleach on everything), and though it didn't alter the skin's colour, it stung where she'd scrubbed it, and her hand has *felt* cleaner ever since. Maybe by tomorrow the bruising will have shrunk enough that she'll be able to put on a clean top and cover her hand with a couple of Band-Aids. Avoid being ridiculed by the boys for being some spaz who wears the same shirt three days in a row.

At breakfast time, she takes a bowl of cereal out on to the porch and sits on the top step. Light flickers through the trees in the park. There's a hardness to the light, something glittery and sharp in the sun's angle; she's briefly blinded when she glances near it.

In the lane, a kid about Gumm's age appears, thrusting himself along on a skateboard. His eyes slide over her as he passes, his flat shadow skimming over the gravel and grass. She thinks she heard him scornfully utter "Ver-Ronnie, Four-Eyes!" But she couldn't see his lips move because of the flash of light. The little creep.

Inside the trailer, they're all crammed into the kitchen, talking about a tree fort.

"We'll build it far away from the path," says Gumm eagerly. "Up on the highest ground."

"It might be private property in there," Marnie says.

"There's no *sign* saying *Private*."

"Anyway, it's a mess. We'd make it look better."

196

Veronica knows the area they're talking about. It's tangly and overgrown, where thin cedar and ash lean into each other, the tallest of them choked with grapevine.

"Remember, son, we'd have to carry up the planks to build it, plus our tools and nails."

"We can all bring things," Gumm says.

"We can make a convoy," Dilly says.

"Veronica can help."

"Me?"

Her mother shoots her a withering look and turns back to the boys. "You might have a problem getting through the undergrowth—there are likely stinging nettles and brambles. Make sure you wear long pants."

There's a soft rolling of thunder in the distance.

Colin says they'd better get started before the rain comes. He estimates it's a few hours away.

"There's some scrap lumber behind the shed. It's softwood, I think. We'll have to work quickly. I'll ask Milton if he has tools and a tarpaulin we could borrow."

"You can help too, Veronica," Marnie says. "It's the least you can do."

"Actually I have other plans."

"But your father's here."

"I know, but I was going to go over to Charlotte's."

Her mother bristles. "Don't tell me you've taken a shine to that girl. Why, I think you have a crush on her! It's unnatural."

Clouds blacken the horizon. Wind plunders the lake.

The pine boughs weave up and down, willow switches shudder and grow still again. Thunder growls like some mythological beast.

Veronica passes the binoculars to Charlotte. "Where do you think the crows go in a storm?"

They're sitting on Charlotte's covered wooden porch, facing her backyard and the lake. A low table and two folding chairs are arranged where the row of trees casts its shade. Between the pine trunks, where the bottom branches have been sawn off, the girls have a clear view of the lake.

"Crows? They probably have some secret gathering place."

"No doubt. I wish the bird books would say more about what they do and where they go."

She jumps as lightning illuminates the dark drama unfolding at the western horizon.

"You're not worried, are you?"

"It just took me by surprise. I'm more worried about the crows than us."

"We'll be safe here," Charlotte says. "And I'm sure all the birds know what to do."

"Yes. Most certainly."

"The crows, I mean. They've survived for generations, they must know places to go to be safe."

"Yes. They probably knew the storm was coming before we did." Thunder cracks, like a gunshot this time, and Veronica feels the thump of it inside her breastbone.

"Seriously. We can go inside if it makes you feel better."

"Nothing I like better than watching a storm," Veronica says, and wants to add *with you*. *Nothing better than watching a storm with you*. But she doesn't. Instead she looks back at the lake and says, "I forgot—my father and brothers went into the woods this morning to build a tree house. I hope they're home by now. Oh, but they must be."

The air grows still while the sky rises and wrestles, rolling over itself in blooms of purple and black.

"Veronica."

"Yes?"

"What happened to your hand?"

"What? Oh, that."

"Wait—look."

Veronica lifts one hand up to touch her glasses, and looks where Charlotte is pointing. She squints. A gathering of clouds seems to be falling, bumping under the canopy of pillowing ink. Something tiny in the distance is spinning itself into a blurry, skittering point.

"Maybe we should go inside." Charlotte gets to her feet.

The first slanted, lazy plops of rain hit the railing.

"Oh … this doesn't look good."

The growing vortex has a menacing air. Descending from its dark ceiling to a point, a spun and still-spinning column, like cotton candy. It slips and twirls sinuously across the lake's surface.

Charlotte's tone changes. "No, we should go somewhere else to be safe."

"Like the admin building, you mean?"

"I think so."

"Is there a basement?"

"I don't know."

"How long do we have?"

"No time. Let's go." Charlotte leaps off the deck and runs to the outside corner of the trailer, looks back at Veronica. "Come on!"

Hail strikes the roof and pummels the ground, bouncing and rolling into the grass. The sky has gone black. Veronica grabs her packsack, hoists it over her head, and sprints after Charlotte.

TWENTY-SEVEN

Somewhere a voice is emitting a monosyllabic note, a noise that bends in Grace's ear like a sneer. Another voice is jabbering words in a watery slip-slide, unfathomable. The third makes a sound that's half-animal, half-human, or half-God and half-Satan. This last one sounds like a cry for help. Her stomach heaves with fear. The Airstream seems to be swaying. What's happening to her?

Grace reaches for Ruby's prescription bottle, grapples with the lid, swallows a pill with a gulp of water. While she's waiting for the drug to take effect, she taps her fingers on the counter and tries to remember her affirmations. She can't think of even one. Her reflection wobbles in the kettle's bright, bulging contour. The woman in the kettle is moving her lips. If she moves her lips too, will the soothing words come back? *I believe in—I am created by—something divine.*

Grace turns on the radio, and the voices that were inside her head get sucked into the transmitter. A talk-radio show is underway. The host is listening to callers who are looking to be reunited with old pals or loved ones.

"—on the football team with me in high school," says a man's timid voice. "After that we went our separate ways but, well, if he's out there, hey, I'd like to know where you are. Can I say—"

"First names only, please."

"Oh. Well, his name is Phineas, so maybe …"

Grace feels awkward, like she shouldn't be listening, for it all feels too private. She has an inkling that her own problems are not so bad. After Phineas' friend has hung up, a woman's voice takes his place.

"I gave up my baby," she says, almost in a whisper. For a while there seems to be dead air, and Grace turns the dial up in case the woman's still whispering. Instead the host says loudly, "Take your time. I know it can't be easy."

The woman tells her story, sobbing all the while, and Grace listens. Finally the radio host says he has to move on.

"I hope we have been able to help, here at Talk Radio 77, and that you'll have a happy reunion with your loved one."

Then Grace is amazed to hear the sound of her sister-in-law's voice.

"My husband and I are worried sick," Becky's voice says, "because we don't know where they are." Her voice is thick and buttery. Her words come out slowly, with break-your-heart sincerity. "We love them so much and would be eternally grateful if anyone who's seen them would ask them to get in touch."

"First names only, please."

"Alright then. Grace, and Ruby. Daughter and mother, they would be together. We would just like to know if they're okay."

To Grace's horror the host loudly repeats their names.

"Grace, you said. And Ruby. Right. Well, if anyone knows of these two, or Grace, if you're listening out there, your loving brother and sister-in-law would love to connect."

When Grace snaps out of her shocked state long enough to reach up and turn the radio off, her hand receives a brief electrical spark. There's a ripping crack of thunder and she jumps; her mind struggles with the possibility that the action of turning the dial triggered the thunder.

There's movement in her peripheral vision. Ruby wobbles in the hallway, both hands gripping cabinet doors. Grace watches her. Has she heard the radio appeal?

"Oh my," breathes Grace. "I thought you were resting. Are you alright? Why don't you come and sit down? That was a loud one."

"I couldn't sleep with that racket."

"What racket?"

"The rain, and the thunder."

Grace listens. Ruby's right, it's raining. The trailer seems to be shuddering with it. Grace ventures toward one of the curtained windows and peers out. Wind is clawing through the willow trees and flinging branches to the ground. She wonders if she should have taken Ruby to the admin building to wait out the storm. It's too late now; they'd be crazy to step outside, given how hard it's raining. Thunder rips the atmosphere again.

"Made me want to crawl under my bed when I was little. Remember?"

"Your two little wide eyes were all I would see. Staring at me from that dusty space. Wouldn't come out for hours. Wish I had a picture."

"It wasn't dusty," says Grace, defensively.

"No. You're right. Gloria used to be scrupulous about dust."

"I remember she wore that little apron."

"That was her idea, you know. She used to work for your father at the club, just devoted. He persuaded her to come to us. Best housekeeper we ever had."

The storm rages outside but now Ruby, lost in memory and nodding, no longer seems preoccupied by it. Grace, still nervous, helps her mother to her chair and continues to make an effort to carry on the conversation.

"What happened to her?"

"What happened to who?"

"Gloria."

"Her husband got sick. She had to leave us to take care of him full-time. Remember?"

Grace remembers. It's been many years since she's thought of Gloria, a name from another lifetime, another world filled with fresh flowers and pressed linens, room after room of bright white walls, formal upholstery, paintings. The shifting crackle of wicker on an airy verandah. Tea trays and dinner bells. A time long before Ruby became senile and unpredictable, decades before Grace started having her breakdowns. Both of them watched like hawks by Craig and Becky.

Becky.

A sudden downpour of rain hurtles over the length of the trailer, thudding on the roof, and frantic rivulets stream down the windows. Thunder rolls past them, sounding to Grace like giant, studded boulders heaving over rocky hills and plains. She opens and closes her fists.

"Gloria didn't have a side to her," says Ruby.

"You mean she was guileless."

"Yes. That's what I mean."

Grace nods. "Reminds me of Veronica, come to think of it."

"Who?"

"Gloria."

"Who reminds you of Gloria?"

"Veronica."

"Who's Veronica?"

The rain lashes and the wind howls outside the Airstream windows. Grace saw a movie with a tornado in it once. It had begun to slip and twirl across a field, then crossed a road to aggress a few houses, its vortex casually stirring up fence posts and snapping trees, peeling off roofs, lifting and carrying farm animals on dizzying trajectories through the air.

"Who's Veronica?" Ruby asks again.

"Veronica Reid. You know, our young friend. The one who came with us to the stained glass lecture."

"I don't know any Veronica." Ruby's fingers close now on her pearls, give a small tug. "You always get mixed up, Gracie. I was talking about *Gloria*."

Grace sighs. She turns to switch the radio back on for any news on the storm, but when she turns the dial, nothing happens. The power has gone out.

TWENTY-EIGHT

Veronica doesn't know how long she and Charlotte have been curled up here on the bottom step of the cellar under the administration building, listening fearfully to the sound of the world above them being ransacked by winds.

They tried the light switch, but it was useless. Then Charlotte called out from the steps, "Is anybody there?" and no one answered. She shut the door behind them, and they shimmied down the steps on their bottoms. In the dark, Veronica was worried about rats, but Charlotte promised her that as long as they stayed on the steps, and didn't set foot on the actual basement floor, they'd be safe from rodents. Veronica believed her. But now she's anxious for it to be over and worried about the others. If only there had been time to warn them.

There are whistling and banging sounds outside, like flapping sheet metal. When the noise stops, the silence feels even more ominous than the sounds of the storm. Veronica imagines the two of them might be the sole survivors, that the tornado might have carried off everyone else in the trailer park except them. They might emerge to find a scene of death and devastation.

"Do you think we should go up now?"

Veronica hopes her voice doesn't sound too wobbly.

Sinewy gyrations of a siren, in the distance at first, grow ever louder and closer. They stare at each other.

"Oh my God. Somebody's been hurt."

Veronica starts to get up just as there's a sneeze behind them, and Charlotte screams. A short, slight man waddles hesitantly out from the darkness.

"Shhh! It's okay!"

The man is in his late twenties or early thirties. Veronica has seen him before: the trailer-park superintendent. A bad smell comes off him.

"I should have told you I was here. I was ashamed."

"You what?"

"I didn't try to help anyone. When I saw that tornado, I ran for it."

"So did we. There was no time."

"Please don't tell anyone you saw me down here. I could lose my job."

They leave him there, hurry up the stairs and out of the building.

Sure enough, it looks like the surroundings have been bombed. Nearby treetops are sheared off. There is debris everywhere. Branches and clusters of leaves litter the park and muddy trailer yards. Rivulets of murky water are coursing down the lane. Further away, a black enamel barbecue is wrapped around a tree. A canvas awning, torn off the front of a trailer, flaps lightly against a broken window.

A trailer facing the lane some distance from them looks like it's had an entire wall sheared off. There's a pile of plywood and oversized splinters of tin. Something pink, a woollen blanket or shawl, half-buried in rubble.

The ambulance has finally appeared, its siren still wailing, though it's stopped to negotiate a fallen tree. Charlotte starts running toward it.

Veronica heads for her family's trailer. People are coming out of their enclosures. Doors are banging. Someone runs past her, legs lifting high, rubber boots plonking in noisy splashes. An old man is using a stick to poke through a pile of rubble.

She steps past a mangled downspout and over a shrub, its root clump torn out of the ground. Then she stops. Near her family's trailer, there's a crowd of people gathered.

Some children start to run ahead of her; Veronica follows them. People are standing amidst the wreckage of lawn furniture. Along the lane, they step over pieces of pink insulation, a broken tennis racket, wet cardboard. A boy picks up a dead frog and handles it curiously.

Her family's trailer has been knocked off its cement-block moorings and the underside is visible, partially tilted up on the lane side. The back rests against a tree that has had all the leaves stripped from its branches. Smashed windows, broken glass. Veronica rushes up and starts banging on the trailer's front end.

"Mom? Dad? Dilly, Gumm, anybody in there?" She leans up to look in the window, scans the interior space. Nobody's there. No mangled bodies, no blood. That's one good thing, at least.

Veronica moves closer to a tree at the side of the lane. Two other trailers that she can see from here rest at improbable angles.

Past the corner, there's a trailer that has a jagged hole punched in its roof from a fallen tree. A torn-off screen door lies in a parking spot, and dozens of plastic beach toys spill from a jumbled heap along the fence line.

A male voice shouts from somewhere unseen, "As soon as I get my bearings, I'm out of here!"

The ambulance, quiet now, makes its way down the lane to the park exit. Necks crane forward; a knot of people approaches the driver's side of the ambulance, shouting, "Who is it? What's happened?" but the vehicle turns and leaves.

There are a few cuts and bruises amongst the onlookers. A woman is sitting on the ground, one of her bare legs bleeding. Someone's stepped forward to offer help; she's waving them away. "It's nothing, I'll be fine," the woman insists.

A woman holding a man's hand hobbles forward. "We sat in the bathroom and held on to each other and prayed very hard. Didn't we, darling."

Behind Veronica, a small boy starts crying in loud, wracking sobs. She turns toward the sound, but his mother is already picking him up, hoisting him to her hip, murmuring "It's okay, baby, we'll find it, shhh."

Veronica wants to find her family, and Charlotte too. She quickens her steps.

The ambulance has gone. The bleeding woman, her children, and the crying little boy are nowhere to be seen. A reporter with a camera hanging from his neck is talking with a couple of people standing nearby; he's nodding vigorously and scribbling notes on a small clipboard at the same time.

"Veronica!" It's Charlotte. They each break into a run.

"Who was in the ambulance?" Veronica demands.

"Mrs Carmichael. Compound leg fracture, apparently."

"Oh, poor Mrs Carmichael!"

"I saw your parents and told them you were okay."

"Oh, oh, good, they're alive then! Did you see our trailer?"

"No, why?"

"Practically knocked over. A few are like that—they must have been right in the path of the tornado! Did you see my brothers?"

"They're okay too. Your dad has a lump on his head, and your mom's pretty shaken up but okay. Everybody's fine. Your dad was glad to hear you were with me."

TWENTY-NINE

The wind soughs and whistles softly. Above the culvert, the rain spatters the earth.

And then it stops.

Hrah becomes aware of the silence outside. He bobs down, leans under the wedged branch, and cocks his head sideways. He can see the sky.

A bird perched next to him vigorously shakes out his wings, and the beating sounds, amplified by the tunnel, echo along the corrugations, rousing those in the middle. Grunts and rasps ricochet between them; an offshoot of the branch starts gently swinging.

Rodents emerge and disappear into tunnels of thatch. Songbirds resume their declarations. Spiders come out to inspect what's left of their webs. Butterflies and moths detach themselves from their moorings and labour into the light.

One by one, the crows burst from the culvert. For Hrah, the four missing tail feathers make flight less intuitive, more of an effort. He has to beat his wings twice as rapidly as usual to stay at a safe altitude, high enough that he has time to brake and steer.

But the air is washed clean. The shapes of the clouds, now traced with silvery light, are reflected in shallow ponds where thickening rows of crops used to flicker and spangle. The shadow of a turkey vulture passes on the sunset side.

Even from a distance the trailer park looks different now. Some of the shelters look like they've been rear-ranged, and most of the trees are ransacked or complete-ly snapped. People are swarming like giant ants whose chambers and tunnels have been clawed at. Sharp squeals and high-pitched whinnies rise from some of them. Only one vehicle is moving below the gliding bird. It scoots along, a coloured light bobbing in different directions like a crazed firefly. It emits a rippling screech that lacerates his ears every time it reaches its highest pitch.

Slowing, the vehicle enters the trailer park, and the crow is relieved when the painful sound stops. He realizes he's lost sight of his kin and calls out to locate them again. There comes one response, faint and far away. He replies. Mutual recognition, followed by reciprocal negotiations about purpose and place. Priorities.

Are we all accounted for?

How many hours of daylight have we left?

The crow turns his attention to the dumpster. Shapes and textures are jumbled about: splintered wood, plas-tic, tangled metal, ripped fabric, torn branches. Most of the things have been dragged over, leaving marks in the gravel. He examines the heaps and some of the objects peremptorily, knowing already there's no food here. He's hungry again.

With his ragged tail he will have a lot of trouble steering; it could be too much exertion to reach the woods.

Which of his closest caches might still be intact?

The white vehicle pulls out of the centre of the park and past the dumpster, this time moving without its keening wail. The crow takes to the air and watches as it follows the road-threads to the west. Sees an arm reach out from it and fling an object, an oily paper bag that could contain something edible.

He lets out two cries on his curved, irregular descent. The missing feathers vex him. He thinks in pictures: a lump of discarded meat, some oil-soaked, soft potatoes smeared with sweet, red paste. He imagines tearing at the paper, which will come up in long, damp triangles.

But there's nothing there for him. The crow paces up and down the gravel strip. Checks the jetsam again and again, to be sure it really is just a bag of burnt segments of cellulose and tobacco. To be absolutely certain there are no morsels of fat or sweetness in there. Two more young crows appear, land nearby, and make slight appeasement gestures, flicking their wings and bobbing their heads. Then they dodder cautiously forward. Ignoring them, the elder lifts off. Sometimes his wisdom is not enough for the new generation. He must allow them time to inspect the package for themselves.

THIRTY

The storm's departure ushers a silence into the Airstream trailer. The shaking and rattling have stopped, the winds have closed their wings, the rain has stopped beating. The soft absence of sound drifts and folds in the kitchen atmosphere. Two broken Minton teacups and their saucers lie shattered on the floor. Grace starts to count her shallow exhalations.

Seconds tick by. Grace lifts her hand to her mouth to bite each fingertip, one at a time. A prickling sensation creeps up to her wrists. She thinks back to the height of the storm when she heard what sounded like a length of chain flagellating a metal pole. Is the siren she hears now an actual siren? Couldn't be a fire. Could it be the police, coming for her?

Grace gets up, leans over the kitchen sink and, with shaking fingers, lifts the window blind to peer outside. There are people near each trailer, picking up assorted objects, stuffing some into plastic bags.

Grace swivels her eyes and sees a crow swoop down to the lane, snatch something white, and lift off again. She drops the blind back down and rubs her eyes.

There's a knock on the door. She jumps. Here it is, they've come for her, she's been taken by surprise after all. Because of the talk-radio program, and her sister-in-law's plea just before the power went out. The Airstream has only one way in and out. If she's caught now, she doesn't stand a chance of getting away. Confusion, fear, and indecision twist into a maelstrom in her mind.

The knock comes again. A man's nervous voice says, "Is everyone alright in there? Does anybody need help?" The locked door handle rattles.

Grace calls out, "We're fine, thank you!"

"Good, then," comes the voice. "I'll just be checking the outside of your trailer for damage, if you don't mind."

Grace opens the door. The superintendent has a clipboard under his arm; he's wringing his hands, darting glances up and down the lane.

"I'm inspecting all the trailers," he says. "It'll just take a minute. Is everything alright inside?"

The man concludes that the Airstream has some minor dents and several scratches yet remains altogether safe and stable. He tells Grace they'll try to have power restored by the afternoon. He shakes her hand summarily and moves on to the next trailer.

Later, stepping down the stairs to the sodden ground, Grace finds herself crossing the lane and walking to the lake. The golden light left behind by the storm is amazing to her, glittering in the very molecules of the air. Flowing sideways in yellow beams, the light melts over the water and dissolves into the astonished atmosphere.

Grace sees a bank of low-slung and disproportionately large clouds illuminated from underneath by the preternatural light. The clouds move from over the lake toward the land, their contours and textures overwhelming the fragile horizon line. The panorama before her gives the effect of a gleaming-wet, top-heavy painting. For a few long moments it seems to Grace as though the whole picture is about to tilt. The clouds will begin slowly to slide off the canvas sky, moving to the north, taking with them the daubed tops of the trees, the paint blending all about her into slick green and grey rivulets.

THIRTY-ONE

The side-swiped trailers, including Veronica's, have been righted. Two have been towed away, and some are undergoing repairs: a splintered railing, a punctured roof, countless ripped-off awnings. The electricity is still out. In Veronica's trailer, two windows are being replaced. Somewhere else in the park is the sound of hammering on metal, like a slow, far-away woodpecker. Near the fence, chainsaws whine. When the heaviest trees smash down, the ground trembles all the way to the lake.

The sun moves in and out of cumulus clouds scattered across an azure sky. Veronica and Charlotte are at the beach to help with the cleanup, raking and picking up debris. The beach is strewn mostly with cedar fronds and small branches, but they're also finding entangled ropes and buoys, weeds ripped out of the lake, splintered wood, an empty oil can. Charlotte wears long sleeves and a hat to protect her from the sun.

They pause to watch a crow perched on a log lying

close to the water. When Veronica moves slowly in its direction, it watches her warily, then springs from the log and tries to fly to the nearest tree. But it overshoots the topmost perch, veers sideways, and ends up landing on the ground nearby. It walks along where some beach sand is scattered thinly over a patch of grass.

"Something's wrong with that one. It can't fly properly." Charlotte says.

Veronica watches the bird, feeling helpless and sorrowful. But as she wonders what they can do, another crow lands nearby. This one ignores them. It's carrying something in its beak, which Veronica sees is a small, light-green crayfish. The second crow hops closer to the first one and drops the crustacean.

Veronica smiles. "The hurt one is being looked after."

The second crow takes to the air again.

"Gone to find more food," says Charlotte.

"Amazing."

They return to their work, then push and pull the burnable portions of the debris into a heap on the beach.

Veronica picks up her rake again, gesturing with it. "All this mess from the storm, here and in the park while, apparently, my brothers' tree house survived."

"No kidding." Charlotte pauses to wipe her forehead with a clean rag.

"My mother says everyone's calling it a miracle. It's so stupid, of course, for there's no such thing."

Charlotte tucks the rag back in her pocket. "How do you know?"

"I just know. Trust me."

Veronica impulsively shows her friend the mark on her hand, now faded from purple to pale green.

"You still want to know what happened to my hand?"

Charlotte nods.

"It was Wayne's doing. He put on his classic gentleman-hero act, when I was at work. He grabbed my hand and he—he sucked on it. All the skin on the back of my hand."

"He did what? And you didn't tell me?"

"I *am* telling you. I tried to cover up the bruise with my long shirt. I was embarrassed because I'm the one who blundered into the situation. It was my fault. Never mind how. A few days before, he made me believe a miracle might happen. So I wouldn't need these stupid glasses. I don't know, I though he meant—I mean I truly believed ..."

"You should have told me."

"I couldn't talk about it. It was so creepy and weird. I was afraid you'd think badly of me, after it all happened. I didn't know what to do. Promise—give me your word you won't tell anyone?"

"Hold still. No. You've got it wrong. Please don't be upset. But we have to report him."

"No!"

"That's a really sick thing for him to do."

Veronica wipes her nose. "Who would we report him to?"

"The police, who else?"

Veronica's head swims.

Charlotte sighs. "I'm not mad at you, honey, I'm mad at Wayne. Maybe they couldn't arrest him for that. But they could give him a warning, or something. That's practically criminal."

Honey. Veronica shuttles the word to the back of her mind to consider later. First, stay safe. Her heart is racing, and it's more from fear than for love.

"No. You can't. Then he'd come after me. He'd know it was me."

A look of concentration passes across Charlotte's earnest face. It's a curative, just to look at her.

"Tell you what," Charlotte says finally. "I don't know what we're going to do just yet, but we're going to do something." She looks at Veronica with a vehement expression. "I'll let you know when I've figured it out."

A worried Veronica sits on the top step of the porch, her knees pulled up and jiggling. She doesn't know if she's ready for this. But her backpack is packed, just in case. For whatever Charlotte's thinking, planning, will be traced back to her. She doesn't know whether to feel miserable or empowered. In either case, she'll likely be a fugitive for the rest of the summer.

Marnie, who's come out to stand on the lawn in front of her, looks down at the garden.

"Weather," she says, her voice low and resigned. "Hailstones or brimstones? Looks more like war."

Veronica watches absently as her mother moves toward the flower bed's only survivor, a weed with a tall stem, somewhat gangly and lopsided. She tugs the weed out, knocks the dirt off its roots, and is about to toss it into the lane just as Saffron happens by.

"Don't do that," Saffron says quickly, stopping abruptly, as though offended. "You can eat that, it's called lamb's quarters."

Marnie shrugs. "But it's ugly. And it spreads."

Saffron glares at her, then snatches it, and her glare turns to triumph. She shoves half of it in her mouth and takes a big bite of leaves, starts to chew noisily. Veronica looks away, then back to her mother. Marnie's dislike of Saffron is thinly disguised.

"Suit yourself," says Marnie, shaking her head in a superior, I-just-can't-believe-it way. "I have better things to do with my time."

"But it's a miracle that this one plant has survived here," Saffron says, her mouth full of wadded green mush.

"I hate to be the one to inform you, but the real miracle is that no people were killed. I think we should all be counting our blessings, not eating weeds."

Blessings. Miracles. Veronica tightens her jaw and fixes her eyes on the park. She wants nothing to do with whatever animosity there is between her mother and Saffron. Veronica imagines launching herself over the landscape, soaring above the willow trees, gliding windward to the hill that conceals the beach where Dilly has gone. Flying over the woods, in which, somewhere, the empty tree house awaits.

"I was just on my way to do some yoga," Saffron

says archly. "I don't know what your problem is, except I think you should stop flirting with my husband." She tosses the remains of the lanky weed at Marnie's feet.

Veronica strides across the park, her yellow flip-flops snapping in the same rhythm as her backpack, which is carrying the collective weight of her notebook, binoculars, *The Plague* by Albert Camus, the reference book on birds, and a bag of peanuts for the crows. It bumps heavily, reassuringly, against her spine.

She turns in the direction of the tree house, or at least what she thinks is the right direction. It might be useful to know exactly, if only as a place to avoid in future. She'll build her own tree house. Without anyone's help. Somewhere she can bring Charlotte, or go on her own to watch birds, or simply to read.

She scans back and forth across the forest's unwelcoming fringe. From here she can't see an opening, just dense thickets of white cedar and balsam fir. Finally there's a narrow seam in the undergrowth that appears welcoming, green bracken swaying on either side. A deer trail? She starts walking. After a while, the woods close in around her. She mustn't lose her sense of direction. Should she keep trying to go forward, or go back and try again? This way, there are too many branches to penetrate. That way, squinting, she thinks she sees an opening in the trees that might indicate a wider path.

The path has a mantle of damp, rotted leaves, and grey, worn-down cedar roots snaking across the surface.

Veronica's shins brush against ferns that yield and spring back on either side of her as she walks. She stops when she hears birdsong and looks up to scan the treetops surrounding her. There it is again, but this time it's not coming from the treetops but from somewhere lower down, ahead of her. A bird, still unseen, that has flown down from higher reaches and must be perched very close by. A thin and tremulous whistle that sounds almost human.

She thinks she sees something move in the woods behind her. Too large for a bird. An animal, a deer? The moving shape starts to separate itself from the screen of branches and leaves. And then a familiar voice.

"My prayers have been answered."

It's Wayne.

Veronica stiffens. "What are you doing—here?"

Instead of launching into his usual braggadocio, this time Wayne's shoulders sag, and his hands hang limply at his sides. "I need a hug."

Veronica doesn't move. He raises his head far enough to make eye contact, lifts his arms forward as though inviting her to embrace him, and moves toward her. She panics and tries to leap aside. But Wayne's too fast and he grabs her by the waistband of her shorts.

She starts to scream, and he deftly claps a hand over her mouth.

"Don't make me hurt you," he hisses in her ear. "All I said was, I need a hug. Are you too *la-di-da* to hug me?"

Confusion and panic swirl together.

He's dragging her into the woods. Her feet kick out,

her protests are muffled under his palm.

His grip tightens, and his voice is like a snarl.

"Into the forest flees a fair maiden, I would never harm her / Does she not know I'm a shining knight, her knight in shining armour?"

Veronica growls, works her jaw, pushes her head forward. Tries to make her legs gallop.

His lips touch her earlobe, and the hand over her mouth squeezes harder. "I will let go if you promise not to scream. From now on, if you know what's best for you, don't fight me."

She stops squirming and stays silent while her heart keeps beating crazily. Think, think, think.

Wayne works her backpack off and tosses it to the ground; he swings her in front of him facing away. His wrist presses against her throat, just enough pressure for her to feel it there. He snakes his other hand around her from behind, fondles one of her breasts, then slides along her waist and down to her thigh, and starts to grope her with thick, insistent fingers. With all her might, she tries to wrench away. Her next scream is clamped by a sweaty forearm; his hard knee presses into her back and the pain makes her gasp.

She fixes her gaze on the trees and undergrowth ahead of her, the woods beyond which somewhere is the trailer park. She wills her heartbeat to slow down, wills time to slow down and give her a chance to think. The way he's got her now, she can't move either of her arms to knock his groping hand away. Don't panic. What would a headstrong, intrepid heroine do? But this, this has never happened to any protagonist she's read about. She's squirming, struggling under his grasp. Sever the mind from terror, think with pure logic. She wills herself not to faint. As Wayne presses her down she hears his growly breathing.

She can't let him wrestle her to the ground. She must employ all her senses, all her abilities, either become an animal or go limp. She tries the latter first: a strategic, pseudo-surrender. Wayne eases his grip for a split second, and just as he's re-clasping his limbs around her, she jerks her head sideways and sinks her teeth into his upper arm as hard as she is able. He howls and lets go.

She sets off running, and Wayne's hand grasps her briefly by a bare ankle—her flip-flops are gone—and in a fraction of a second she twists and wrenches her foot under his fingers and pulls free. She imagines she's a leaping deer, a dashing fox, finds an agility she's never had before. The ground is uneven, and she can barely see. Scuttling hands and bare feet encounter rocks and prickly junipers, and she has to duck to avoid the climbing grapevines. Don't look back. Blind instinct drives her.

Veronica trips and falls heavily on her side, scraping her thigh. Stunned and immobile for a second, she realizes that all is quiet now. Pain throbs in her back. Crouching, balancing with one hand on the ground, she dares to look behind her. She brings her free hand up to her face. Her glasses! They're gone. Her mother will be apoplectic.

She can't think of that now. She needs to concentrate. Squinting, she can see for a limited distance only.

Instead of moving quickly, she must focus on moving quietly. But which way is the lake? Has she been going in circles? Which way is the trailer park? Even if she could figure that out, where should she head? What if he's still following her, hiding somewhere, watching and waiting? Her fingers scrabble at the ground, and close on a rock. She pries it up, lifts it carefully, quietly. Larger than her fist, it barely fits into her pocket.

In the distance Veronica hears the sound of a motorboat. She listens hard. The lake. Maybe there's a chance he can't swim. Would she be able to get the attention of a boater? How long could she hold her breath under water?

Veronica stays still. The silence is almost more terrifying than Wayne's howls were. Which way to turn? Where's the sun and what time is it? She's not safe yet. She must concentrate on how to become safe. She shifts her weight, begins to move in the direction of where she thinks the lake might be. Stumbling forward over alder suckers and past a clump of burdock, she regains her balance, and then she sees it. To her left, a rope ladder rests against a tree trunk. The ladder leads up to a wooden platform, the edges of which she can barely make out amidst the blurred foliage. She springs for it. Now she's a monkey, a swift sailor-boy, climbing up and into the tree.

Veronica pulls the rope ladder up to the tree-house platform and stows it beside her. She still has the rock. If she hears Wayne, she can throw it. If he could somehow shimmy up here on the tree trunk, she could swiftly kick him away. She practises how she would sit:

hands anchored, knees bent, her legs ready. She imagines the force of her hard kick. She imagines how he would fall backwards, his body spread-eagled in the air, his face contorted in disbelief.

Veronica's breathing slows down. She should feel a sense of relief, she thinks, having gotten away from him. But instead she feels sullied, broken, helpless. How will she ever deal with this? Who can she tell, who will understand?

Write, write about it. Tether it to a page with words, keep it under control.

Write? Her notebook! She doesn't have her backpack. Her binoculars, a gift from her father. The Camus novel, and the reference book on birds that the librarian will want her to pay for now. Wayne has them. She starts to cry, then swiftly wipes her eyes. She needs to be vigilant to stay safe.

The shape of the platform, uneven and indistinct as it is, reminds her of a ship's bow. At its pointed end, there's a jutting branch that looks as long as a bowsprit would be. If it were a real bowsprit, surely she could rip it off and use it as a sword and stab Wayne with it. He could fall overboard.

Veronica imagines a network of rigging pulled taut through the dense umbrella of foliage, the different dappled shades of green. Imagines a mast breaking through the tops of the trees, and a small able seaman clambering to the top to affix a flag. Or to stay up there as a lookout in the crow's nest, as the Vikings called it. The crow's nest.

How extraordinary.

Where are her crows, now?

Corvus brachyrhynchos. Common crow. Large, black perching birds with strong bills; genders alike. Often gregarious. Considered nuisance birds; vermin to farmers. Habitat: woodlands, farmland, agricultural fields, rivers, shores ...

She can hear them.

Voice: a loud caw or cah or kahr. Hrah.

They're coming closer.

Corvus brachyrhynchos. Common crow.

Veronica's father, calling, finds her in the tree house. She's lost her sense of how much time has passed. Her knees shake when she climbs down the ladder, and her legs want to buckle when she reaches the ground.

"You're hurt! What happened?"

Veronica looks at the dried blood on her leg, then at her swollen feet.

"Veronica! What were you doing up there?"

"Hiding." Her voice is small.

"Tell me what's happened. Did somebody hurt you?"

Uncharacteristically, her father puts his hand on her shoulder. She flinches.

"What's the matter? Where are your glasses? Where are your shoes? Oh, Veronica, now, don't cry. We can talk about it later. Let's get you home."

Her bare feet are too sore to walk on, so her father takes his own shoes off and gives them to her. They flop loosely on her feet, but she is grateful to have them.

Colin picks his way carefully in his socks. Twice Veronica thinks she sees movement in the woods, but when she looks again everything's blurry and obscure. Two months ago, she got along fine without glasses; now she feels blind without them.

Finally, they are out of the woods. There's light, open space. Her body gives an involuntary jerk. She feels cold in the bright sunlight, and realizes she's shivering.

Colin awkwardly puts his arms around her. "Veronica. Tell me, have you hurt yourself? What happened to you?"

She tries to look at him. Inside her head there's a whistling sound, like wind, like the sound of the ocean contained in a seashell.

"Where are your glasses? Did you have your backpack?"

"I don't know. My glasses …"

"Does your leg hurt?"

"My back hurts."

Colin has to bend his head down to hear her speak.

"He grabbed me," she starts.

"Who? Who grabbed you?"

"Wayne."

Haltingly, miserably, she tells him what happened.

"Oh no. Oh my, my. Oh, no."

Colin removes his socks and puts them on Veronica's feet. Then he slips his own shoes back on.

He walks her back to the trailer park like this, straight to the admin building where he uses the pay phone. He makes her wait with him in a room off the hall for twenty minutes, until a red-faced, heavy policeman arrives to talk to her.

The constable removes his hat, and Veronica's father gives her a gentle nudge.

"Go ahead. Tell him what you told me. I'll be right outside."

Veronica feels shaky.

The door clicks shut.

The policeman pulls up one of the metal folding chairs. "Why don't you start from the beginning."

But Veronica can't think where the beginning is. When Wayne sucked on her hand? Was that against the law? It was all just too bizarre to talk about. Might the constable conclude Veronica had caused everything? Had she asked for it?

Dirty, bruised, and damned. Numb from the neck down.

"Where exactly did the incident take place?"

She doesn't know where. Surely she's not expected to lead him there.

"Woods. Somewhere." Her mouth feels dry. Her knees are bobbing up and down of their own accord, and she keeps trying to tuck her hands under her thighs, but they keep wanting to fly out.

"What were you doing in the woods?" The constable balances a notebook on his right knee and is leaning forward with a pencil poised over it.

"I don't know."

"You lost your glasses, didn't you? If you don't know

why you were in the woods, do you know *where* you were when your glasses came off?"

She shakes her head no, and tries to lick her lips. Her tongue feels thick. The policeman's black shoes are shiny, and reflect a slowly-lurching ceiling fan.

"What happened first?"

"I don't remember."

"Your Dad says your backpack was stolen? How did that happen?"

"Yes. I don't know …"

"So … tell me again, what you told your Dad."

She feels herself shrinking. All those things he's going to ask her to talk about.

"Please speak up, Veronica."

And then she is crying again. In the centre of another storm, she the cause of it this time, a lightning rod for unspeakable things.

Afterwards, she can't find her father in the hall. Instead he's outside. The officer holds the door for her. She sits on the step and clings to the metal railing while he and her father talk in low voices. She hears resistance, agitation, annoyance, all mushrooming into anger.

Finally Colin bursts out, "Is that the best you can do? I don't fucking believe it. That sanctimonious bastard gets away with it! Is that the best you can do?"

She turns her head away from them, never having heard her father swear before. Has anything ever been as it seemed?

Flashbacks bring thrusts of shame that undermine her

232

entire previously-understood version of the world. It feels like she's clinging to this railing to keep from slipping off a pitching deck, the wind caterwauling in her ears. She feels sick.

Veronica sees the shapes of Gumm and Dilly materialize in the road and turn their bicycles in her direction, slowing down to a stop in front of the building. They try to intercept the bulky constable.

"Can we see your gun?"

"How many bullets are in it?"

"Are you going to shoot somebody?"

"No, son, I'm not going to shoot anybody."

"More's the pity," her father retorts.

The four of them watch and listen as the police car turns the bend and disappears slowly. Toward Wayne's motorhome. Veronica pries her hands from the railing and stands up.

Dilly says, "What did Veronica do, anyway?"

THIRTY-TWO

Grace keeps peering out the window. She hasn't left the trailer, she can't remember in how long. Each day that passes following the radio call-in show, it's less likely that she will be discovered and exposed. But after exactly how much time should she feel spared from her brother's attempt to find them? A week? Ten days? Ever? She has to remind herself that she hasn't done anything wrong.

Every time Grace tries to probe what Ruby remembers of the injustices done to her, Ruby doesn't seem to get it. Her rheumy eyes light up every time Grace mentions her brother's name. Sometimes she wonders if her mother remembers more than she's letting on. Whenever Grace mutters, "I'll never forgive Craig for what he's done," Ruby replies, "You have to let each one go to the devil in their own way."

As usual, Grace has been keeping her blinds closed, though lately she's been making sure the windows are all the way open so she might at least hear approaching danger. She fears the sound might come in the form of authoritative voices, or boot steps marching over the gravel, or more sirens.

Her mind ricochets from despair to hope to certitude to confusion. Is it possible that no one in the trailer park actually heard the call-in show? How many people know her name?

She fingers the blinds once more, scans left and right as far as she is able, and freezes. It's a police car coming her way. It's moving so slowly along the lane that it sends shivers up her spine. She turns and reaches for Ruby's open bottle of pills. Seizes a glass of water. Her hands are shaking so much when she lifts it, the edge of the glass strikes her hard in the teeth and water sloshes up her nose.

The slow sedan quietly crawls past her trailer and keeps on going. She heads for the farthest window to see where the car might stop. She enters the bedroom, but before she gets to the window she doubles over and expels a slurry of pills and watered saliva onto her bedspread.

As soon as Grace can breathe again, she stands up and reaches for the window blinds, keeping her other hand on the wall for support.

After a moment, she slips outside and conceals herself in an opening in the lumpy hedge behind the Airstream, where she looks past the backyards and through a space between two trailers.

A uniformed officer stands on the doorstep of a motorhome, and a man in track pants is standing just inside the open door, gesturing with his arms, shrugging, his palms up. Looks like Wayne.

Grace watches them for several minutes. At one point the officer turns his head in her direction and she ducks down. Then she crawls to the corner of the Airstream and lifts her body up slowly, flattening herself as best she can against the side. In the thin sliver of vision allowed her now she sees the officer rest one hand on the gun in his holster, and lean close to Wayne as though to say something in his ear. When he straightens again, he points his finger at Wayne, says something that Grace can't hear, and walks back to his car.

THIRTY-THREE

Veronica is soaking her ragged feet in a bucket of warm salty water, which stings but feels good at the same time. Marnie has given her an Aspirin for her back. The boys linger at the edges of the room in silence. Colin announces that they're all going to pack up and go home.

Marnie and the boys groan in protest.

"Colin," her mother says, "we both know Wayne should be the one who leaves, not us. Why should we be punished for what he did? We're on Veronica's side after all. The law has run its course, it seems. That's what the officer said, isn't it? That he gave Wayne a stern talking-to?"

Veronica lifts her right foot from the water and begins to blot it dry with a towel.

Marnie asks, "Will you tell us what you want to do, Veronica? Stay or leave?"

She's fearful of staying, as long as Wayne can't lawfully be forced to leave the park. But the thought of being away from Charlotte and possibly never seeing her again is even more upsetting. Grappling with the injustice of it all, teetering between propriety and defiance, instinct and indecision, everyone waiting for her to speak.

"May I think about it?"

On the question of sleeping arrangements for that night, Veronica tells her uneasy father that she'd rather have a sense of confinement, to be locked in the storage shed, than to sleep in their trailer's living room in view of the door. The lesser of two evils, she calls it.

On the first night, even with a foam mattress, sleeping bag, two flashlights, spare batteries, novels, and paper to write on, the lock being on the outside does feel a little bit creepy, almost medieval, like she's in jail or something.

"If we can't come up with a better solution," Colin says, "we'll get you a lock to put on the inside."

The next morning after breakfast, Colin agrees to walk with her to Charlotte's trailer. He makes her promise that Charlotte will walk her back.

Charlotte is quiet for a long time when she hears what Veronica tells her. Then Veronica reveals what the burly constable had told her father: that he'd looked inside Wayne's motorhome and found nothing suspicious.

"I don't believe it for a second," Charlotte says.

"What do you mean?"

"Because I was speaking to Grace, and I got her to tell me what had upset her at the slide show. She's certain he was there, committing—well, an indecent act. Second, she didn't know why, but a police officer recently went to Wayne's and seemed to question him. They stayed talking outdoors, never went inside."

"So the officer was lying? And Wayne was lying, too. Does everybody lie?"

Charlotte flexes her fingers, her classic water hands, the ones she said she long ago tried to scrub the freckles from. Her green eyes have little sparks in them.

Finally she says, "If *they* won't make him leave, *we* must."

"Charlotte, please. Whatever you do, he'll know it was me."

"We have to show him we're not afraid."

"He'll come after me. He will."

Now Charlotte focuses her eyes on Veronica's. "That's why we have to do it right."

Veronica hesitates, then fills her lungs with air.

Charlotte unfolds her hands and says, "You have to be brave."

Veronica nods.

Charlotte says, "The right thing is to make him leave. Something else Grace told me. She said she saw Wayne shaking a broom at a crow, to make it get off his lawn. Apparently he kept thrusting the broom, then dancing back and protecting his head, like he was scared it might attack him."

"Do you think he heard about Gumm?" Veronica ventures.

"Maybe."

They decide they'll write Wayne an anonymous threatening note, using cut-out letters from old magazines.

Veronica's beginning to like the idea; flares of hopefulness and daring dart up through her apprehension. They find some outdated copies of Chatelaine magazine in the laundry room and smuggle them back to Charlotte's trailer.

"What shall it say?"

"Something to scare him into leaving."

"Make him think he's being watched."

"Make him know, you mean, that people are watching him."

"And crows."

"Great. Here, let me just—"

Charlotte pulls the cap off a black Magic Marker and opens her sketchbook to a blank page, where she swiftly draws the shape of a crow in the upper right corner. Veronica composes the note and calculates how many of each letter they need. Six E's, three L's, two A's, two P's. They find and cut the letters out carefully, then glue them to the page, one at a time. When all the words are in place, Veronica adds a thick black arrow pointing to the crow. Charlotte adds a few more details to the crow sketch.

When it is finished, she hands it back to Veronica. The note reads,

Go AWaY Or ELSE hE
wiLL PecK oFF YOuR pECkeR !

Suspended in the upper corner, a crow comes down to land, tail feathers low down and splayed, its shoulders lifted, wings outstretched with the tips curled upwards,

240

one claw held higher than the other. Head thrust forward, a lifted eye, a sharp beak.

"Are we really doing this?" Veronica asks. And then, when Charlotte nods, she adds, "Thank you."

It feels like they've made a pact. Like Charlotte has made a pledge to protect and defend her. As though she's taken Veronica under her wing.

Charlotte will deliver the note in the darkest hours, sometime between midnight and three. She will come to Veronica's locked sleeping-shed to tell her it's done. The code: three scratches on the shed door.

Worried for Charlotte, that night Veronica can't sleep. She lies on her back, so both ears are free to hear the slightest sounds. She slips in and out of an unfamiliar, panic-stricken state. She feels lost. Ruined, undone, at thirteen. All her resolutions are trapped bubbles in deep water that want to zip straight for the surface. Instead, images of gargoyles with giant phalluses make their way into her consciousness.

She lifts her head from the pillow and switches on her flashlight. Her surroundings are intact, though indistinct. She focuses the circle of light on the shed door boards, where there's an infinite series of tiny versions of herself, each smaller than the next, all flailing in unison, as though seen through binoculars held the wrong way around. Binoculars. In her backpack, gone.

The next morning, Veronica's father calls her to come with him into town. But things go wrong before they even get to the car. They see the park superintendent in the lane, and her father accosts him.

"Do you know," he says, "it's not safe here for children? This one," he points at Veronica, "wants a lock on the inside of the shed. And you people should pay for that."

The superintendent begins to tremble, looking up at Colin. "Did you say the lock is going on the inside, sir?"

"That's right. One of your tenants molested her yesterday—"

Mrs Carmichael, labouring past them on her crutches, sends Veronica a sympathetic look. Veronica's father waves her away, as if to say, "We'll take care of this."

Hot flames of distress climb Veronica's neck to her forehead. The superintendent is wringing his hands.

"Sir, any tools you'd like to borrow," he says finally, "you're welcome to. And I'll even give you a lock and key. But a lock can only be fastened on the outside. It's a storage shed. Those are the regulations."

Clutching her arms tightly to her waist, Veronica funnels all her fury at the man.

"I think," she says, "you can make an exception in this case."

The superintendent licks his lips.

"Alright," he says finally, "but don't tell anyone I let you. And you must remove it when you leave for the season."

"Fine. In my opinion," her father continues, "you should tell that degenerate, Wayne, tell him it's time to leave the trailer park. That he's not welcome here."

The superintendent nods, gulps, and says, "Yes, sir."

"That so-called manager is useless," Veronica's father mutters grimly as he climbs into the car. "Between him and the police, a person doesn't have a prayer in this place. Put your seat belt on, will you?"

Colin's impatience is new. He jerks the car past the skateboard park and the edge of the open area with the swings. Veronica squints. A new pair of glasses has been ordered, and they're supposed to be in next week. Veronica looks away from where the woods bristle, the forest full of climbing vines and blinking eyes, where she imagines Wayne is reading through her notebook, smearing his thick fingers on its pages.

The car has stopped.

"Are you coming?"

She blinks and looks out the window, shades her eyes, and squints. They're not at the hardware store, but the library. She hesitates.

"Don't you want to come in and pick some new books?"

"No. I can't even see where I'm going."

Her father says, "We have to tell the librarian what happened."

He lets her take his elbow to go up the steps and into the library.

Colin offers to pay for the stolen books, but the librarian refuses to consider it. Without her glasses Veronica can't see whether the woman is looking sympathetic.

The librarian says she believes the missing volumes might yet turn up, so they should leave it until the end of summer to report them stolen.

Next they stop at the hardware store to buy a lock, a hasp, and a swivel plate. "Once both parts are screwed to the wall, it will be very secure," Colin assures her.

Veronica finds a combination lock with a red dial. Then, across from the end of the next aisle, the bird-feeding section, a bag of peanuts. She's decided she's going to tempt the crows to come to Wayne's trailer. Peanuts, bread, Saltine crackers with Velveeta cheese smeared on them, cut-up hot dogs, all heaped on the roof of his motorhome in the dark. She'll even track down some roadkill and throw it up there, if she has to.

The lock will enable her to live her new life. Charlotte's plan to scare Wayne away gives her fresh courage. Veronica will summon her wild, survivor side. She will come and go as she pleases. Crepuscular creeper, creature of the shadows. Woman of the night.

THIRTY-FOUR

The days are getting noticeably shorter. The sun doesn't come up over the woods until 7:05 a.m. now, assuring Grace, murmuring to her, coaxing her awake. This time she thinks she can hear the sound of someone yelling. She sits up and takes a look past a pinched pair of window blinds, searching down the lane.

She quickly gets dressed and slips outside.

What now? Once again, it's Wayne reacting to some crows. He's jumping up and down on the grass facing the back end of his motorhome, waving his arms, and yelling. The man must be deranged. He's holding the broom again. He heaves it into the air, striking the wall above a lashed-on aluminum ladder, runs away, stops, goes back to retrieve the broom, and tries again. The next time he tries to slap the broom at the roof, it becomes caught on a roof rail. He bellows and jerks at it, holding one arm protectively over his head.

Grace looks up. A murder of crows is circling above

the roof of his motorhome, flapping and squawking. She shivers and pulls her sweater tighter. The crows keep wanting to come back to the motorhome, but Wayne curses at them and waves his arms.

Grace watches the crows finally disperse. Whenever they gather like that, there's evil afoot. Is the moon full or something? Her heart contracts with fear. Wayne lets out one last agonized roar and marches back inside, slamming the door hard after him.

THIRTY-FIVE

At first there were only peanuts, Hrah noted, then a sweet crust of bread appeared, and a nest of too-bitter tent caterpillars. Two days later, there was a stack of square crackers and strips of raw calf liver, dripping and fresh and unbelievably delicious. After that, a dead fish, more peanuts, then a flattened chipmunk carcass infested with plump, wriggling maggots. And now, every night, on the same nondescript roof in the trailer park, a new banquet materializes.

Hrah and the other crows come to find the morsels in the early morning, before any of the humans have yet stirred. Sometimes there's a mantle of mist over the trees. Sometimes their arrival sends woodpeckers, grackles, or blue jays scattering, smaller birds who've been there for the nuts since dawn.

The crows mean to land quietly, but usually there's a bit of squalling from the jays as they relinquish their positions. The birds' claws scratch for a hold on the slippery fibreglass roof. They're instinctively wary, but Hrah and his family find the temptations irresistible.

Most often he comes with his spring-fledged young. Once he shared a scattering of hot dogs and sardines with them, and when the feast had been almost all consumed, one of the nest-mates whom he'd not seen in eight months had alighted on the spire of the spruce tree across the lane from the motorhome, his familiar appeasement gestures triggering jumping, shrieks of recognition and acknowledgement.

There's a mound of raw ground beef on the roof today. Even as he seizes and gulps, the elder crow keeps his hackle feathers stiffened, stops to look around between every other jerking swallow. This morning, it's misty and still, all the humans concealed and sleeping but for one, an adult figure who walks under the willows and down to the river, where she pauses.

They take turns over the meat. His right eye spies a lean tabby cat emerging from under a trailer across the lane, and he shrieks out a warning. Beside him, one of his kin stops feeding, suspicious of a trick, but another steps nearer and turns to look. The cat slides purposefully in their direction. Hrah visualizes launching himself off the roof, dive-swooping over its head to drive it away.

He leaps, lifts, and flies up, up, a few short flaps. Alights at the top of the tree across the lane from the motorhome, up here to gain a better perspective. Two more crows are coming.

He stretches his body up and back again with each

utterance. "Hrah! Hrah! Hrah!"

Injury and death are daily realities that must be guarded against. Constant vigilance is the price of survival.

The last elder in the family was dispatched by a short-eared owl, which they know because another crow eventually found his bones in an owl pellet by the lakeside. That elder's mate expired not long after, one of her ankles having become caught in a long ringlet of coloured string hanging across a tree branch. The others heard her distress calls and when they found her, tried fruitlessly to pick the tangle from her ankle, each jerk unfortunately drawing the string tighter. Her stiff body had hung upside down in the tree for days. The funeral observance for her (one that preceded Hrah's mate's by two seasons) was especially fraught.

Two more crows land expertly at one end of the motorhome roof, and Hrah watches from the treetop as the yearlings size them up, strut about, and assertively greet them. One begins inspecting the latest offerings. Hrah looks down. The cat has slipped into the dark space under the motorhome.

THIRTY-SIX

Grace fills the kettle, squinting and keeping her eyes averted from her smeary reflection. When she reaches for the teapot, she sees a fly and snatches her hand back. Then she notices more flies: the kitchen is full of them. Black and shiny, some buzz about her, others investigate the empty tin cans, more are climbing up the cupboards over the sink, exploring the dirty dishes with their sucking mouth parts, twitching across the stained counter on their hairy black legs. When did it become so bad in here?

Oh—oh—obsidian. Diabolic. Some of the flies are climbing on top of each other. They're energetic, lecherous, coupling. Grace wrings her hands while a twosome buzzes like a burdened helicopter past her elbow. Another one strikes her forehead. It's not enough that they're ubiquitous, they have to be defiant as well. She snatches up the fly swatter and starts to swing at them. Cutlery clatters as she misses, again and again. She turns in circles until she's dizzy.

Ruby's voice warbles cheerily from behind her

bedroom curtain. "I know an old lady who swallowed a fly."

Grace stops the swatter in mid-air. Her mother is still in bed, waiting for Grace to bring her tea. Are there flies in her room, too?

"Did you say you swallowed a fly, Mother?"

A fly rummages in Grace's hair. The swatter falls to the floor as she starts to smack at her head with both hands.

Could Ruby really have swallowed one of these evil things? Will she get worms? Should she induce vomiting?

"I don't know why … she swallowed a fly … I guess she'll die."

"I'll be right there, Mother. I'm coming!"

Grace retrieves the fly swatter and sets it across a stack of plates. With two fingers, she fishes yesterday's tea bag out of the little teapot, drops in a new bag, and pours the boiled water. She rinses yesterday's cup and saucer and balances them next to the teapot on the small painted tray.

Ruby continues singing.

"I know an old lady who swallowed a spider, who wriggled and jiggled and tickled inside her."

Grace gets it. It's a nursery rhyme.

By the time she reaches her mother's room, she's recovered herself.

Ruby's room seems free of flies.

"I must remember to clean the kitchen," Grace murmurs as she lifts the curtain aside and sets the tray on her mother's blanketed lap.

"Gracie, this tray is filthy."

Grace grimaces. "I know. I'll get to it, soon. But your cup's clean. That's what really matters."

With a shake of her head, Ruby lifts the teapot with her shaking, lumpy fingers, and starts to pour.

"I'll have to speak to Gloria about this."

Grace sighs, straightens up and, just as the curtain drops, she happens to look down the hallway through the back window and there sees someone walking briskly, purposefully toward her trailer. She panics. It's Sylvia from next door, Ruby's one-time caregiver, Sylvia, who knows both their names, of course, and probably listens to the radio. Sylvia has a look on her face that's impossible to read.

Grace springs down to the floor, quickly crawls on her hands and knees to the door, and confirms that it's still locked. Then she crawls back to her mother's room, ducks behind the curtain, and sits on the bed, careful not to rock the tea tray.

"Mother," she says quietly, "we're going to play a little game."

Ruby frowns, slowly setting her tea down. Her tongue seems to knead the inside of her mouth.

"What did you say, Gracie? I can't hear you."

Grace brings her finger to her lips.

"Mother? Let's see how *quiet* we can be."

A knock comes on the door.

Ruby's pencilled eyebrows shoot up, and the teacup rattles in the saucer. "Gracie?" Her eyes are huge and round.

"Shhh. We're going to pretend—"

Sylvia knocks again, quickly and more forcefully this time.

Grace leans in and lowers her head to her mother's ear. "We're going to pretend we're not here."

Grace sits back. They hold each other's gazes as Sylvia's voice shouts, "Hey! Hello! Anybody home?"

Grace moves her head back and forth. "Not a squawk," she whispers.

Ruby smiles and looks at Grace, radiating complete trust. She stifles a laugh, managing to lift a pillow to her merry face and stuffing the corner of it into her mouth. She says something that's muffled by the pillow.

Grace keeps her voice low.

"What did you say, Mother? I can't hear you."

Ruby removes the pillow from her mouth, beckons, and Grace leans in close to her again.

"A mouthful of feathers," she repeats, and chortles.

"You're funny," Grace says.

"I know an old lady who swallowed a bird. How absurd, to swallow a bird!" Ruby starts to giggle again.

Later, much later, Grace is still sitting on the end of her mother's bed, her back propped against the wall. Ruby is fast asleep, the tea tray aslant her lap; a few drops of tea stain the coverlet. A clear glass of water with a set of teeth and plastic gums on the night shelf. A fly on the rim of the glass.

Grace waves the fly away, a movement that seems to jog her brain a little. She doesn't know how much time has passed since Sylvia's near-intrusion. Surely by now the woman has left.

Ruby snores softly.

When she rises from the bed, her mother doesn't stir. Grace recovers the teapot, cup, and saucer, sets the tray down in the hall. She crawls closer to the kitchen, where the flies seem to have doubled already. She can hear them plotting in their buzzy voices, some smoothing out their wings, others rubbing their greedy little forelegs together.

Grace eases up slowly to peer out from the bottom of the window, which is also crawling with flies. She strains to be able to see the front doorstep. There's no one there.

She stands up carefully. A fly is on its back on the counter, vibrating so fast it's turning itself in circles. It stops abruptly, then starts again. It's a coded message. They're preparing to go on a rampage, and she has to get out of here. She has to get out of here, or the flies will drive her crazy.

First she shakes out and swallows another of Ruby's pills.

"I know an old lady who swallowed a pill," she murmurs to herself. "I don't know why she swallowed a pill, perhaps she's ill ..."

As Grace is closing the door behind her, she hears a woman's voice shout, "There she is!"

From the corner of her eye, Grace sees a scuffling motion. It's Sylvia, and someone else, a man, coming for her. Medium build, black round-rimmed glasses. Grace bolts. She aims away from the voice, makes an explosive run for it. Takes the nearest corner as fast as her legs will carry her, heads for the far end of the park limits, where she sets off a volley of barking that makes her abruptly change direction. Finally, she ducks behind a hedge to catch her breath. Where is she? Doubled over, gasping, her leg muscles burning and her lungs bursting.

When Sylvia said there she is, who was she talking to? Could it really have been Craig?

No one seems to have followed her. From the other side of the hedge there comes no sound, there rises no shout. All is quiet. Of course. Why would they bother following her? They'll be waiting for her return. They know she wouldn't—couldn't—leave Ruby alone for long.

Grace considers her options. As of today, her mother could be removed from her care and put in a home. Craig would have all the legalities worked out and papers ready to sign, ultimatums in legalese. Grace will be out on her ear, as Ruby might say. What will she do now?

A dragonfly lands on the inside of her forearm, and she starts in alarm.

This time, when she runs, it's more spasmodic, with her fists opening and closing at each step. She is single-minded. The only thing that matters is to put as much space as possible between herself and all the flies and their ancient dragonfly ancestors and the Airstream and all who surround it. Find somewhere to pull herself together, where she can think and not go back until she's ready. A voice in her head says, "Go, Grace, go! Trust me! I'll tell you when it's far enough, keep going!"

How much time has passed? Hours? Her surroundings

have become completely unfamiliar. The ground between the trees and the shoreline is strewn with boulders and sharp-edged rocks, and she's not wearing the right shoes. The long effort is starting to wear on her. There's a sharp pain in her breastbone, and she feels dizzy.

Maybe this is all for nothing anyway. Maybe this is useless. Or maybe the pill she took is starting to do something. Did she take one, or two? She'll just rest here a bit.

But there's something odd just out there, in the water. A sagging lump of blue cloth, almost submerged, but not quite. She hesitates, afraid she'll twist her ankle between here and there. Then she wades out to recover it.

When she pulls at the blue cloth, the lake water is reluctant to release it. She lifts with both hands, and, as it comes free, it sheds water copiously. Grace struggles with it back to the shore. Oddly enough, it's a backpack. She's seen it before: it appears to be Veronica's. But how did it get in the lake? Does she dare look inside it? What if there's something gruesome in there, like a head? She drags the bag over and heaves it up on a large boulder. Her fingers probe the outside of the bag first. Feels like books. It has to be Veronica's. She unbuckles the top flap, loosens the drawstring tie. Too bad the books are wet. There's something else underneath: a pair of binoculars. Her right-hand fingers close on the rubber-coated handgrip, and she wrestles the awkward shape of the binoculars against the opening of the bag, tugging at the wet canvas with her left hand, yanking the binoculars free—and just then feels a hand on her shoulder.

In a fraction of a second, Grace knows it's her brother

Craig, who must have followed her here after all. In the next fraction of the same second, her arm blindly swings out and arcs without stopping, her hand still gripping the binoculars. Adrenalin and fear propel her movement, and the heavy weapon meets a sudden resistance—a deep, dull crack to the skull—followed by a sickening thud.

Grace casts a quick sideways glance as she steps back. Craig's body lies unmoving on the rocks, as though he's sleeping. She can't see his face. She's knocked him right out. She didn't mean to. He surprised her; it was an in-stinctive reaction. She stares at the binoculars in her hand, and then with an anguished groan she heaves them as far as she can, into the lake.

At the sound of the splash, all the warmth is sucked out of the air. Grace begins to shiver violently. She hugs the backpack against her body, but it's still releasing water and her shirt is soaked in no time, making her feel even colder. She takes a few steps toward Craig, her feet mov-ing carefully, staying far enough away that he can't reach out and grab her. She gasps when she sees his face. Not Craig. Wayne. And blood, lots of blood, seeping from his head all the way down the side of (and starting to pool under) the rock on which his skull is impaled.

Still clutching the dripping-wet backpack, Grace stag-gers away from the terrifying scene, her teeth chattering. She slips, catches herself, and totters between the rocks, trying to make it safely to the firmer ground ahead. She's headed in the direction of home, to the trailer park and the Airstream. To Ruby.

THIRTY-SEVEN

Veronica and Charlotte have just stopped in the lane in front of the Reid family's trailer.

There are words Veronica longs to say, but she can't. Words like, You're the most loyal friend I've ever had. I can't believe you stayed with me through the whole afternoon shift. I am forever obliged to you for escorting me home. In a way, it feels like you've saved my life.

Parting, the sweetest sorrow.

Veronica steals a glance at their elongated shadows, which stretch from their feet in the dusty lane across the grass to the fence. When she squints, she can see their silhouette-heads almost touching. Avoiding Charlotte's eyes, she tries to project a casual nonchalance.

"Hey," Charlotte says swiftly, "isn't that your backpack?"

Veronica follows her gaze; she takes in the shapeless bundle on the trailer's verandah, uncomprehending. She squints. Then she claps her hand over her mouth.

She flies at the bag, Charlotte close behind her. This means *he* must have been here. Veronica reaches for the buckle which flaps up, undone. The canvas feels wet. In fact, she realizes, the whole backpack is sodden.

She's struck with the thought that Wayne's given it back in this condition as a message. A threat. With shaking hands, she tugs the drawcord all the way open and looks inside. A drowned bird-identification book: the cover warped, the pages probably stuck together. She roots frantically inside the bag. No binoculars. Another message: he's watching her now with her own—

"Binoculars," she wails. "They're gone!"

"Let me see," says Charlotte, tugging the bag from her hands. She retrieves Camus' *The Plague*, shakes its pages open.

"It's no use," Veronica sobs, "It's completely water-logged. It'll never recover."

"You're right, there aren't any binoculars," Charlotte says, quickly adding, "but there is something else." She pulls it out.

Veronica snatches her notebook from Charlotte's hand and clamps it tightly under her arm, where its dampness starts to spread into her cotton T-shirt. Will she be able to restore it? But Wayne might be watching her right now, while without her glasses she can't see anything clearly in the distance. She directs a desperate whisper to Charlotte.

"He could be watching us right now! That creep! I want to kill him!"

Fury and fear corkscrew themselves tightly into

Veronica's chest. Her breath comes fast.

"Hang on," Charlotte says. Her deep voice sounds calm, but her frown betrays grave concern. "It's not necessarily like that. He could have taken the binoculars to sell. I mean, they're something he could turn into cash, right?"

Veronica presses her hands to her face while Charlotte continues.

"We could tell the police he brought the bag back, and they could search his place for the missing binoculars."

Veronica looks again at the wet copy of *The Plague*. She grasps it and at the same time reaches for Charlotte's arm.

"No. I have a better plan. Come."

Veronica guides Charlotte around the back corner of the trailer, and they squeeze in between her sleeping-shed and the hedge. She keeps her voice low and close to Charlotte's ear.

"We're going to make masks, to wear, out of papier maché, I mean, to fit over our heads. How long do you think that would take, start to finish, to be dry enough for us to put on?"

Charlotte says, "What are you talking about?"

"The masks will be crows."

She holds up the book to show Charlotte. "See? In medieval times the plague came, and all the doctors, in order to treat the sick, would dress in long black gowns with masks that looked like crows' heads. They believed the masks kept them from being afflicted with the plague themselves."

Charlotte is faintly nodding as Veronica goes on.

"We'd need balloons to make the form, chicken wire for the beak, newspaper to rip into strips, and flour and water. And black paint."

Charlotte looks directly at her, their faces inches away from each other. Her eyes are close and in focus, pale green, attentive. Her eyes ask, "And then what?"

"Wayne's scared of crows, right? So we amplify what he's afraid of. We haunt him, terrorize him. At night. Under the lamplight, across from his trailer. First, we make some noise to wake him up. Better yet, light a fire in the lane."

Charlotte shakes her head. "We couldn't do that. A fire would bring too much attention. But it is an intriguing idea. There are balloons at the tuck shop. We could make the masks in my trailer. That would work. I do have black acrylic paint and a can of latex primer. For the glue we'd need flour and salt."

"We have ample flour," Veronica says. "Newspapers, too, and I saw some chicken wire in my shed. Do you know where we can procure some cardboard?"

"Sure. Tuck shop. There's loads of it."

Scarcely an hour later, they've assembled everything in Charlotte's trailer. When Veronica tries blowing up the first balloon, it bursts, and she jumps.

"Sorry. Oh but wouldn't *that* be a grand way to wake up Wayne in the night. Burst a balloon outside his window?"

"Careful you don't make yourself dizzy," Charlotte cautions. Then she lifts the bag of flour and tips half of it all at once into the bowl of warm water. Reaches for a box of salt and dumps some of that in as well.

"The salt," Charlotte explains to Veronica, "will help harden and preserve the mixture."

They agree they'll make four masks—no more trouble than making two, and in case some break and collapse, they won't have to start all over again. With intense motions, Veronica rips the newspaper into long thin strips that spool down into a growing pile on the floor.

They dip the strips of newspaper into the bowl of thickened paste, and use their hands to smear the first layers over the top two-thirds of each balloon. They are careful to leave openings for the eyes and a space to affix a beak. Charlotte uses her hair dryer to hasten drying each layer. Veronica cuts the cardboard into the shape of enormous beaks and tapes the pieces together.

From time to time Veronica trains the hair dryer on her notebook, the pages of which she peels apart, one at a time, wherever they stick together.

On the morning of the second day of working on the masks, Veronica goes home for lunch to find that her replacement glasses have arrived. She slips them on and looks around; she can soon see her mother ladling warmed-up canned stew into bowls, her brothers coming into the kitchen, laughing about something. At once she's suspicious of their intentions and glances at them, but she now can tell by their expressions that it has nothing to do with her. She relaxes.

When they sit down to eat, Veronica's hands keep

touching the frames as though to make sure they're still there. Her mother reaches for her drink and keeps her eyes locked on Veronica as she lifts it to her lips. When Marnie starts to swallow Veronica can see her top teeth magnified through the glass, pearly and gleaming.

That afternoon, back at Charlotte's trailer, the third layers of papier maché are dry. Charlotte takes a pin to burst the balloons. Veronica attaches the cardboard beaks to the head-forms, and folds and clamps the chicken wire over the two parts, pinching it into place.

"What will we use for cloaks?" asks Charlotte.

Veronica is gathering the strips of newspaper and poking them into the glue.

"We could keep checking the laundry room washing machines for dark towels and sheets," she says.

"You mean steal them?"

Veronica giggles. "No, well, I mean, technically, borrow them."

Is she happy because she's been spending so much time with Charlotte, or because she has her notebook back, or because she's about to do something so terrifying and dramatic?

She thinks about it after she's locked herself into the shed, sitting in her forepeak bunk with her flashlight, her collection of stones in the corner, shadowy bulwarks hunched protectively nearby. Here in her shelter she can smell the oiled sailcloth and candle wax, hear the bilge water slapping against the cross beams beneath the floorboards. There's the reassuring creak of the boom rubbing against the mast. The sound of the rain striking the fore-hatch. The sturdy anchor chain holds fast, fathoms and fathoms down. The certainty that she'll see Charlotte again tomorrow.

After nine applications of gluey strips of newspaper over three days, the masks are finally dry, primed, and ready for painting. They look magnificent: the shapes are well-proportioned; the first black brush strokes turn the rough eggshell-coloured surface into glossy, rippling feathers.

It doesn't take long for all four masks to be painted, and when the last one is placed next to the others to dry, collectively they look formidable.

They discuss their plan while the paint dries. They try on their makeshift cloaks. Veronica's is a crocheted black poncho borrowed from the laundry room; Charlotte's is a dark purple tablecloth.

Veronica touches the drying paint surface lightly with her fingertip. "I wish I'd thought of fedoras."

"Fedoras! And cravats maybe."

"And big black boots with pointed toes."

When the masks are ready to try on, they practise walking in the small space inside Charlotte's trailer, moving their heads back and forth and side to side. They clasp their hands behind their backs. Each step is an exaggerated shift of weight from one foot to the other.

"Veronica? Are you afraid?" Charlotte's voice sounds hollow inside the mask.

"Of course. Aren't you?"

Charlotte's large, absurd beak is nodding up and down.

The plan is that Charlotte will come and knock on the shed door at midnight, and together they'll walk back to her trailer to pick up the masks. They'll make their way there behind the trailers, avoiding the lane, then don their disguises to begin their clandestine mission. Veronica trembles with excitement. Her feet are light as she skips up the steps and on to the verandah where she used to sleep.

As soon as she enters the trailer, she's aware of stoppered laughter, quick movement, a rearranging of arms and legs. Then she sees them: her mother half-kneeling on the floor, and Milton on the bench behind her. Milton is fumbling with something in his lap. Marnie is smoothing the pleats of her skirt over her thighs.

Milton starts stuttering.

"It's not—not what it looks like. Your mother was showing me, what someone—a lady, did to her one afternoon, and then—we had another drink, and one thing *almost* led to another—hey Marnie, we're lucky Veronica came along! You've just saved us from ourselves, young lady! Somebody give that girl a medal!"

Marnie gets to her feet, her laugh sounding more like a bark. She reaches for her drink, strides to the kitchen. She nudges the ice cubes with a plastic sword. When she lifts the sword, gesturing, some of the drink splashes on the wall.

Milton mumbles something more, stands up from the bench, and hobbles unsteadily to the door. He has to stoop to step out, and the door closes flatly after him.

Marnie turns to Veronica.

"Don't look at me like that. You have no idea what I go through."

Veronica stares at the tiny plastic sword pinched in the air between her mother's thumb and forefinger.

"And you, holier-than-thou, Miss Praying-for-a-Miracle, you never have desires?"

Affixed to the sword is a pierced olive. Marnie brings it to her mouth and pries it off with her teeth. She starts to chew. Veronica imagines a tiny pirate, a swashbuckling figure running along a heaving deck, the sword held forward, about to perfectly impale a tiny plastic woman with red daubs of colour on her cheeks. Who's still standing there jabbing the miniature sword in the air.

"I've hardly seen you," Marnie says. "For days."

Then Dilly's calling out from the front yard. "Can we come in now? Mom?"

Her mother swallows the olive and drops the sword in the garbage pail.

Veronica says, "You've read my notebook? Before it was stolen? Or after I got it back and dried it out?"

"It's my right. More importantly, it's my instinct to protect you. And that's the only reason why I know for sure what you've been up to. You're hooked on that girl, aren't you."

Hooked. She says it with disdain. Hooked. The word is sharp; the condition, irreversible. There is only the sound of the ice cubes nudging the inside of Marnie's glass.

"Mom?" comes Dilly's voice again. "Now? Can we come in?"

Veronica abruptly backs out the door and closes it behind her.

"Not a good idea," she says to Dilly, marching forward, taking him roughly by the upper arm. "Let's go somewhere else. Where's your brother?"

Dilly points, and Gumm comes out from a hiding place, close behind the trailer. Has he been listening? What are they going to do now?

Veronica considers her options, then makes up her mind.

"Can you keep a secret?" she asks them, and they both nod. She walks them across the lane to stand under the mountain ash, where Veronica's bird feeder used to hang. "I must have your word on this, your sealed bonds," Veronica says to them seriously. "This is a sacred trust."

The boys exchange glances. Dilly looks worried.

"Do we have to cut ourselves and mix our blood?"

"No. Don't be ridiculous."

Dilly looks so relieved that Veronica softens.

"How would you like to pretend you're crows? Let me hear you caw. No, wait, not here." She lowers her voice. "But do you think you can caw, like a crow, really loudly?"

Dilly looks at her as though he's intrigued, but Gumm's expression has turned skeptical.

"Is this a game?"

"It's not a game, no. I'll explain it on the way."

When she goes back later to pack their things, Veronica

is prepared to confront her mother but instead, finding the trailer empty, she leaves a note saying that she and her brothers are together, that they've gone on a sleepover. Into a garbage bag she stuffs sweatshirts and long pants for her brothers. The sweatshirts are black with white designs on them. She rolls up their two blankets. Any more and she won't be able to carry the bag.

She arrives back at Charlotte's trailer with the boys, who crowd into the doorway beside her.

"Charlotte, I'm sorry, but I had no choice," Veronica says. "The good news is they've promised to help us."

Charlotte crosses her arms across her chest and looks at them with a mock-skeptical expression. "Help us? How?"

"You'll see," Gumm says earnestly.

"I've sworn them to secrecy. Charlotte, please, I had to tell them. Everything. It'll be alright." Veronica pauses. "Do you mind, really?"

"Of course not."

Dilly sees the masks for the first time and makes a bee-line for them.

"I don't know exactly what you want us to do," says Gumm. "Remember, crows don't like me."

"Caw, as loud as you can. Let's hear it."

Gumm takes a breath. But it's Dilly who caws, not one but three short cries, and the sound is so convincing that Veronica bursts out laughing.

"Save the rest for tonight," she says. To Gumm, she adds, "If you can't caw, you can walk back and forth, or just stand still, like a silhouette, in full view of one of his windows. "If Wayne comes out, he won't chase us. But if he does, we each run in our separate, appointed directions. Got it?"

Dilly tries on his mask. He holds one of his eyes against an eyehole. "Can I keep it for Halloween?"

Charlotte and Veronica exchange glances.

"Got it," says Gumm.

"One more thing," cautions Veronica. "Once your masks are on, there's no taking them off till we get home, unfollowed. This is a secret mission which means we can't let anyone know who we are."

Afterwards, they build a fire outside, and when they get hungry Charlotte cooks sausages and warms up two cans of beans over the coals and gives each of them a spoon.

Later, the boys are asleep on the kitchen benches, the table having been clamped back up to the wall. Veronica finds Charlotte in her bed; she moves over to make room. They lie fully dressed under a blanket and whisper, going over their plan again. Charlotte soon falls asleep, but Veronica is restless. She has goosebumps; she's preoccupied with trying not to accidentally touch Charlotte under the blanket. There's the scent of her, like lavender, and something else she can't identify, something sweet and smoky that seems to rise from that abundant mass of red hair that she's tried to loop at her neck.

Finally, it's time. They rise quietly and pull extra clothes on, keeping their voices low in the dark. "Here. Blow this up," Veronica whispers, handing each of the boys a balloon. "And tie a knot, you know how."

"Why are we bringing balloons?"

"Never mind why."

"I know." Gumm cups his hand and whispers in Dilly's ear.

"You should have told us," Dilly says, looking at Veronica. "Silly. We have firecrackers."

"You do? Where'd you get those?" asks Charlotte.

"We traded some comic books for them." He pulls his hand from his pocket and extends it toward his sister, in his palm at least a half-dozen red firecrackers. "See?"

Charlotte grins. "Don't forget matches."

Veronica and Charlotte don their cloaks. The boys are wearing their sweatshirts inside out so they will blend better into the darkness. Once outside, gathered behind Charlotte's trailer, they solemnly lift their masks on.

Veronica hears Dilly, his voice muffled and echoey, say, "Looks like we've got us a convoy."

"Too bad we don't have walkie-talkies," Gumm says.

"Maybe next time."

No stars are visible; no moon appears. There are no signs that anyone's up, no sounds other than the trilling crickets and their own mismatched footsteps bruising the grass.

They reach Wayne's motorhome. The boys dig into their pockets and head to the back window.

A dog inside a nearby trailer starts to bark. Veronica watches as her brothers freeze, knees bent in crouched hesitation, unlit firecrackers in hand. Then she sees the sudden flare of the match, their trembling readiness, the fling, their sprinting away.

With eyes and beak forward, Veronica watches as her brothers scurry back to her. She and Charlotte move their body disguises simultaneously to enclose the pale shaft of lamplight across the lane.

A succession of rapidly exploding firecrackers breaks the stillness, and for a stunned space of time afterwards there is nothing: no dogs, no crickets, just silence. A string of miniature white lights on the edge of the nearest trailer blinks on and off.

Then the dog starts barking again.

Veronica is pleased to see that, in their disguises, with the effect of the darkness and the shadowy light winding loosely between them, Charlotte and her brothers look truly like giant, restless crows, readying to converge.

Veronica turns her head inside the mask and peers out the opposite eyehole at Wayne's motorhome. Is that movement at the bottom corner of a window?

THIRTY-EIGHT

Grace feels queasy as she pushes Ruby's wheelchair along the lane in the dark. Ruby is humming "Till We Meet Again," the warble of her notes sliding under the wheels crunching along the uneven gravel.

The knowledge that she has to leave the trailer park is a heavy lump that has been turning and writhing in Grace's belly for three days. If it were up to her, they would have been gone by now. But when she'd returned from that fateful run to find her mother missing, only to discover her later at Sylvia's, sitting under the awning no less, the two of them seeming to be chatting amiably—that changed everything.

"I'm sorry we got off on the wrong foot," Sylvia said, turning to Grace, "I must say your mother really is quite delightful."

Grace, suspecting irony, had narrowed her eyes and tried to calculate what had happened. Sylvia must have knocked on the door again, and Ruby must have let herself out. The memory of Sylvia striding toward her, and Craig at her side, now fills her with anxiety and confusion. Where is her brother now? It was just hours ago. Is this little charade, this subtle manipulation, how the two of them plan to ambush her next? Obviously Sylvia knows everything about them, has probably pumped Ruby for the inside story, and now is waiting to report back to Craig.

"There's a real sense of community here," Sylvia then said. "Don't you find?"

Grace didn't have an answer.

Then Sylvia said, "One of these days I'd like to meet Gloria."

Before Grace could take her mother home, Sylvia was insisting that Ruby promise to come with her to the sing-along event a couple of nights later. And after that, it was all that Ruby could talk about; what she would wear to the choir, as she called it, became her chief preoccupation. Most of her blue clothes—for she still wouldn't wear any other colour—were too worn-looking, she complained. Much as Grace tried to persuade her to wear her green serge suit with her white blouse, Ruby was adamant.

The whole situation is as frightening as it is absurd. Grace is terrified that Sylvia and Craig have cooked up some plan to trap and detain them at the singalong. But, of all the things she might have been doing next, Grace found herself calling a taxi and taking Ruby shopping to find a new blue dress.

Everything that matters is now packed up and ready to go, except for her mother's pearls, which have gone missing again. The Minton and Limoges china, Ruby's photos or what's left of them, their deck of cards, the kettle, some clothing, the pills—all packed. After tonight, as of now, Grace feels freer to leave, but she can't call a taxi to come at two in the morning without stirring up other suspicions. The taxi driver would be interrogated later.

Then again, she can't go hauling their suitcases out in broad daylight, attracting attention to herself with everyone around, and having to make something up to explain, and all of it being remembered later.

For it's only a matter of time before Wayne's body is discovered, and then the police will be knocking on doors. It's a miracle she's had so long to hatch a plan.

They'll have to leave at night, that much is clear. Her mind clutches at possibilities. Hare-brained schemes, her mother would say, if she knew what she was thinking.

Ruby stops humming and kicks her heels against the footrests.

For the last two nights after Ruby's fallen asleep, Grace has crept nervously out to examine Wayne's motorhome for signs of life, and she's quite certain he hasn't been back. Once again there are no lights on; no sounds emerge. She wonders if there is any food inside. On this, the third night, she's determined to try the door. If it's open, it will be the perfect solution for them. And if the key to the motor is in there, then she and Ruby are home free.

"Home free," Grace says out loud.

Ruby tilts her head back until it's upside down, looking at Grace, and gives her one of the widest smiles Grace has ever seen.

Grace helps her mother into their trailer and goes back outside to fold up the wheelchair. It's just past nine o'clock. She looks up in the direction of Wayne's motorhome, out of sight past the corner. If she can pull this off, it will be the most daring thing she's ever done.

Grace heats some milk on the stove for her mother, reaches for a box of digestive cookies, selects two of them, sets them on the last unpacked plate.

"We might go on an adventure tonight," she says brightly, as she pours the heated milk into her mother's favourite china cup.

"An adventure, you say?"

"If things work out, yes. I may have found us a way out of here."

"That's nice, Gracie," Ruby replies, reaching for a cookie.

A few hours later Grace quietly slips out again.

If all goes well, if Wayne's door is open, and the keys are there, she will pocket them and return to the Airstream to collect their things. Then she will use the wheelchair to take their two suitcases and one taped-up box over to Wayne's motorhome, and go back once more with the wheelchair to fetch her mother and the last duffel bag. First she'll have to wake Ruby, then she will have to to persuade her to come. It's a tall order. What awaits them is an impossible series of improbable events, any one of which could trip them up.

It's gone past midnight.

"I am created by divine light," Grace whispers. "I am protected by divine light," she breathes, as she creeps past the side of her trailer and scurries forward to crouch in the next shadow. "I am ever growing into divine light."

So far she's not been seen.

She stops whispering. Now she's particularly nervous, because she has to sprint across the partially-lit lane to get to the next cluster of shadows. But just as her feet take flight, she hears three gunshots fire in rapid succession. She halts in the centre of the lane, her knees bent, in full view of anyone who might be looking. Yet who might see her is now her least concern. Beyond the dark screen of trees ahead, Grace has caught sight of a group of gigantic crows, oversized and sinister with beaks like black chisels, the birds converging across from Wayne's motorhome. Four moving silhouettes, grown almost human-sized, four black, evil crows, strutting and swaying and cawing and flapping, and one of them flaps and lifts into the air and hovers there before it lowers itself again, slowly, and takes a few hops along the ground. And then the trees spring up to surround Grace, their limbs like tendrils winding tightly into each other, and collectively they bear down in a leafy, unstoppable whirl, and spin her feet out from under her.

THIRTY-NINE

Not a movement, but a strangled cry. Veronica tries to turn toward it, but she wrenches her head too fast inside the mask and it slips across her face. She lifts her hands up to straighten it.

Coming from the right, Charlotte's voice is barely audible. "Did you see that?"

"Pardon? See what?" Veronica swings her head again.

"Somebody fell. We have to do something."

Veronica, peering through the left eyehole, allows the shapes to separate themselves from each other in the dark surroundings, and spots the unmoving form slumped across the lane three trailer-lengths away.

"What about Gumm and Dilly?"

"Tell them to wait here. Stick to Plan A."

Veronica summons the boys and explains.

"Be careful," she says. "There's no knowing what Wayne will do. Don't take any chances. Fly off in different directions if he comes out."

"Very funny," says Gumm.

"I'm serious. If you have to fly to save your lives,

you fly. Caw as loudly as you can."

"I'm scared to do it without you, Veronica," says Dilly.

"You'll be fine. Go on now, make us proud."

Charlotte's already reached the prone figure. When Veronica gets there, Charlotte has her hands on her mask and is about to pull it off.

"Stop!" Veronica hisses, pulling Charlotte's arm down. "You can't. You'll be recognized. Someone could be watching."

"I can't see, though."

"Charlotte, oh my God, it's Grace. We have to help her. She must have seen us and been frightened."

Veronica looks around to get her bearings, and realizes Grace's trailer is not far.

"We must get her home." Once again Charlotte starts to remove her mask.

"We can't carry her and the masks at the same time! We can take the masks off once we get her home."

"She could have died of fright. Can people really die of fright, Veronica?"

The thought makes Veronica have a sudden flush of panic. She presses her fingers to the side of Grace's neck. "I'll see if she has a pulse," she says. It's weak but steady.

They manage to lift her up to a sitting position and prop her up between them. Grace is surprisingly slight. Her head lolls.

"What have we done?"

"Let's just get her home."

The rest of the way to the Airstream they are both

silent as they stagger along, half-dragging Grace. Finally, they reach the lot and they pause. For a while nothing stirs; the trailers nearby remain dark and silent. Then from the direction of Wayne's trailer they hear a crashing noise and the sound of loud cawing, the thump and vibration of running feet.

"Don't drop her! We'll check on them later. We can't just leave her here!"

Getting Grace's body up the steps is the hardest part. After some unsuccessful tries, Veronica holds her semi-upright while Charlotte props open the door. Veronica can't hear her brothers cawing any more. She looks in the direction she thinks one of them fled, but sees and hears nothing.

"They're fine," Charlotte says. "They're survivors. Help me here."

Grace moans; Veronica looks at her through the eye-holes in her mask to see if she's coming round. She lifts Grace's wrist, but it flops back down.

They carry her into the trailer slung between them and manage to set her down on an upholstered bench. They kneel down next to her on the carpet and take their masks off.

Inside, surfaces are clean, and there is a smell of bleach clinging to the kitchen. The macramé owls are not where they used to be, nor is the larger piece that Veronica remembers. The walls are bare. There are packed suitcases and a taped-up box taking up most of the living room.

Charlotte rests their masks on top of the suitcases.

Veronica brings her face close to Grace's and holds her head near to Grace's lips.

She's still breathing, but it's barely discernible.

"Grace?" Charlotte pats her hand. "Can you hear me, Grace?"

"Who are you two, and what are you doing here?"

Veronica twists around to see Ruby.

She stands up. "I'm sorry, Mrs Urquhart. Don't be alarmed. I'm Veronica, do you remember? And this is Charlotte. Grace took a turn. She had a sudden spell—"

"Grace felt ill," Charlotte explains. "We brought her home."

Ruby steps forward, fumbling with her housecoat sash. Veronica and Charlotte stand aside to make way for her approach.

"It's the middle of the night, isn't it?"

"Yes."

"What was Grace doing outside?"

"Don't know, Mrs Urquhart."

"And you? Not sleeping? What were you two *girls* doing outside, in the middle of the night?" Ruby regards their clothes, their dark haphazard capes, then glances at the masks propped on the suitcases. So she *has* noticed.

Veronica gambles on the truth.

"We were trying to frighten someone into leaving this place. Not Grace. We didn't know she was there. Someone else, a very bad man. You know, the one called Wayne, who keeps preaching to people about salvation? We were trying to haunt him, trying to give him a scare so he would go away."

"Mercy. Go on."

When Veronica hesitates, the old woman blinks. "Did he interfere with you?"

Veronica nods.

"Scum of the earth," Mrs Urquhart says.

"I got away," Veronica tells her. "But the police didn't—weren't able to—"

As if Ruby has just remembered her daughter, she moves closer to her, bends over slightly, and places one hand on Grace's forehead.

"Poor girl," she says, and looks up at Veronica. "My daughter has a very delicate constitution. She has her troubles. Always did. Thank you for bringing her home."

Grace moans again and, this time, turns her head in their direction. They all watch her and wait. Seconds pass: Grace's eyes remain closed. Mrs Urquhart glances at the masks that rest on top of the packed suitcases, and she lifts them awkwardly, one at a time, hands them over.

"Take these. They'll upset Gracie. You should go now."

As they leave, Veronica catches sight of Ruby, a bony, forlorn old woman stooped over in a dressing gown and slippers, rubbing her daughter's arm.

"Gracie, you just had a hard day at the office. There, there. Don't open your eyes until you're feeling better. We've got an adventure to go on tonight, remember? I'll help whenever you're ready. There, there now. You're fine."

FORTY

The girls find Gumm and Dilly cowering in the bedroom in Charlotte's trailer. They leap up with relief when they see it's Charlotte and Veronica.

"That guy's a maniac," says Gumm.

"Who is? Wayne?"

"No, the guy in the trailer across from his."

"Told us to scram or he'd shoot us."

"Gumm went one way, and I ran the other way."

"I hurt my elbow."

"I scraped my knee."

"We cawed, just like you said."

"It worked. We heard you."

Dilly looks up at her, his brown eyes radiating loyalty. Gumm has a look of pride, and when he meets Veronica's gaze she realizes he's grown taller since they last stood face to face.

In the morning, Wayne's motorhome is gone. There's a dry, abandoned space where the vehicle used to be, the grass all yellowed up to the shadow line, a bare scattering of gravel next to the back hedge, a rusty bicycle lying in the corner. The four of them stand in the lane, the dust still settling around them from their sudden halt.

"It's a miracle," says Charlotte.

Dilly whoops, dashes over to the empty lot, starts running in circles about the space. He stops and bends down to pick something up, then runs back to Veronica and hands her a crow feather.

She takes the feather, feeling dizzy with exhilaration. There's something about the abandoned space that has a feeling of permanence about it. She, Veronica, has been an agent of Wayne's removal. She sweeps her eyes once again over the empty lot and notices the details: the rusty bicycle has a flat tire, and the white blotches that outline the dry rectangle where the motorhome used to be are bird droppings.

She looks thoughtfully at the feather in her hand. She and the birds, and Charlotte, and her brothers, all made him leave.

Gumm gestures at the point of the quill.

"If you want I can make a pen out of this with my penknife. People used to write with feathers. Before there were real pens."

Veronica grins at him. "How do you know that?"

"There's a picture in *David Copperfield*."

When Veronica and her brothers get home, they find their mother kneeling next to the shed, where she appears to have been trying to transplant a shrub that was damaged in the storm. She's wearing her gardening overalls, and her shovel is lying on the ground beside her. But as they get closer Veronica realizes, to her alarm, that her mother is praying. When she sees Veronica and the boys, she unclasps her hands, still clad in her gardening gloves, and starts to get up.

Marnie holds out her arms to Dilly and embraces him. "Did you have a nice time at your sleepover?"

"We went on a secret mission," Dilly says.

Veronica glares at him but their mother laughs.

"Did you, now? You must tell me all about it. But first, come see what I found."

She straightens, pulls a glove off and crams her clean hand into her pocket. Veronica and Gumm gather closer as their mother opens her palm to show them: a scattering of silver and copper coins, and a medallion. A Jesus medallion.

Dilly looks at the shovel and the freshly-turned earth. "Buried treasure?"

"Pieces of eight?" asks Gumm, reaching out.

Veronica says, "Oh no. Mother, what have you done?"

The next morning, Veronica sees the park superintendent with Sylvia and a man she's never seen before. All three are engaged in putting up posters along the fences. From a distance Veronica can see the word *MISSING* in big letters across the top of each poster, and a black-and-white picture beneath. She's suddenly frightened. Must be about Wayne. Does someone know what happened, about their

284

trick? Are they going to be in trouble?

She walks across the lane to the fence, ambling as casually as she can toward the nearest poster, and casts a look. It's not a picture of Wayne; it's Grace and Mrs Urquhart, looking about ten years younger than they are now.

How can they be missing? What terrible thing could have happened to them? In the photo, a smiling Mrs Urquhart is sitting at the head of a fully set dinner table, and Grace is beside her in the next chair, looking away from the camera, her eyes half-closed. They are each wearing tissue-paper Christmas hats pulled over old-fashioned permed hairdos. Veronica peers at the picture, comparing their younger faces to their older ones in her mind's eye.

A man's brusque voice. "Do you know them? Have you seen them?"

Veronica turns from the poster and sees the stranger in a smart business suit, with black round-rimmed glasses.

"Why, what's happened?"

"It's very important that I find them. It could be a matter of—well, it's very important. Well? Do you know where they've gone?" The man tugs at his tie and waits for her answer.

Veronica thinks, If Grace is gone, then she must have good reason.

She says, "I haven't seen them, no."

"If you do, would you contact me, please? Here's my card."

She takes the card. It says, *Craig Urquhart, Esq., Barrister-at-Law.*

Veronica steps into her shed and locks the door.

First I was naive, then I became embittered. Now I trust no one.

I have been dragged into some kind of altered world, through a portal whose door was in the woods. And now I can't go back. Neither to the woods, nor to the girl I was before.

Before, my life was merely joyless and inconsequential, but now it's become something else. (I know not what.)

Hope, fiercely guarded, is beginning to beat again in my secret heart.

I liked being a crow inside the costume. It felt like I was enigmatic, inviolable.

Bird droppings, where the motorhome used to be.

Word droppings: scat that one examines for clues.

We hoodwinked Wayne. We did it together.

Tomorrow, I will make ink and use the crow-quill pen to write Charlotte a letter, for what could be more meaningful and romantic than that?

Ink, think.

Sacred, scared.

Verse, subversive.

Armour, amour.

The next day, Veronica empties half a bag of peanuts into her backpack.

She needs to ask Charlotte if she can make ink out of some of her black paint, and if she should add water or turpentine to it. Charlotte's scheduled to be working today. But as Veronica comes closer to the canteen, almost jogging along in her enthusiasm, she perceives that there's nobody behind the counter. Then she hears voices, and muffled laughter, so she creeps around to the back of the trailer, prepared to surprise her.

Instead Veronica comes upon Charlotte and Jeremy, their arms sliding around each other, Charlotte's head is tilted to one side, and Jeremy's face is nuzzling her neck. When they pull apart a second later they open their eyes simultaneously and see her.

"Veronica?" says Jeremy. "Yawright?"

There are no tears, just a leaden, deadened feeling that is slowly consuming her from the inside. Even now, having found her way blindly here, looking up at the tree house with her glasses on, Veronica sees nothing; all is smudged and indistinctly grey. The tree house—a safe place to find her way to, now that Wayne's gone—was the only place she could think of, in her distress, where she could be alone. Her backpack on her back, still half-full of peanuts.

She tugs at the climbing-rope and lifts her foot to the first rung.

How long will she be able to survive up there, with only rainwater and a few peanuts?

Care, scare. Scar. Love, dove, rope, dope.

The words spin in her head, and the letters get all mixed up and push behind her unseeing eyes as she climbs.

There are crow droppings on the tree house platform. Veronica pulls herself up on her elbows and knees, then squats and hauls the rope ladder up, hand over hand, until it rests in a heap on the deck like a coiled hawser.

She opens her backpack and meticulously aligns peanuts along the railing, fiercely keeping her mind on the task at hand. When melancholy crests over her like a wave, she curls her body up in the corner. She considers throwing herself overboard off the platform. Only she might merely break something, like Mrs Carmichael did, and be in agony. But this is another kind of agony. Better to hang herself by the rope ladder. She adjusts her position to reach for it. She might be able to undo some of the knots, make a noose. She would still have to jump, of course. But it would all be over in a second, and she would no longer feel this raw, excruciating despair.

Veronica hears the call of a crow nearby, followed by the echo of another. At the edge of her vision, there's a swift movement of black feathers. She quickly squeezes her body into the corner of the tree house platform. And when the crow alights on the railing across from her she watches as he picks up one, then two peanuts, before he briefly glances at her with one black eye, then shoulders himself into the air, beating for the space between the uppermost branches and away. The moment he is out of sight, Veronica becomes aware of another bird lifting from the treetops, heading out to follow the first one.

She'd been in the company of crows all along.

Colin comes home a few hours later that afternoon, and from within her sleeping-shed, Veronica hears his footsteps and his voice. He enters the trailer and calls out a greeting. A few minutes later, he comes out again and knocks on Veronica's door, asks her to join him at the picnic table where he's already opened a beer.

Her heart has been cracked wide open, and her limbs feel heavy and sore. Can he tell? Does he know?

He asks her how her mother's doing, and without meeting his eyes she says, "Fine."

Veronica then hears his sharp intake of breath and she looks directly at him. He's leaning far over to one side, to avoid a wasp. Finding his balance, bracing himself, trying to get up from the picnic table, but his legs won't co-operate.

She shoos the wasp away from him with her arms, and her father dances away backwards, making odd squealing noises. The wasp makes off in a zooming trajectory for the park, headed straight toward Saffron, who Veronica can see is going through her yoga poses on the hill again.

Her father swivels his eyes from Saffron to Veronica.

"Thank you."

"You're welcome."

The commotion has brought Marnie and the boys outside. They come up behind her father, who's still standing there, as though he's too uncertain to sit down. Finally, he comes closer to the end of the picnic table and looks at Veronica, his words reaching them all.

"What I was about to say, was that I've just spoken with the librarian who said to tell you not to worry about the reference book. They have a fund for things like that, so they will simply order another copy from the publisher's agent."

"Thank you."

"You're welcome."

"I have good news for you, too," Veronica says. "Wayne's motorhome is gone. Looks like permanently."

Marnie's eyes dart from Veronica to Colin and back again.

Colin doesn't look surprised; instead, he raises his eyebrows and nods.

"It worked, then," he says.

He stuffs his hand into his pocket, and waggles his fingers through his change, creating a rich jangling sound, as though he's weighing palmfuls of golden sovereigns and doubloons.

But now Veronica's confused. She looks at her brothers. Did the boys tell him about the crow costumes? Gumm shakes his head, no, then gestures at Dilly, who shrugs.

Veronica says, "What do you mean, it worked, then? What worked?"

"I think you should tell her, Colin," Marnie says gravely.

"Tell me what?"

Colin stops moving the coins in his pocket, and then there's no sound at all.

Veronica bobs somewhere over an ocean of space between dread and hope. She watches her father's face. There's something about the set of his jaw, his expression both defensive and defiant, the way his eyes blink hard and open again to meet hers.

"Last weekend I spoke to that degenerate myself," Colin says. "Man to man. I said to him, 'I am a peaceful person.' I said, 'You have to leave this place.'"

Marnie turns and looks at Colin.

"And? Go ahead, tell her what else."

"I also told him that if I had to, I could find some people who would take care of him. Permanently."

"Me," says Gumm.

"And me," says Dilly.

Veronica is dumbstruck. She buries her face in her hands.

Their mother says, "You see, that's all it takes sometimes, to get along. Being reasonable. Your father is a good example."

FORTY-ONE

For a long time, a thick vapour, fragrant and clammy, hangs over the countryside.

Hrah wings his way along the lake's edge. At this lower elevation, he can recognize the familiar shapes and textures on the ground. As long as he keeps his extended body gliding within the same horizontal ribbon of air, his right eye sees atmospheric gravity waves suspended in overlapping arcs, visible today because of the linear diffraction of the light. With both ears, he can hear the vibrations of infrasound, the movements of the distant air currents, the profound music of charged particles from the sun crashing into the earth's magnetic field.

The fog seems to curdle around him, and his wings begin to feel heavy. Hrah drops his shoulders and tail to decrease speed and bring his body down, slowly, until the treetops are close again. He skims above the crowns until he sees the tree he's looking for, a half-rotted Manitoba maple. He flies past it and circles back, tracing a spiral before arching his neck, flapping to maintain his balance, and touching down with his claws extended. He shrugs his shoulders and shakes out his wing feathers, hops twice, and folds his wings back again.

He plucks a fat brown spider off the branch he's standing on and swallows it. He sidles sideways along the branch, nearing his caching place. When he is sure he's not being watched by another crow, he inspects the hollow crevice. Pokes into the top of it, rearranges a few shards of coloured glass, discards the red poker chip, and nudges the string of white pearls out of the way.

He singles out a pair of peanuts, pinches them in his beak, and lifts off toward the lake.

His flight muscles get very warm from the effort as he tries to stay alight in the thickened, heavy air. His tailbone itches, next to where the new quills—to replace the feathers he lost in the storm—are growing in.

Hrah reaches the flat rock, looks around to make sure he's still alone. He releases the peanuts and looks around again. He nudges one closer to the small cleft in the rock, holds it down with his claw, and punctures the shell. He crushes the nuts into fragments before swallowing. He defecates.

After a drink he rises back into the air—into the density of white fog—and flies from tree to tree. He turns his head from left to right, trying to make out what's on the ground. He must be well out of his territory. Where the mist touches the flora in this place, Hrah can almost taste the sticky sap oozing from the spruce trees.

As he climbs above the mantle of fog, he sees he is no longer alone. At a higher plane there are several larger birds, five turkey vultures and a pair of ravens, none threats to him. The crow turns and glides past them in an arc while he regards them, sailing their proprietary circuit. It means something's down there that wasn't there before. Under the fog there's something promising that they can smell and he can't.

Hrah descends into the fog, feet first, head down, outstretched wings beating swift backward circles to slow his descent. The fog thins and the tops of trees come into view. He sees he's at the far edge of the forested land past the point, and well away from human habitation. There seem to be sacks of cloth here, left on the rocks. He lands, looks at the cloth, and takes two slow steps closer.

Then he lifts from the ground again, regains a safe height and regards the carcass and its surroundings from the air.

He flies away from it, over the trees, then changes his mind and circles back, banking, his wingtip almost grazing the water. He comes to a running landing, and then hears the others. A freewheeling flock of crows who claim this territory as theirs.

The clan comes for Hrah, screeching, flying noisily at him and showing their underwings. He tries to signal his intentions by hopping back, averting his gaze, vibrating his wings and tail to indicate he means not to threaten them. But they chase him anyway.

He flees upwards, angling for the canopy of trees.

Before he gets there, one of the resident crows zooms in to stab at his straining shoulders, and another lands well-placed kicks at his tail with her claws.

He forms his body into an arrow shape and dodges them, swiftly weaving in and out of the edge of the forest in the direction of his own territory, eluding them until they give up and turn back.

Hrah alights on the lowest branch of the oak tree that looms over the spruce and cedars that mark the edge of the trailer park. Here he rests, preening his feathers while the lake nudges the beach and the last tufts of mist slowly roll up the distant hillside to vanish.

ACKNOWLEDGEMENTS

On crows and crow behaviour, I consulted many books and individuals for help. *Gifts of the Crow* by John Marzluff & Tony Angell, *Mind of the Raven* by Bernd Heinrich, and *Corvus* by Esther Woolfson, were particularly helpful. I am indebted also to Kevin J. McGowan at the Cornell Lab of Ornithology at Cornell University for fascinating webinars on the nature of crows.

Susan Wylie, Executive Director of Le Nichoir Bird Sanctuary in Hudson, Quebec, offered suggestions that much improved the crow sections of the book.

Artist Susan Valyi kindly created a papier maché crow mask for me.

Mom Carolyn, brothers John and Stephen, and sister Susan, I am grateful to you for believing in me and in this book. I wish my Dad, Robin, could have lived to read this; it was he who first set my imagination alight when I was four, and he showed me where the crickets were hiding.

John Burge and Linda Thompson, extended family,

you keep me bolstered as well as balanced.

Thank you Bonnie Laing and other Ottawa Fiction Writers' Group members for invaluable feedback. Likewise, the ongoing advice from Catherine Purdie, Elizabeth Sellers, and Leah Smith was inspiring.

Jackie Newell and Audrey Wall, your support was vital and your comments uncommonly generous.

Thank you to publisher Linda Leith, with whom it is such a privilege and a pleasure to work, and my gifted editor, Elise Moser, whose skill and conscientiousness has brought much clarity to the pages. Credit also goes to Alexander Chalk who has meticulously guided the fine-tuning.

Most of all I'm ineffably grateful to Elisabeth Skelly, whom I cherish, and whose love and constant encouragement continue to sustain me.

Karen Molson
Dalkeith, Ontario

RECYCLED
Paper made from
recycled material
FSC® C100212

Printed in March 2016
by Gauvin Press,
Gatineau, Québec